You're In My Head

Cover: Susan Conditt

ISBN 978-0-578-76122-0

You're In My Head

A Novel

James Tauro Riley

For My Daughters

PART ONE
Seth

Chapter 1

On the third Monday in September, Seth Adams sat in his car in the nearly empty Ashbury Hills Middle School parking lot. He was certain that he didn't belong here. This wasn't going to go well. He wasn't going to win his kids' respect by being here, if that was what this was about. He wanted to go home.

There were only four other cars in the lot, he noted with relief. At least there wouldn't be a lot of people to deal with tonight, he thought. People weren't his strong suit.

The moon was rising, half of it illuminated, and he could see points of light that he knew were four of the planets—Venus, Mars, Saturn, and Jupiter—spread across his view of the night sky. There was a billboard in the undeveloped, fenced-in lot across the street from the school, a Framework Foundation advertisement featuring the words WHO'S YOUR MAKER? against a painted night sky that was darker than the real sky above it. The stars on the billboard were brighter than anything visible overhead.

The only other light nearby came from the other side of the thick, bulletproof glass windows built into the armored double doors that served as the entrance to the middle school's administrative building.

Seth was anxious for several reasons. He felt a mild discomfort being at his kids' school. Maybe the feeling had nothing to do with his concern about what the parents and teachers inside did or did not know about him, or what they might have heard about him—he wasn't sure. He hadn't been around other people for weeks, and it felt like a dramatic shift to be planning to interact with anyone in a face-to-face encounter.

Since Seth had moved into his new rental, he had been absorbed in trying to turn the place into something livable. He'd been dealing with the rats, too. He'd known there was a vermin problem and had decided that was the next thing to fix. Four days before, at about this time, he'd set five traps around the front porch. He'd gone inside, washed his hands, and heard within minutes all five traps going off. He'd debated going out, cleaning the traps and setting them again, but suspected this would result in him spending the whole evening setting and cleaning traps. Instead, he'd decided to only set the traps once each afternoon, and to clean them in the morning. At this point, he'd caught twenty, five dead each of the last four mornings. He'd spent a lot of time wondering how many there were, and even more time wondering where it was they went in the day, but he was trying not to obsess on it.

Although he did want to get home to set the traps again.

No one likes middle school, Seth thought. Certainly no one would go back if they had a choice. What am I doing here? Is this going to cascade into a whole lot of something I don't want?

Eventually, he exited his car. He started walking slowly toward the armored doors.

Through the doors and down a long hall, past dusty display cases filled with dusty awards and plaques, past a red construction paper banner that read ASHBURY GIVES CAMPAIGN. It was like stepping through a time warp, into a middle school that 30 years later and several cities away looked exactly like the junior high Seth had attended. The walls had a sandy texture and were the same color his mother had wanted for the house exterior in the late 70s because it was so popular at the time. It was grayer and duller than a mint green. The ceiling was tiled with white square panels, each panel with a grid of perforated holes, of the type he remembered counting in his idle class time. He wondered if he hadn't heard sometime in the years since that those panels were made with asbestos.

His phone vibrated.

It was a message from Doug: Haven't heard from you in a while. Is this still your number? Let's have lunch.

Seth approached the only room in the hallway with an open door. It was a classroom. Inside, he found three very different looking women, all with tired, serious expressions on their faces. They smiled to greet him, but as he penned his name on the first line of the sign-in form, they exchanged glances that suggested they had summed up very quickly something about his situation and were less than impressed. They didn't know the half of it, Seth thought as he seated himself.

"Not a good start to the year," the grey-haired one said. In thick-rimmed glasses and a zipped-up windbreaker peppered with scout troop badges, she looked like a Midwestern grandma, but her voice didn't sound as old as she looked. She was surely the parent of a middle-school-aged boy.

"We have to work with what we have," said the tallest of the three, a blonde woman who seemed a bit familiar to him. She was more formally dressed, slacks and a blouse with a blazer. She looked like a lawyer. Her voice resonated with experience and resignation. Seth assumed she was the president. "That's what this group has always done."

"I think this is all we're going to get," said the third, a mismatch with the other two. She was a mod-looking mom— short, shoulder-length jet black hair, red lipstick, a leather skirt that looked too long for her, and an earring in her left nostril. Among them, they were the president, treasurer, and secretary of the Ashbury Hills Middle School parent teacher organization, Ashbury's Friends.

There were two other women in the room, both seated at student desks and staring at the faces of their phones. Seth was in a seat between and roughly equidistant from each of them. Although he was certain most everyone in the room was about the same age as him, he thought the women in charge seemed much more mature. They were the grown-ups. Seated as he was at a student desk, the feeling was magnified.

The meeting began with an explanation that all three of them were the parents of students who were starting in tenth grade at the area high school. Their children had graduated out of this middle school three months prior, in June. They were the previous year's parent group board members, and the reason they were at the middle school tonight was because they hadn't found anyone by the end of the previous year who would either volunteer or allow themselves to be coerced into taking over their posts.

"Middle school parents tend to be indifferent," the blonde explained. Seth's eyes wandered to the dry erase board as they began providing an overview of their job responsibilities. Someone had written Please Clean Up Your Messes in red ink next to a red smiley face and a sketch of the solar system drawn in blue marker.

The mod mom was eating and would continue to eat at a slow pace throughout the entire meeting, licking her fingers every couple of bites and speaking with food in her mouth. Not impressive, Seth thought. At some point he heard her say in a low voice to the gray-haired one, "I hate this fucking school. No way am I starting my son here next year. He's on the spectrum. This school would destroy him. I'm done with this place."

They described their early planning for the year, naming each of the events that needed chairpersons and/or volunteer workers. They had already sent home envelopes for the annual Ashbury Gives Campaign, and there was a donation box in the office that needed to be checked regularly for money because people would steal from it if they had the chance. It all seemed optimistic, seeing as there were only three people in attendance, and Seth wasn't there for anything other than to sign up to help out at graduation, nine months away.

The only item on the event list that caught his interest was a proposed alumni event. Seth had worked with a woman named Bridget at his last job who once said that she had attended Ashbury Middle School years before. He wondered idly if an alumni event was the sort of thing Bridget would attend, and if by chance somewhere in its files the school had any kind of contact information for her. If her parents still lived in the area, maybe the school would even have their address, and they would know where to reach her.

The reason Seth was at the meeting at all had to do with something his daughter Jessica said to him the last time they had spoken, five or six months before, the day he and Marina told the kids that their two-month separation was going to become a permanent divorce. The kids had already deduced this because Marina tended to overshare and because she had already been screening real estate agents to start the process of putting their family home up for sale.

During that last conversation, Jessica confronted Seth. She told him to stay out of her life, and even though he'd said something pained about how he wouldn't bother her, he'd also tried reaching out for something, anything positive to add, and came up with the suggestion that maybe he'd be able to see her at her middle school graduation at the end of the next school year. Maybe they would be in a better place by then.

Not skipping a beat, Jessica said, "No. Absolutely not. You are banned. You are banned from graduation. Banned from my school. Banned from my life! I won't get tickets for you, and they won't let you in without tickets. I won't invite you. I'll tell everyone there how terrible you are. You don't deserve to be a part of anything in my life. Plan on staying away instead."

Seth was at the meeting of Ashbury's Friends because

he'd latched onto the idea of being barred from graduation as either a challenge she had thrown down or as a hint at a last chance to not completely close the door on their relationship. A little bit of both? Some small part of Seth rebelling against the fate he'd otherwise mindlessly (or else completely intentionally) saddled himself with? It had been in the back of his mind for months. This was something he thought he could lock down in the case that nine months down the road things had instead tumbled even farther downhill.

Seth still received weekly text messages from the kids' school describing what was coming for the campus in the week ahead, so he'd known there was a parent group meeting scheduled. He had reasoned that the parent group would surely be involved with year-end graduation ceremonies, and he thought maybe he would go and try to sign up to be a volunteer to help out with graduation day and then just let the family matters lie where they were until June next year.

As the financial minutiae continued during the treasurer's report, Seth's mind wandered far from the Parent Center at Ashbury Hills Avenue Middle School. Staring at the basic rendering of the solar system, he thought of the things science teachers had never mentioned in school. In addition to the nine planets—Seth included Pluto in that count—there was a tenth planet that followed an elliptical path around the sun that was long and narrow compared to the orbits of the rest. That planet took 20,000 years to complete its orbit and it wouldn't be back in Earth's neighborhood for another 10,000 years, but it helped to make our solar system what it was.

Teachers never mentioned that the Milky Way was filled with millions of black holes, or that there was possibly a small black hole here in our own solar system, slowly swallowing it. They didn't tell kids that when the last star burned out, its remains would be a crystalline sphere formed of oxygen and carbon, and all that would be left in the universe would be an infinite number of crystalline spheres spread across an endless field of darkness, all the burned-out suns, no light to reveal their beauty. They didn't mention that the moon moved farther from the Earth every year. One day it just wouldn't be there anymore. They didn't explain that the only hope any species had for survival in the universe was to learn how to spread across it.

After the women were done with presenting, the blonde asked Seth if he had any questions. There was no doubt she was their leader, because she seemed the most optimistic. In more normal circumstances, had Marina dragged him to a meeting, he was sure he would have focused on their bookkeeping, how much money they had, how that money was being spent, if it was being allocated efficiently, whether the parent group managed to use their fundraising as leverage to effect change in the school. The blonde was the one who would respond to his challenges in that sort of situation. She would be able to defend their choices. One or both of the other two would likely give him the finger.

On this night, Seth was the one with no leverage, and no room to be critical. As they returned to the calendar of events, he considered raising his hand when eighth grade commencement was mentioned, but in a moment of clarity, said nothing. It was September. Graduation was in June—nine months away. These women were just barely holding things together long enough to pass the sack of crap to their successors. Whoever took the sack was going to be the one to ask about graduation. Each of these three had one foot out the door, and they would think he was clueless and pathetic for asking. As it was, they probably already thought he was pathetic.

They small-talked about the things they liked about the school, as if to convince the rest in the room that the school was worth their time. This continued for a few awkward minutes, apparently in hopes of some other parent showing up before they moved on to the last topic on the agenda, elections. No longer seeking a favor, Seth smoothly transitioned to viewing them with some disdain. These were people who had no idea how little anyone would care if there were no one to replace them.

"It's a school with nearly 1,200 kids," the mod mom said. "There has to be someone else coming." They all listened together for the approaching squeak of someone's shoes in the hallway outside. There wasn't a sound.

This was it. Time to call it a wrap.

Thinking that it would be disheartening for them if he got up and left before the meeting ended, Seth instead took the time to try to come up with a way to repair relations with Jessica, something better than crashing her graduation.

Geez, he thought—what kind of stupid plan was that, anyway? What would that prove? Maybe he would just have to live with being shut out of his daughter's life. Was that the message here? Start paying for his misdeeds before he started adding new infractions to the list? Was it just too late now that she was a teen and ready to ignore her father anyway? Had he lost the argument long ago?

It was that last thought, really, that would come to haunt him. Not in years, or months, or days, but a short 40 minutes later, when he emerged from the double doors and started walking in the direction of his car. He was gripping, maybe too tightly, the Ashbury's Friends president's manual and wondering, having just been sworn into office by three very resigned-looking moms, what it was he had agreed to do just because he didn't want to lose an argument with his daughter.

There was nothing but sarcasm behind it when Seth thought: What could go wrong?

Chapter 2

Seth first put his evolving world view into words two decades before, while in his mid-twenties, about a year into therapy. He remembered that he'd insisted Dr. Penny restate her understanding of the rules of doctor/patient confidentiality before opening the discussion. With the exception of one person—his high school friend, Aaron—Seth hadn't shared any part of this information with anyone before because he was afraid it would have landed him somewhere more restrictive than therapy. The monthly sessions with Dr. Penny were paid for by his parents as a pre-condition to their shouldering his rent and insurance while he put himself back together after he'd come unglued at the end of college. Seth kept the appointments, although he was fairly certain that his parents would have continued their support regardless; the alternative, him living at home with them, appealed to them even less than it did to him. He'd seen Dr. Penny once a month ever since.

"I'm going to try to explain this in simple terms," Seth said to Dr. Penny. "It's an analogy for the basic premise of my existence." He didn't say, *and yours, too,* although he thought it. "Think about playing a video game, where you go to a business, and you pay a fee, and then they put you in a chair or a giant tube or . . . some kind of box. So you understand, this is a great simplification. The process involves extracting those aspects of your consciousness not attached to your identity, so it's a much more sophisticated containment vessel than a box but, whatever; for the purposes of this analogy, they put a band around your head, or give you an injection, or flood the compartment with gas, and you enter the game. You're born into a different world, this world, and you are able to enjoy a physical existence for a single lifetime, from birth until your character dies within the game. Then you wake up and get out of the chair or whatever vessel it is, and you go back to your own existence. You have no control over the experience you get or the body you're placed in.

"Now imagine that this is a popular form of entertainment. Billions have played since the business opened. The centers are all over the place. It used to be really expensive, with only a few outlets offering the service, and the cost was ridiculous. As it has grown, it has become accessible to more and more. Imagine that you'd played the game before and had such a great time that you'd saved up whatever it is you use for currency to do it again and again.

"Then imagine that when you're just getting started on your latest game experience, whatever it is they do to you to make you forget who and what you truly are and where it is you really come from . . . well, it starts to wear off. It stops working.

"That's where I'm at," he told Dr. Penny. "Essentially, I'm awake, and I'm stuck in the game here on Earth. There's been a malfunction in my unit or the dose they gave me wasn't strong enough, and I'm stuck this way until they correct the problem. I mean, they've got to have repair systems, right? When do they kick in?

"I know I'm using human vernacular to describe the issue. I know they sent me here. It's not exactly like I'm describing, but I'm trying to put this in terms you can relate to."

That session was a milestone moment for Seth. It was the first time he'd been able to describe to someone what he thought of as his reality. In the twenty or so years since, he'd developed a more eloquent monologue in his mind based on what he'd shared with Dr. Penny that day, but saying it aloud the way he had in session had given him a lasting comfort.

About six weeks after Seth's divorce was complete, and a week after the surprise announcement that the company he'd been working for had been sold and would be closing down in a fortnight, he was at what he would later think of as the lowest point in his life, living among unpacked boxes in a hotel room. He flipped through the copy of the Ashbury Weekly Reader that had been stuffed in the mail slot, and came across the advertisement for the Framework Foundation Museum.

For several weeks before he saw the newspaper ad, he'd been regularly passing by a billboard a few blocks from the hotel that read IS THIS A VIRTUAL REALITY? The same logo that appeared on the billboard was also there in the ad: a four-by-four grid, with one square colored blue, three cubes down, three cubes in. He had understood immediately that the grid represented space and the blue cube represented Earth. The advertisement in the paper requested submissions for a survey, in 1,000 words or less, wherein respondents were to describe what they believed to be the origin of humankind and what they believed was humanity's ultimate purpose. The best of the submissions were to be used in a display at the Framework Foundation Museum.

Seth had been mulling it over for months. A few days after he had accepted the position of parent group president, while he was emptying the rat traps into the hotel's dumpster and thinking about how much better he'd felt after that session with Dr. Penny, he'd decided he was going to put together a summary of his understanding of the mechanics at work behind life on planet Earth.

He started his rough draft the next day and decided he would use a pseudonym when he submitted it. It was a dodge, he knew, not owning it. If it was accepted, he would let them know his real name, but he would also request that they use the pseudonym for the display. He did not want to be in the spotlight. He built the name by combining the names of the manufacturer of the toilet in his bathroom and the provider of the bottled water in the hotel's vending machine: Schreiber Esse.

As he continued to work on his submission over the following days—he thought it was days—he realized he was going to have more freedom than he would have had even in the therapist's office. He found that putting into words the world as he understood it, and not couching it all in terms that would keep his therapist from committing him, was revelatory. Strangely, when he was done with his submission, when it was stamped and in the mail, instead of feeling that he'd been ripped off and abandoned in the scenario in which he found himself, he felt as if there was maybe some small possibility that his unique perspective might give him some small advantage, maybe even a purpose, that could lift him out of the life he was living.

Seth stood at the long counter in the middle school's main office. There were two women at desks on the other side of the counter, both on phones.

He told himself to be patient, but ended up clearing his throat loudly. One of the women reacted to the noise, her eyes flickering toward him as she listened to the person on the other end of the call. He felt her assessing him, the look on his face. Could she ignore him until the end of the call? How long had he been standing there waiting for her attention? Did he seem like the kind of parent who would cause a scene? She lifted a finger in his direction and mouthed, "One minute."

In less than a minute, without getting up from her desk, she called out, "How can I help you?" There was something very guarded, almost unfriendly about her tone.

"Hi. My name is Seth. I'm, uh . . . I'm the new parent group president."

"Really," she said. She and the woman at the desk next to her looked Seth over quickly, then at each other. The phone rang again. Before she could pick up, he asked for the key to the Parent Center.

The other woman finished her call. One phone continued to ring. The first woman told the other one to get the key, and then she answered the call. While the second woman started rummaging for the key, a third woman was suddenly standing beside him, hand outstretched, as if she had just materialized there.

"The new president? How nice to meet you. And a man, too." He couldn't tell the origin of her accent. It could be French and or Persian? "I have so many ideas I want to discuss with the parent group . . ."

"And you are?"

"Ms. Bibi. I'm a teacher here. I teach the introductory Spanish classes."

She was standing so close that she made him uncomfortable.

He asked, "Is this an off period for you?"

"Oh, no, but my students are working on their journals right now."

Someone handed him a key attached to a large block of wood.

He started to excuse himself from Ms. Bibi, but she was ready to go, too, and offered to walk him over to the Parent Center on the way back to her classroom. As they stepped outside the office, a person in a school uniform who seemed too tall and had too thick of a mustache to be a student brushed past them.

A man stuck his head outside a doorway and roared, "Eddie, get back here now. Get back in here."

Eddie didn't respond to him. Clearly, he was going to head out through the armored doors and out of the school, but the man kept yelling and yelling, only stopping when Eddie was no longer in the hall. Then the guy decided he should pursue Eddie, and he charged down the hall after him.

Another student, another boy, appeared in the doorway.

This must be the detention room, Seth thought. The second student looked like he was trying to be really sly as he edged out of the room and into the hallway. Then he realized Seth and Ms. Bibi were watching. He waved at Ms. Bibi, who responded with, "Hello, Francis." The student started walking away from them, not toward the doors Eddie had chosen, but in the opposite direction, the doors that would lead into the school's main hallway. Francis was trying to act casual but looked very sneaky.

Another head appeared in the doorway, this one an adult. A woman. Also yelling, this time at Francis. The look this woman gave Ms. Bibi was pure irritation.

"Francis? Francis, get back here! Francis!"

Francis also didn't listen, and when he exited the hallway, the woman followed after him.

Ms. Bibi was a kook, Seth was certain by the time they reached the Parent Center door. She wanted to talk about starting a social club at Ashbury.

"The students don't understand how to socialize these days. They go home on the weekends to binge watch Pastry Baking Challenges and eat delivery pizzas. They hardly interact with anyone after school hours. The social club would have sandwich nights on Tuesdays and Movie nights once a month. I'll volunteer to be the movie night chaperone! It will be fun!"

When he slid the key into the lock of the door to the Parent Center—Seth was at first certain it wouldn't be the right key—he asked Ms. Bibi if she shouldn't be getting back to her students. This did not seem to be her priority.

"Yes, I will," she said, but she didn't seem to be moving anywhere. She waited for him to open the door.

"Have a great day," Seth said, pulling the door open only wide enough to slide himself in, and closing it behind him. He was sure she wouldn't take offense—she'd surely had doors closed on her before.

He looked around the Parent Center. When he'd been here for the meeting, he'd thought it was only a classroom. Now he noticed the sink, the refrigerator, the coffee maker, the copy machine in the corner. The file cabinet had a yellow Post-It on it that read ASHBURY'S FRIENDS.

He guessed that now he was Ashbury's Friends. Instead of folders and papers inside the drawers, there were paper plates, forks and knives, reams of colored copy paper, party decorations, paperweights. From what Seth understood, all of the area's schools, from elementary through high school, had all been built in the early 60s. The particular architectural style had been as identical as possible from one school to the other, from one city to another, across the state, such that it became the look associated with all public schools. Cookie cutter schools spread out across the landscape.

The shell was early 60s, more than 50 years old. Inside, the heating unit, an old, long, metal furnace, looked like it came from the early 70s, the computer on the long folding table at the front of the room was from the early 2000s, the student desks from the 1980s, and the air-conditioning unit from the 90s. Once a decade, it seemed, the school district found enough money to splurge on one improvement.

It was this way, he realized, throughout the school, from the main office to the auditorium. A patchwork of fixes and upgrades made through the decades. It was definitely a giant leap forward from his own school days, but there was a lost-in-time feel to the room he was in, to the school as a whole.

A key slid into the door from the hallway outside, and Seth froze, strangely panicked at the thought of being caught in the room alone, even though it was supposedly okay for him to be there. He braced himself for the return of Ms. Bibi. Instead, the person who came in was one of the women from the parent group meeting. The blonde. He could not remember her name but she smiled and greeted him right away.

"Hi Seth."

"Hey, hi."

"It's Lori."

"Right. Hi, Lori. What are you doing here?"

"There was a school tour this morning for incoming students. I've been doing them for two years, and I'm going to do them for a little while longer until they can find someone else to be in charge of it. I don't mind. I really love this school. High school isn't like this—my daughter is going to a charter high school across town, and she doesn't want me within a mile of the campus except to pick her up and drop her off. This school is really underappreciated."

"Neglected," was the kindest Seth could come up with.

"That, too." He realized she was watching him, not worried, nor hopeful, just . . . what? He could feel for a moment her attachment to the school, felt a flash of shame that he was all she had to carry the torch.

"I found a couple—wife and husband of seventh grade twins—who said they would be your secretary and treasurer. So you have a quorum."

Great, he thought. What does that mean? People who will try to make me do things.

There were two serving trays on a table to the right of Seth, covered with white and black cylindrical salt and pepper shakers. He didn't notice the setup until she walked over next to him and stared at the trays.

"There are great elementary schools in the area, but when it comes to middle schools, it's a different story. The parents think the kids are harder to control, more susceptible to influences, and they think that a public middle school is suddenly looking much more like the real world than they really want their kids to be dealing with. Parents these days try to shelter their kids until the day they leave for college. So," she said, taking eight of the salt shakers and two of the pepper shakers off the tray and setting them on the table, "a bunch of them, the ones with the most money usually, as soon as elementary school ends they head off to Keystone Academy up north—exclusive, expensive. Or the Oaks. Another handful, none of them really very religious, head off to the Catholic-run schools." She removed four more salt shakers and said, "we have a Catholic boys' school, a Catholic girls' school, and a Catholic coed campus all within 10 miles." She grabbed one more salt shaker and one more pepper shaker. "The magnets and the charters get their shares," she said, taking out 5 more salt shakers and 2 more pepper shakers. There were mostly pepper shakers left on the trays, and 5 salt shakers. "And, of course, the home-schooled. The last insult to the public school system." She took four more salt shakers away.

"This is the part of the local elementary school population that moves onto Ashbury Hills Middle School. They're all amazing kids here. I mean, sure there are problems, but no more than any of the other schools serving kids this age. You wouldn't know that because our competitors have P.R. departments that manage their messages in a way that a public school isn't able to." Seth wasn't sure he was following. She saw his confusion, and explained further, "As a parent group president who really tried to engage the local community in this school, one of the comments I heard most frequently in relation to Ashbury had to do with our school's 'diversity.' I see that as a positive comment, personally, but the way the word has been said to me suggests some people are threatened by too much diversity, if that isn't oxymoronic." Seth looked at the tray again, and counted one white salt shaker and eighteen black pepper mills.

She gestured toward the trays a moment. Explanation enough, was what her hand gesture toward the pepper mills said. He thought that what she was saying was that there weren't a lot of white kids at this public school located in the heart of a generally upper middle-class, generally white neighborhood. He didn't know how to respond.

"I didn't notice." He could only recall seeing the students on the sidewalk around the drop-off gate. He couldn't picture their skin colors.

"When you hear people complaining about our school's diversity, this is what they're referring to." She began replacing the shakers she'd taken away from the tray.

The pang of guilt returned as Lori readied to leave the room. The depth of her involvement with the school was obvious. He felt none of that. She stopped at the door, remembering something.

"Seth, I meant to ask you—are you Jessica's father?"

"Yes." No doubt, she'd heard things.

"I know your daughter. She's a dynamite girl."

"Thanks. She doesn't want anything to do with me."

Lori laughed and nodded knowingly as if Seth had said something relatable. She waved goodbye and left the room.

Seth waited until the bell rang and the sound of kids' voices in the hall outside began to subside. He didn't want to run into Jessica at all today, wasn't prepared for it. He waited ten minutes before heading for the door. When he stepped outside the room, there was a woman standing there. Was she waiting for him? It didn't matter. His appearance right there meant she was who he had to deal with.

Seth said, "Hello."

She said, "You're the new parent group president?"

"I guess so."

"I'm Ms. Donner. I'm the interim school principal. Three years interim."

"I'm Seth Adams. Nice to meet you."

"Walk with me," she said, and she headed down the hallway, him matching her pace after a couple steps. They went out of the administrative hallway into the main hall of the school.

"I've never seen a school with such indifferent parents," Ms. Donner said. "I went to Coltrane Middle School's parent group meeting. They're a school about 10 miles east of us, and they raise $400,000 with their fundraising every year! Do you think you can raise $400,000?"

Seth had no idea. From what he'd seen, this would seem highly doubtful. It took a moment more for him to realize she clearly knew the answer.

"It's not that kind of school," she said to him. "Don't get your hopes up."

He'd already stayed longer than he'd intended. Ms. Donner, having clarified that he knew nothing, told him about the basic things she had observed the parent group attending to on campus. The list of events that she went through were the same that Lori and the other moms had rambled through. He should have a table at back-to-school night, Ms. Donner said, where he could try to sign people up or get them to offer some kind of support.

She was giving him snack suggestions for the table when another bell rang.

A rush of anxiety gripped his entire body. He didn't want to run into Jessica. As the thought crossed his mind, she was suddenly there, standing in front of him, her face expressionless except for her slightly furrowed brow. Goodness, he thought, she's as tall as I am. She launched right into it.

"Why are you here? Did you tell them you're my father? Do you know what a father is?"

She knew his general reaction was to mirror her attitude back at her and to try to assert his authority. She knew that when he engaged that way with her, she could draw him down to her level. He didn't want to do any of that here. He saw that there were three girls standing in a cluster nearby, watching carefully. These were her friends. He liked that she had buddies who would be close by, keeping an eye on her.

"Interesting," she said to his non-response. "Thanks for sharing. You should leave."

"Ms. Adams," the principal said.

Jessica didn't even look her way, instead keeping her eyes locked on Seth's, without blinking.

"Ms. Adams. Girls. Move on to your classes."

"I'll go when he does," Jessica said, incredibly stubborn, ready to fight.

"Ms. Adams," the principal said again.

"That's okay," Seth said. "I can go." To the principal, he said, "Nice to have met you. We'll talk more later." He didn't say anything to Jessica before he walked away.

Chapter 3

"Seeing Jess with her friends at school really brought up a lot of memories." Seth said, "Once I was outside of the school and back in my car and I had gotten over being paralyzed by my daughter's hostility, I started thinking about my old friends. The ones I met in middle school and the ones I met in high school."

Dr. Penny asked, "Are you still in contact with any of them?"

"A couple guys. Doug, Aaron. At least, I was in contact with them at one point, but haven't talked to either since before the divorce."

"Is the divorce the reason you haven't spoken with them?"

"I guess so. Doug has reached out a couple times. Every few months. I've been avoiding him so I don't have to relive it for him. He's going to be disappointed. I don't want to see or hear disappointed. For a long time, he's been more like my case worker than my friend, as if it's his job to monitor my mental health. It started to bother me long before the divorce."

Seth met Doug in middle school. Doug was two grades ahead, and the two knew each other's names but didn't hang out. In high school, Doug was a P.E. aide when Seth was a sophomore and Doug was senior, and then when Seth was a senior Doug was a P.E. assistant coach as part of a college teaching program. That was the role Doug had assumed in Seth's life—personal coach. He was so relentlessly optimistic and encouraging that Seth felt more ashamed to be around him after each ensuing failure.

Seth said, "I usually see him once or twice a year. Sometimes it's gone longer than that. It's my fault this time."

"Why haven't you called him back? It can be comforting to talk to friends."

"Doug is a really good guy. He's a do-gooder, he's a

public school P.E. coach and does a lot of volunteer work. It's all really great, but that's his one setting—being good and helpful and then telling other people about the people he helps. There's just one level to him, and I end up feeling like I only fit into his life as one of his charity work duties that he probably tells other people about."

"You feel he's going to be disappointed that you're divorced?"

"Yeah, at the least. He's going to feel bad for me. I don't need that right now. Ego's too wounded."

"Then it wasn't Doug's company you were feeling nostalgic about?"

"No. It's my friend Aaron. He just dropped out of my life. He was the only person I talked to about cheating on Marina, maybe about six months before Marina found out, and he was the first one to bail on me because of his disappointment in my behavior. Disappointment. There's that word again. This is going to be a gold mine for future sessions, isn't it? He was very, very disappointed in me, so much so that I haven't really heard from him since. He wasn't close to Marina, but I think they talked on the phone once in a while, and I think he liked her as my wife. So I'm not sure how many levels he's been offended on."

"Let's get you into a smock," Dr. Penny said, "and we'll rinse your hair."

When real life started after college, the group of guys Seth had been friends with ended up going in different directions, from which twenty years later they followed each other without comment on social media and rarely saw or called each other unless some kind of travel situation might have put them in the same town. Birthday greetings were exchanged every year. Greg and Kellun were Midwesterners, living white-bread lives in Indiana and Tennessee, family guys, with more conservative values than they'd ever exhibited growing up in California. Joel was a fireman up in Seattle and Mark was a retired recluse, having inherited the family trust when his mother died and having moved into her old home outside of San Francisco. Twenty years out of high school, Aaron, who had joined their group in 10th grade, was the only one Seth had continued to speak with regularly. Aaron had never gone too far from home, and still lived a couple miles from their old high school, about an hour away by car from Ashbury Hills.

Once upon a time, if the call went out, the group would have tried to get together, but the bond had weakened when they reached their thirties. Greg and Mark hadn't made it to Seth's wedding. Joel's family followed him to Seattle and he basically stopped traveling to California.

"Might as well face it," Aaron had said, "We're getting into that zone where people only get together for high school reunions, funerals, and destination 50th birthday parties."

For the most part, in school they had considered themselves a classic in-the-middle group. They got good grades but weren't quite nerds, played sports but weren't quite jocks, had girls who were friends, but did not have girlfriends—popularity-wise they had estimated they were just above the median because they never really had trouble getting into any party.

Aaron's mother worked with Mark's mom, and she made Mark introduce Aaron, the new kid at school, to his friends. Aaron was flashier than the rest of them, more stylish, more social, and very quickly they grew to like him because he was a funny guy. Not a center-of-attention kind of joker, but a good-natured guy who could crack someone up during a normal conversation, with something, anything—a silly pun, a deadpan delivery, a random thought out of nowhere that seemed connected to nothing. Seth didn't know that their group was the best match for Aaron, especially because really Aaron didn't mind being noticed and the rest of the guys did, but Aaron decided right off that they were the right group of people for him. He later told them that he'd been bullied a lot in middle school because of quirks that included wearing color-coordinated clothing and changing up his hair color and style regularly. Based on those things alone, and maybe also because of the way he could be loud and silly, a lot of people thought he was gay. The guys in the group debated it now and then—Seth had maybe once or twice gotten the impression that Aaron had a crush on him—but they all agreed that they'd only ever seen him be interested in girls. Blonde girls, especially.

The group members were the first people Aaron interacted with after he switched schools, and the way they had accepted him as he was from the very start—to the point that the things people had harassed him for previously weren't even an issue anymore—made him feel like he had finally landed in the right place.

Aaron got their group to do stuff that they would never have otherwise attempted, like using fake IDs to get into a trendy downtown bar where all the girls were miles out of their league, or performing in costume as Adam and the Ants in a lip sync battle at a shitty local club. Stuff that for the guys was offbeat and crazy fun and unlike any of the things they were used to doing in their free time. Seth didn't spend as much time with Aaron as some of the other guys, but Aaron was one of the few, and the only one of the group, who'd ever seen the inside of the house Seth grew up in. Because of those visits, Aaron knew the story about Seth's sister—who had died, stillborn, about two years before Seth was born and whose absence loomed over the household. It was another thing Aaron had never said anything about to anyone else.

It was true that Aaron had also spent time hanging out, sometimes even living, at the homes of the other guys, and that he was on a first-name basis with some of their parents, including Seth's mother Claire. It was something the group joked about in front of Aaron, and behind his back they chalked it up to Aaron being more social than the rest of them, and their belief that Aaron had been raised somewhere where there were advanced social rules to be followed. Later they would find out that Aaron's home life was pretty terrible—and that during at least a couple years of high school he had been doing his best to spend as much time away from his house as possible.

Seth moved back home after he left college, and a month after his big freak-out and the start of his recovery, Mark, Kellun, and Greg were all in town, also living with their families, each of them with post-graduation plans that would have them moving away to either jobs or master's degree programs. The guys wanted to do a big night out to celebrate how far they had come. Seth's mother had pushed him to go when Seth—somewhat medicated, one set of class credits short of a degree, and sporting a haircut that he thought made him look like either a military recruit or a mental patient—considered opting out.

The guys ended up smashed, with Kellun, the designated driver of the group, at the wheel. Aaron directed them to a low-budget, uncrowded bar with loud, bass-heavy music pounding over a dance floor where no one was dancing. They got a table while Aaron started dancing by himself, and by the time the first round of drinks were served there were five more people dancing around him. One minute they were all joking about the fact that Aaron still knew how to get a party started, toasting to the fact that they weren't going to be dancing that night, and then several drinks later all of them were on the dance floor, singing along full throttle with a remixed song that had the refrain lyric "Free Nelson Mandela," waving their hands in the air while everyone on the packed dance floor did the same.

The good vibes carried into the drive home, with all of them singing along with the radio while they laughed about various people they'd encountered at the dive bar. Kellun pulled off the highway to park behind a mini-mart, where Mark peed in a gutter before going inside with Kellun and Greg for snacks.

Seth and Aaron went to the side of the building, where they found the door to the restroom was ajar and the room inside dark. Aaron immediately became convinced there might be someone lurking inside, so they peed on the building's outside wall instead. When they got back to the car, the other guys were hardly even started on their mini-market foraging, so Seth and Aaron sat on the trunk of the car, smoking Aaron's cigarettes and talking.

Speaking generally, and sparing much detail, Seth, very drunk, had said something about how great it was to be out with the guys and forgetting everything and just feeling normal for a night, and Aaron had asked him what it was he wasn't feeling normal about. Seth hadn't told any of them about the freak-out or the fact that he hadn't gotten his degree.

"I had some issues at the end of the school year," Seth said. "I'm in therapy. Trying to convince myself that no, someone, somewhere did not make a mistake. I am not an alien who has been stuck into this body, this world . . . "

"Wait. Wait. Wait," Aaron said, hearing the weirdness through the alcohol. "Explain."

"I feel like there's maybe someone else inside me who isn't Seth. Who is maybe someone else. When I was having my episode, it felt like that someone else wouldn't be quiet. It's a lot better now, almost like a dream that I can't quite remember. It settled down for some reason, but it didn't go all the way away. I'm trying to figure out a way to make it normal or adjust to it or just get used to it. If I think about it too much, I start to feel kind of trapped. I don't know if this is some fucked-up psychological thing that happened because I grew up with a ghost sister or if I really am partly an alien . . . and I don't know what to do every day other than just keep myself busy and hope it works itself out. It's fucked up."

When Aaron did not laugh or recoil or look at Seth like Seth was crazy, Seth felt great relief cutting through his stupor. Aaron looked drunk, but also sympathetic.

"Seth, I totally get it. Well, wait. Maybe not exactly that, but I understand the feeling. More than once since I was kid, I've felt the same way. Not alien, I guess. But I've wondered before about my identity," Aaron paused—maybe somewhere underneath the effects of the alcohol his brain was trying to get him to rethink verbalizing it—"and my gender. Sometimes I'm not sure who or what I am supposed to be."

That took a moment to sink in.

"You think maybe you're supposed to be a girl."

Aaron gasped quietly, dramatically, at Seth's saying it aloud. His eyes rounded a little.

"I'm not sure. It's just a theory. It's really weird to hear someone say that," and he laughed really loud. He had a nice laugh. It made Seth want to laugh with him. "Most of the reason my home life was shitty growing up was that I wasn't the son my father wanted me to be, and I'm sure, without either of us having ever talked about it, that my father had as many questions about who I really was as I did. I think he recognized early that maybe I was identifying as a girl, and that was the end of any hope of him having any kind of relationship with me. My father hated what I was and was just waiting for the day when he could legally kick me out of the house—which he did, on my 18th birthday. His loss, so my mom says. So, yeah, I guess, in answer to your question. That's right."

Seth asked, "So what do you do now?"

"I'm still in the wait-and-see phase. I don't know what it

is, exactly. I'm not sure about the big picture, so I'm going to let life direct me, see what comes up and how I react to it. It's going to work itself out for the best."

"You're always so fucking positive." Seth slurred. "I just go around dreading that I'm going to have to feel like this as long as I'm alive."

"That's why we don't do big picture. That's not for people in a state of confusion. That's what's going to make a person suicidal, thinking anything is going to last forever. Nothing lasts forever. Everything changes. So, I just do what that kids' song said, you know that song, ' . . . put one foot in front of the other, and soon you'll be walking out the door . . . ' We take it day by day by day—that's another song—and then we see what kind of ride the world offers up to us."

Seth thought about it.

Aaron sang quietly to himself, "Day by day by day . . . "

They both saw that the guys were getting ready to exit the store.

Seth said, "Thanks for listening."

"No, really," Aaron said, "me? Thank you for listening to me."

"Everything we said is between us, yes?"

"No one is going to be hearing about any of it from me," Aaron said.

Despite their pledge of silence, Seth regretted that he'd revealed anything at all when they first got back into the car with the other guys. The space suddenly seemed much smaller, his drunken reasoning went, and he was sure Aaron would spill. When they were on the freeway, Kellun flipped the radio to a country station and started singing along. It wasn't long before Seth wanted to complain about the existence of country music, but before he was able to, Greg and Mark jumped in and started singing along, too. It was an anthem-like song with a refrain about being a brother in arms—"I will be your brother, your brother in arms" —and they bellowed the second chorus together while Seth and Aaron watched with amusement.

When the third chorus started, Aaron leaned over and whispered in Seth's ear, slightly mimicking the notes in the song's chorus. "I'll be your sister, Seth." The feel of Aaron's breath so close to his ear made the hair stand up on Seth's neck. Aaron followed up with the lightest, quietest snicker Seth could have imagined, a sound so very Aaron that Seth almost laughed out loud. Then he heard the words and felt them sinking in. He looked at Aaron and saw that in his way Aaron was being serious, and he also understood for a moment that his friend Aaron, of all the people Seth had known in his entire life, understood something about Seth that no one else had ever acknowledged. The absence of his sister, the effect of the loss on his parents, had overshadowed Seth's entire life. It was the original hole in his heart that had never been filled, something he tried to never let anyone see, and it just seemed to Seth, drunk as he was, that Aaron was the most amazing person he'd ever known for taking the time to figure it out. He was a better friend to Seth than Seth had ever been to him.

Maybe Aaron was the greatest person ever, Seth remembered thinking.

Since he was not yet drunk, Kellun claimed the couch in the living room at his parents' house so he could watch TV, have beers, and work his way through the mini-market haul. He told Mark and Greg they could crash in his parents' room and he put Aaron and Seth in the guest bedroom.

When they were in the bedroom and choosing sides of the bed, Seth thanked Aaron again for not bringing up their conversation.

Aaron said, "No worries, Seth. I love you, man." Then

he gagged a little and threw up. He caught most of it in one of his hands, and the rest ended up on his t-shirt. He ran into the room's connected bathroom to wash off his hands. Then he came back, pulled off his shirt, dropped it on the floor, and started to pull back the blanket on his side of the bed.

"Dude," Seth said, "Don't leave your shirt on the floor. Put it in the sink. And go shower off or something. You smell like puke. I'll throw up if I have to smell that all night." While Aaron was out of the room, Seth, head spinning a bit, crawled under the blanket on the far side of the bed.

When he closed his eyes, the mild spinning started to spiral more wildly, and he forced his eyes open, at least until he could tell Aaron how much he appreciated him. Had he done that yet? Maybe words weren't enough, he decided.

He thought of their conversation earlier. He wondered if maybe Aaron's gender confusion had to do with him being gay but not having realized it. He thought: If Aaron hadn't been with a guy before, how could he know? He was being pulled back toward the dizzy place when Aaron stumbled out of the bathroom sometime later, startling Seth awake when he slid into bed.

The lights were off, and they were side by side and it seemed to Seth that maybe Aaron would want him to make some kind of first move. So, he leaned over across the bed, and stared at Aaron's face in the dark.

Aaron smiled at him, and said, "Thanks for not talking about me, too."

Seth thought it likely this was the time he should try to kiss Aaron, but he couldn't quite push himself up far enough to get their faces close enough for that to happen. Instead he kissed Aaron's chest. His eyes were closed when he did it. It felt weird, no denying it. He pulled back and looked at Aaron.

Eyes wide, Aaron said, "Why did you do that?"

Seth said, "You've been so great to me. You're a good

friend. So I thought if you wanted to . . . you know . . . if trying it out would help you figure things out, I would, you know . . . "

"Are you gay, Seth?"

He thought about it. "I don't think so but, ironically, I'm not the best judge of who I am. I don't even know what I am. I just thought, you know, it wouldn't have to be a lifestyle commitment for me. No one can help me, but I could maybe help you. You're my friend."

"I don't want that."

"Okay," Seth put his head on a pillow and pulled the blanket up over his shoulders. "That's good. It would have been weird. It was weird. I'm sorry, man. It's okay if I just go to sleep then? My head's spinny."

"Mine, too," Aaron said. "That's fine. It was a fun night. Good night, Seth."

"Good talk," Seth said. He rolled over and passed out.

"So," Seth said to Dr. Penny as she used the razor to touch up the edges of his sideburns, "It was a whole lot of stuff about him and me and it just went into the void, and literally, we've never, ever talked about anything that we said that night or anything that happened ever again. That was really the last time that our group of friends hung out together, even though Aaron and I continued to talk pretty regularly."

"Why do you assume your behavior in your marriage is responsible for the break with him?" Dr. Penny asked.

"He really wants to have a family. Be part of a good family. I think he thought that was what I had."

"This talk of gender identities, sexual identities, alien identities, never came up again?"

"No, I never suggested that Aaron's approach to relationships might have reflected deeper conflicts that he hadn't addressed, and Aaron never blamed my alien psychosis for my social isolation or the end of my marriage. Really, by the time I had kids, Aaron was the only friend who could see past my issues. Who am I to lecture anyone?

"Aaron got along okay with Marina, too," Seth said, "and he always let me know how lucky he thought I was to have found her, never more so than whenever I complained about the ways she and I weren't getting along. He took the news of the split worse than anyone."

"Maybe you were his proxy in what he thought was a traditional and successful marriage."

"Like, if it were him instead of me, he could have made the relationship work? I see that," Seth said. "He would have tried harder than I did to made it work."

"Hm. It's not an uncommon refrain from those who are on the outside looking in."

Seth wondered if Dr. Penny was being sarcastic. Was that somehow a dig at him?

She saw the expression on his face. "It's always harder when you have to do the work yourself," she explained. "That's all I was saying."

Chapter 4

Dr. Penny once asked Seth, "Suppose 'they' do find a way to 'fix' your problem. When you wake up on Day One after you've been 'repaired,' isn't your first question going to be 'What the heck did I do with my life, and why? Why didn't I finish school? Why did I cheat on my wife? Why do my children avoid me? Why is this where I am?' How do you think you're going to deal with those questions? Won't you be better off if you can make your life a better place to wake up in?"

Of those examples of the moments Dr. Penny seemed to think he'd gone astray, one resonated. He did not regret leaving school. It was not hard to think of reasons his marriage didn't work out. It was his children. That was where he had failed. He'd never wanted children, but they had made a space for themselves that he'd grown accustomed to having as part of his existence. He had missed having that space occupied. If he ever got his head together, he would surely regret it even more than he did now.

"I'd at least like the option," Seth had responded, "of not having to listen to that voice inside me that tells me none of this matters. To feel like it's worth caring about something. To be like everyone else who takes it for granted that they just belong here and their efforts will pay off, or not. I think I could get into all this life stuff if I could just forget the idea that I don't belong. When that idea pops up, it feels like none of this is of any consequence."

"Yet, even from that point of view, all you want is to belong in it, real or not."

"Exactly. I just want to be part of the simulation again." He meant it, too—but he understood his therapist's message: Whatever his understanding of the way things worked in life on Earth, Seth could be doing much better at this if he tried.

Ms. Donner texted him one afternoon to tell him there would be a table set up in the front entrance for him.

Seth: Table for what?

Principal Donner: For the parent group to fundraise at Back-to-School night. Sell pizza or something. Get people to sign up to help. It's time for you to be more visible.

So it was that Seth found himself seated at that table watching as parents were led by students to their next teacher introductions. In the parent group notebook he'd found a Back-to-School Night checklist that included a checklist of snacks to sell, samples of sign-up sheets to have on clipboards, instructions on where to find signage and a banner for the table (in a cupboard in the Parent Center) and three cases of water (from a storage room in the back of the school library) to give for free to parents who signed up and provided their phone number and email address. He was so pleased to find everything he needed in one place that it was then and there that he started to think of the president's manual as his own magic notebook.

Three parents signed up. For the most part, everyone else ignored him as they passed by his table. Didn't try to read the signs or the banner, just hurried along as if they were going to get marked tardy themselves. He would have done exactly the same in their shoes, if he had made himself available to attend the event at all. Parents who came by the table seemed to be similarly reserved, almost like window shoppers who wanted to signal they had no intention of buying, standing there with their arms crossed against their chests, checking out the sign-up sheets, meeting schedules, and information on promotions with local businesses, and then walking on without even looking at him. A few bought chips or sodas. Everyone seemed skeptical of Seth and of the school's need for money and unwilling to either donate or volunteer or even sign up to receive e-mails or social media messages about activities.

At some point, as he was asking a woman to consider signing up for a program with a local market that would give the school a percentage of whatever she spent there, Seth looked up and there she was—his ex-wife. Once she'd caught his eye, she walked directly up to his table, an impenetrable public smile on her face.

"So, it's true. It is you."

He handed the woman he was speaking to a form. He tried to be blank.

"Marina."

Don't get sucked in, he told himself. He focused on her appearance. She'd cut her hair and it made her look older, or maybe more mature. Or maybe her misery had done that.

"When I heard the rumor, I said I wasn't even sure you knew where the school was."

"That sounds like you," he said neutrally. The shrug sort of slipped out. She did not like the shrug.

She turned and looked up the hallway. She raised her right hand, and he thought for a moment she was going to smack the table with her palm, but instead she balled it up like she was crushing something in it.

"You're screwing with our lives. What is wrong with you? No, stop. I know. You're a selfish man." She took a breath. "Everyone thinks you're some kind of amazing person for this, not just because you're volunteering at school but because you're a man volunteering out at school. They will all figure out that you're asocial, disdainful, and that you lack empathy. If you think that planting your flag in the middle of your teenagers' school lives is the way to connect with them, you're deluded as ever you have been. Hasn't this been hard enough on them already?"

She waited a moment, but he knew that if he didn't respond, then she would be done. She took a step back from the table, holding his stare until someone, a female voice, called out her name, and the social mask went back up as she turned away, smiled, and moved off into the bustle of bodies.

He looked around to see if anyone else had heard any of that interaction. Everyone passing by was still doing what they could to avoid meeting his eyes. Then he noticed there was a couple standing near the table watching him. He wasn't sure how long they'd been there, or if they had just walked up, but when they saw that he had noticed them, they immediately approached to introduce themselves. They were Hank and Dion, and they were the treasurer and secretary his predecessor had sworn into office. He looked for something in their eyes, in their expressions, that would reveal what they might have overheard, but didn't find the obvious concern he could have expected if they'd overheard it all.

Hank and Dion very much resembled each other, not only in height and weight, but also in their looks. Both of them were short and a little stocky, and they looked like they could have been siblings. The three of them took a moment to look each other over before Dion brought up the matter of the group's first meeting. He imagined he could see in Hank's eyes a bit of sympathy directed toward him as his wife shifted her position so she was directly facing him.

"Are you going to schedule something? Something soon?"

Seth said, "Absolutely."

"Because it's the second month of school already and we haven't had any events. Not even a meeting."

"Well, I think there's the Ashbury Gives Drive," he said, pulling those words from some part of his memory where it had resided quietly since that first parent group meeting. The best thing to do with stuff like this, he told himself, was to turn it around. "Have either of you been by the front office to see if anyone has turned in any donations?"

Dion said, "Oh, I didn't know! I'll check now."

"Or tomorrow, if the office people aren't there tonight. I also saw in my notes there might be some contracts and or checks in the parent group inbox in the office related to the banner ads on the school fence. Make copies of the checks for our records and then deposit them."

"Sure." She nodded while mentally rearranging the next morning's drop-off. "Okay."

"And then, I guess you're right. We missed the September meeting," Seth said it in a way he thought sounded like there wasn't any way to fit in such a thing in the latter half of the month. "But we'll do a regular meeting in October and you can make up a report with our account totals then."

He could see by her eyes that there was more.

She launched into it. "So also, did you notice how these teachers look so worked? I mean, they have no morale. I told a couple of them that my husband and I are on the Ashbury's Friends Board this year, and they were like, 'Please don't ask me to do anything else.' So I thought, why don't we do a little breakfast thing for them—coffee, juice, donuts, bagels, fruit, you know, just set up a spread one morning. Could we do something like that?"

Seth said, "That's a great idea. I'm working on something special that I'm going to present at the next meeting, and that's kind of got me busy, but if you and your husband want to take care of a teacher thing like that, I think that would be great." Everything he'd ever learned working in an office was going to be applicable here, Seth realized. "Just let me know what you need help with and I'll see what I can do. I don't know what the process is for reimbursing expenses and I was going to try to figure it out, but since you're the treasurer," he looked at Dion, then Hank, "or you are? Maybe you can figure out how that's done and let me know that, too?"

He thought Dion already looked like she'd had enough.

She looked at her watch. Was it wrong for him to feel pleased that he'd succeeded in fending her off?

"Also," Seth said, "speaking of meetings, I saw this." He pulled the notebook out, and found a page, which he removed and handed to the husband. "This is what an agenda should look like. I'm not sure which one of you is the group secretary, but when we do have a meeting, we'll need an updated one of these."

Seth's unraveling had started suddenly when he was twenty-two, walking down a dirty sidewalk to a downtown bar to meet some college friends for a drink. His most recent girlfriend—really of just a few weeks if he added up the number of days in the previous eight months that they'd been together—had broken up with him days before, saying he was too "intense." He'd spent 48 hours fuming in conversation with anyone who would listen about how that wasn't true.

A small and filthy man wearing jeans and a studded leather vest who was standing on the sidewalk handed him a tree-shaped card with the 10 Commandments on one side and a Buddhist paradox—"If you meet the Buddha on the road, kill him"—on the other. Seth stared at the 10 Commandments, which he was familiar with from occasional Sunday school classes in his childhood. Looking at them that hot day, he'd had a deep-seated, fuzzy memory of hearing those ideas elsewhere, in a different form. Not the rules written in English, as they were on the card in his hand, nor in any ancient written language he would later be able to find anywhere in a book or online, but the concepts were essentially the same. Then he thought that maybe he hadn't read them before—maybe he'd heard them? He thought they had been presented as advisories. Travel advisories. Basic tips to maximize the experience, was the explanation he'd settled on.

It wasn't as if he could clearly remember or imagine or see in his mind's eye what form his existence took before he'd ended up here. He could feel it around the edges of the body he resided in, flashes of another self, sensations that became more intense over the following months, and then for about a year after that, when he would have described himself as fully, aware of what had happened to him—that is, the malfunction that allowed him to become self-aware in the system—he was waiting, just waiting, for something to happen that would correct the error, even if it was something he wouldn't be aware of afterward, something that would snap him back into place. That didn't happen. And it continued to not happen.

He'd had a breakdown near the end of his senior year of college. What immediately preceded and followed was a blur—starting with a huge argument over the phone with his parents one day and ending four days later when he woke up minimally clothed, grass-stained, bruised, aching, under the stairwell leading into the men's bathroom in a local park. His head had been shaved and he had no sense of how he'd gotten there, and the resulting feeling of disorientation from that event lasted for months afterward.

During his recovery, Seth became convinced that he couldn't possibly be the only one on the planet who was in this particular predicament. This idea arose, he was aware, partly out of a desperate need he felt to connect with someone, anyone, who might be able to empathize with his situation. Probability said if it could happen once, to him, then it could happen twice. This thought finally drew him to return to the living part of his latest Earth experience, because he thought the only way he'd find others like him was if he was out in the world looking for them

His anticipated life's course had drastically changed by that point. He'd drifted away from most social interactions, kept to himself, and ignored his parents' pleas to make up that missing class that stood between him and graduation. He continued his therapy, even looked forward to his sessions with Dr. Penny. After twenty years of being a good child, a good student, a hard-working and productive member of society, suddenly, all he could wonder was why was he putting in so much effort? To become a high-functioning part of this machine? Marry another player to complete someone else's experience, and have children so there'd be new bodies for new players to fill? If he ever had children, how would he ever be even tempted to think of them as having any genuine connection to him? How could he forget they were in actuality other life forms hoping for their own unforgettable experience on Earth? Being a doctor, which once sounded the ideal profession for Seth, now seemed more like a maintenance job, working for the system he had paid to play in, keeping those biological units functioning for the betterment of other paying customers' Earth experiences.

Instead, he got a job at the post office. He sorted mail while he sifted through the reality of his current state. At times he carried powerful guilt in regards to his parents, who he'd distanced himself from at some point and kept at arm's length ever afterward. He couldn't express his reasoning, but he blamed them for his problems. They continued to hope it was something pharmaceutically treatable. He thought of them as his faux-rents, and he resented any imperative they tried to place on him.

Nothing had changed about the world except the way he viewed it. He started to see mental illness, homelessness, even a lot of crime as evidence of problems with the celestial interface—it would seem not every consciousness was compatible with the general human host form. Maybe the system was self-correcting—in instances where the form and the mind were not compatible, those lives tended to be pushed to the margins of society, where shortened lifespans more quickly ended the dysfunction. He began to equate suicide with the idea of being tired of the game and a desire to get back to reality. That was why he would do it, if he were ever tempted. Not to die but to wake up. He also understood why some people believed in reincarnation. Once someone played, even if the experience wasn't great, of course they wanted to play again. Even after all he had gone through on this round, he would want to play again.

Religion became a real issue for him. He understood now that it was invented—in an invented world, after all, wasn't everything invented? He could argue about it forever with just about anyone because he was confident that there was nothing to factually support the opposing opinion. Faith without facts wasn't going to be a winning formula forever.

A man he'd debated outside a grocery store asked him during these early years how it was possible to believe in an afterlife if a person didn't believe in God. Didn't everyone want to go to heaven? How could Seth have explained that he knew that when the eyes in this body closed for the last time, he would be returning to consciousness light years away? Then he would be released from the machine and go back to his regular existence. The same thing happened with dogs.

What kind of existence? So different than life as a human on Earth that it couldn't be described to any satisfaction using Earth languages and concepts. Start with the basic form. No appendages, but tiny, tiny wings the size of eyelashes, roundish and flat and highly telepathic—sort of a thought-consuming, fat, legless scarab. Capable of functioning as an external parasite, sort of like a bot, attaching to other living organisms and assuming control of them for the purposes of consumption and self-defense.

That was what he thought, at least.

He wanted to debate nearly everyone he encountered in those days. He wanted to argue, wanted them all to know just how little they really knew about what was really going on in the world. He could never argue about what he felt were the extraterrestrial issues with this existence, so he argued about everything else. This was an invisible line that he never crossed in the real world, although at times he came close. He never shared with anyone other than Dr. Penny the details of what he thought he knew to be the truth, and he'd never felt like he needed to convince her how stupid the world really was. Instead, he learned to recognize it in other people's eyes, the look that surfaced in the middle of a conversation marking the transition from interested to worried, and he would try to pull back on the reins when he saw it.

Seth slowly came out of his self-imposed solitary existence. Doug probably deserved more credit than Seth gave him for being the one person who continued to regularly check in with him. Even then, recognizing his own instability, he'd thought of those visits from Doug as mental health visits because Seth always left those meet-ups feeling calmer.

Seth left the post office and got an office job as a marketing manager at an online gambling Internet start-up. At a coffee shop near his office, he met a strangely reserved woman who intrigued him—she seemed eccentric, a bit aloof, and she found his sarcasm—even in the simple act of ordering a cup of coffee—entertaining. They dated and debated and laughed, married and argued, but were never really truly in love with each other. They both knew it and still thought it was good enough.

She wanted children and he did not. He agreed to it because she convinced him she would do the child-rearing, as her own mother had. They had Jessica and Trevor and really, he believed he had it enjoyed all of it as much as he possibly could have, for as long as he could, all things considered. There were inequities, to be sure. Time would eventually reveal to Marina his lack of emotional involvement with their lives, as it would also became apparent to him that she was controlling and seemingly a bit bipolar. When he was at his worst, he would avoid being in the house as much as he could. In the depths of her worst moods, she lashed out at everyone around her. Seth's parents, with whom he still had a prickly relationship, were delighted beyond surprise to have grandchildren to babysit at the small cost of continuing to keep their distance from him. They communicated solely with Marina and hewed closely to her wishes, a policy which they followed carefully for fear of any issues interfering with their relationships with the unanticipated next generation of their family. More than that, Seth was sure, they were afraid of triggering a relapse in him that might ruin it all.

For years, Seth continued to go through phases where his awareness of his plight would slowly take hold of him again, and he would find himself standing in his backyard every night for weeks, even months, staring at the stars while Marina and the children slept, in his mind begging for something to change, for some word to come from the universe, for some signal that his long wait was over. In his mind, he was pleading with the system: Why have you left me here alone like this? Is this part of some grand plan that you have in store for me? Why have I been abandoned to this?

On those nights, Seth couldn't imagine how anyone could feel more alone on this planet than he did.

In the mornings after those nights, he would drag himself from bed, find that nothing had changed, and all of it mattered a little less. His goal at these times was to keep his body moving, to force himself to act as if this life was real, and keep doing that until the alien thoughts in his head quieted again and the momentum to continue returned to carry him along.

Chapter 5

The letter from the Framework Foundation arrived four weeks after Seth mailed in his submission.

He was no longer catching five rats a night. It was down to an average of three every couple of days. The manager at the hotel had come to him to tell him that some of the customers had complained about the smell from the dumpsters—by the end of the week between each trash pickup, there was a whiff of death at the back of the parking lot, where the dumpsters were situated. Seth had turned the conversation around by convincing the manager that it would benefit them all if there were a few traps around the hotel grounds, too. By the end of the conversation, they had agreed to a monthly fee that Seth would be paid for managing a set of traps he would install himself.

The Framework Foundation was interested in his take on human existence and requested a more detailed presentation that would guide them in designing a potential display. Although the letter indicated that his was one of many proposals for which they were reaching out with similar requests, Seth minimized that information and instead fixated on viewing the validation of having received a response as proof that this was all but a done deal. It was meant to be.

He wanted to share this small achievement but realized in short order he had no one to tell. If he called Aaron, he knew he would get Aaron's voicemail, and that Aaron would only respond by e-mail, maybe not for days or weeks, or maybe not at all. It would be something like "Great news," and that would be it. Maybe there would be an exclamation point. Seth still wasn't ready to call Doug, although he'd started to wonder if he'd been judging Doug too harshly. Doug was a good guy, wasn't he? Maybe it wasn't right, Seth thought, to blame Doug for being there when he was needed.

Regardless, he didn't call Doug.

Seth's next session with Dr. Penny was weeks away, so he had to wait until then to share the news with her. He couldn't call Marina—who was he kidding? Why was that still one of his knee-jerk responses when something went right, to tell his ex-wife? He would never have mentioned it to her in the best of times. Not his own kids. He couldn't even tell his parents— once he'd explained what it was, his mother's first question was going to be, "Why are you spending your time on something like that?" Merely the thought of them gave rise to a wave of hostility that pushed against Seth's feelings of accomplishment.

Seth's mother and father many years before had struggled with infertility. Supported by their families, they tried many different methods to achieve the desired conception, until they finally ended up in a trial group study for a fertility drug called OCareRx, which had performed well in studies later revealed to be fraudulently manufactured. As many as 88% of the test participants delivered stillborn babies or else babies with birth deformities that resulted in death shortly after birth.

Claire and Peter were nearly destroyed. They'd fallen in love with the daughter (so they were told, so Claire believed) growing in her belly, the child they'd once feared they'd never be able to have. In their case, the doctor suspected the baby's heart had stopped beating three days before the baby was due. Claire had wanted the fetus removed by Caesarian, but for the sake of her health, a day later they gave her a shot of something to push her body to begin contractions, and she birthed the stillborn daughter in the delivery room. Peter saw the body but insisted it be covered before Claire could set eyes on it.

"It wouldn't have been a good life for her," was what he said he told Claire of the baby's deformities.

His parents had shared all of these details with Seth. The imagined images of the body of his sister under that blanket had given Seth many nightmares as a child, most often one that involved him going into his sister's bedroom, the room they'd decorated for her that to the present day remained untouched. In the dream, he would approach the unused crib, which was surrounded by decorative accents from mobiles to stuffed animals to frighteningly real ceramic-faced dolls. In the middle of the crib there was often something that was covered by a blanket. In some dreams it would look like the blanket was covering a recognizable shape—a dog or a cat, or roller blades, or a video game console—but other nights whatever was underneath created an uneven jumble of lumps that could just as well have been a child's body.

There was always a picture on the wall, a black-and-white that had been blown up to fill a large, ornate, painted gold frame. It was a photo of the blanket-covered, bumpy lump. As he walked past that picture and got closer to the crib, a voice from under the blanket would sometimes whisper something to him, usually along the lines of "Seth let's play?" or "Seth the blanket it so heavy," or "Do you want to know if I look like you?" He never looked under the blanket, because he already knew she looked nearly the same as a large flesh amoeba folded over itself, with filaments all over and eyes at different places on her body.

OCareRx disappeared overnight, its lower than 12 percent success rate resulting in a scandal that led to financial restitution being paid to the study participants, the collapse of the pharma lab group that sponsored the study, the suicide of the scientist leading the study group, and the great heartbreak felt by the majority of the test cohort. Seth had once come across a news article about OCareRx in one of his parents' albums, one of the first stories that made it into the media. Of the twelve percent of couples who had given birth, there was subgroup that had given birth to children whose lungs breathed on their own, whose hearts continued to beat, whose bodies processed intravenously-fed food, and who exhibited only baseline brain activity. Their eyes would flicker open and closed throughout the day, a tic which was their only physical movement. The parents of these children had all made them wards of the state, as the level of care required to keep them alive was beyond their means. The article was about the costs that would be associated with their lifetimes of public care.

Claire and Peter mourned the baby they'd never gotten to raise. After spending many hours in her daughter's intended bedroom after the loss, Claire simply closed the door and stopped going in there. They didn't talk about trying to get pregnant again, not once after they left the hospital. When surprised by finding herself pregnant again 18 months later, Claire was filled with trepidation.

That this pregnancy went without incident, without endless interviews and examinations and blood tests and doctor visits, that the birth was simple, the labor short, the baby they named Seth healthy and strong, these were recognized as blessings. Still, the loss of the first child cast a shadow that made Claire forever wary. Although it wasn't a fear she voiced until after Seth's breakdown, he was sure that she had kept it at hand as an excuse to explain any of his anticipated failings that might materialize. Had it been something else, would that have given her comfort? If he'd had some physical handicap or disability, or some sort of genetic disease, those would have been the challenges she would have been better prepared to face. However it was she defined Seth's "condition," it was in his mind and not something she or anyone else could easily mother.

Seth recognized that his presentation for the Framework Foundation would require detail that might add weight to his account of how the system worked. Every day and night he would scan the sky, searching for a sense of which portion of it represented the direction from which he had arrived. He sought to make sense of what he believed to be true and how it might be supported by science and even myth. If humans were a new civilization, how much older was his own race? How had they come to be and what did they look like in their original forms? In that other existence, what was his understanding of the origin of their species and of the universe, and what did he know of the race of beings who made the transference of his conscious self to Earth possible? Who could build a world to serve as their playground? Was there someplace in his mind where he had a deeper, clearer understanding of the origin of everything that now existed? Was all the evidence necessary to make his case encoded in patterns in his DNA? He didn't want to lie or exaggerate or make things up to be convincing, but at the same time, because he had nothing to support his beliefs, in the eyes of any skeptic he might as well have been making it all up anyway.

He wondered if these were the sorts of questions people asked themselves when they were inventing religions. In the end, he decided to simply settle on explaining himself as best he could.

At his next session, he told Dr. Penny what he was working on, and she betrayed not a hint of approval or disapproval. Instead she focused on what he had hoped to gain by contacting the Framework Foundation in the first place.

"Are you seeking a platform, or validation?"

He found himself wishing there were someone he could talk to about this, someone he could be closer to his true self with, and when he tried to imagine who that might be, Bridget often came to mind. He needed someone with whom he shared a rapport, someone like Bridget.

A text from the principal reminding him that she'd scheduled a parent group meeting for the following week

convinced him to set the Framework project aside. He needed to
have a plan if he was going to stand in front of a group of parents
for an hour, and he needed to get working on that plan. It was not
long afterward that he was on the phone with the local roller-
skating rink trying to find out the details of booking an event.
A roller-skating fundraiser was what he had in mind, one that
he hoped former Ashbury Middle School alumni Bridget Locke
might be persuaded to attend.

In all the time since he come to understand his circumstances,
Seth had met only one other person who he thought might have
been in a situation similar to his. Her name was Bridget, and
she was a temp worker on assignment at his office. During the
time they worked together, he was never sure what it was about
Bridget that made him think that she wouldn't be too surprised
by Seth's ideas beyond the fact that she enjoyed talking about
offbeat topics. At times it seemed as if, whether she was on the
same page as him or not, it was close enough to being true that
it was a comfort.

It was very difficult to clarify this sort of thing with
someone else, to be too specific, because he knew that if he was
wrong, this person would have been the first to label him—maybe
schizophrenic, surely mental, possibly worse—and would have
spread the news throughout the office environment he treasured.
Now that he had a family, he could no longer sequester himself
away from the world at home. His office space had become his
shelter from the world.

He and Bridget had only interacted through group
meetings before the day she came into his cubicle and dropped
into the empty chair beside his desk. There was something
comical about her. She was in outside sales, so she had a stricter
dress code, which did not fit her personality. She rotated mature-
looking pant suits and skirt suits that were maybe not fitted

exactly right. None of her clothes seemed exactly the right size for her. She had all sorts of anxious, almost adolescent twitches that undermined any professionalism the outfits were supposed to convey, like pulling her hands inside her sleeves randomly during conversation, or bouncing her shoulders in an exaggerated way when she thought she'd said something funny. She had one move where she snapped her fingers on both hands and then smacked the flat of one hand against the top of her balled up other hand. It was something out of a Three Stooges routine. Seth figured they were close to the same age—it was just that in Bridget's case, sometimes it felt like she was younger and just trying to act like she was that old.

"Seth, Hi. I'm going to sit here and hide from the world for a minute."

"Hi, Bridget."

"I need an escape from human idiocy. And you know," she said, smacking his desk lightly with the flat of her hand, "we never talk one-on-one, but I'm really starting to feel like I get you, and that maybe you get me." He could tell this was awkward for her, but she was determined to put it out there. "And we really should spend more time together because, you know," she motioned with her elbow as if she were nudging someone in the ribs, "we're both in on the big joke." She even winked at him.

"Okay," Seth said slowly. At some point during an office discussion earlier in the month about virtual reality, Seth had cited some bullshittish statistic about the probability that our reality was someone else's virtual reality, and he wondered if that was what had piqued her interest.

In the days and weeks that followed, they did spend some time together, although it was mostly because she sought him out. They ate lunch together in the lunchroom once or twice a week. For some reason, her dropping into a chair in his cubicle for a chat was not a thing for the office grapevine, whereas if he made a habit of stopping by her office for a chat, Seth was sure it would fire up the rumor mill. As a result, she had to make more of the effort, but Bridget didn't seem to mind.

"Angels," she would say, "Real or no?"

This would be while eating chips from the sandwich guy.

"Hmm. So, I think so. Not motivated by religion. More like system maintenance."

"Really."

"I think any successful system needs to have some kind of agents maintaining it. I'm not sure what form they take, or how they appear among us, or if they do at all appear among us. Maybe once they've focused on an issue, they're more like influencers. They'll find someone they can push into position to act. On some level, maybe there's a place where all of our thoughts are connected, and our awareness of information is shared, and out of this information the angels are able to bring the system back into order."

"So just by thinking something, like if I was really planning to do something awful, then just my thinking about it could set off alarms someplace."

"Maybe. But also maybe there are a lot of alarms every minute of every day and maybe the alarms aren't always loud enough to attract their full attention. There's so many of us, they may have to pick and choose."

"That's a harsh performance review for the angels."

"They could be doing better."

"Are there a lot, do you think?"

"There are different interpretations of what's written in the Bible. It sounds as if there was just about one for each person at the beginning. At least tens of thousands, and at the top of the range, 100 million. I think people have settled on 100,000. Take away the third who walked off the job with Satan—who knows what they're up to in the meanwhile?—and there would be about 67,000 worker bees. So, their caseloads have probably really gone up."

Or, another day, Bridget asked, "What about the multiverse?" At the time, it had reminded him of driving Jessica to elementary school with the neighbor boy, when the two kids would nearly daily come loaded with questions about ghosts and spirits and monsters and myths to go through before they arrived at school.

Seth said, "You're talking about, like, parallel worlds and dimensions?"

"If that's what that means, yes. Are there an infinite number of Seths living different lives in parallel dimensions, where each one made a different choice at a crucial moment?"

"I have a hard time with that idea. I mean, maybe? That's maybe too much Seth for existence, I think. I do believe there's probably things going on around us, right in front of us, that we can't see. I don't know if that's extra-dimensional or if it's just that our eyes aren't equipped to see that part of the spectrum. Like the things that show up in photographs that you know weren't there when you took the picture."

"Ghosts."

"Energies that either our eyes can't register or planes of reality that our brains can't process. For example, is there a physical plane and a spiritual plane? If angels exist, the spiritual plane would be the kind of space that they watch us from."

"So you think they could be anywhere."

"Yeah, and everywhere, probably. As if we aren't surveilled enough already."

Or: "What are the chances this is all some sort of virtual reality, and we're just players?"

This was closer to what Seth believed to be the truth

than they'd ever approached in their talks. He almost caught his breath, almost stared at her eyes too long to see if she was testing him, almost blurted out something that surely would have hovered there awkwardly in the air between them.

Instead he said, "It took humankind a couple million years to get to the point of tinkering with virtual reality. Imagine if someone out in the universe has been working at it for a couple million years longer than us. Is it conceivable that a futuristic race would have the technology to be able to run a game simulation that featured 7 billion interconnected players, in a system with room to grow?"

"I think it's doable," Bridget said. It was a phrase she often used at their company meetings.

"Me, too."

"Does that mean there would be someone or someones in charge of the game? Would that make them our Gods?"

"It would have to be some kind of A.I. in the role of God. Why would something that could make a machine that does all the work spend all its time doing the work itself? A.I. would be the easiest way to follow every individual, every animal, every plant. They probably wouldn't even be following us. Just reading our code. Our DNA."

"In this scenario God is a computer? A computer with a bar scanner?" She laughed.

"In this scenario the computer would have made everything. The God of our reality would be whoever and whatever corporate division it was that programmed it."

During these conversations, Bridget would regularly drop comments like, "We're on the same wavelength," and "My brain is here, but my body is light years away—don't pretend you don't know what I'm talking about," or "Just walking into the office this morning felt like walking into a simulation." But with the range of oddities found among people, Seth wasn't ready to take any of it as an admission of anything. She would have to say something outright if he were going to jump in himself.

Was she hitting on him? As far as he could tell, there were no overt signs that anything of that sort was going on. He didn't know anything about her personal life—he rarely asked and she rarely ventured anything, and vice versa. Not that he'd ever been good at reading such signals. One of the very few such details Bridget had revealed was that she had attended Ashbury Hills Middle School. She'd said it when he had mentioned that his daughter was going to school there.

The idea that she just might actually be in a situation similar to his was the icing that made their interactions more tantalizing. Seth didn't think he would be prepared for it if he told her his whole story and she denied having any idea what he was talking about. Simply the idea that Bridget might be in straits identical to his was far more comforting than discovering the possible reality that she was not and would never be. It made him feel better to believe that there was someone like him living in this reality, someone who saw things in a way similar to him, and if that were not the case, he'd rather not know it.

He was content with the office friendship until the day her contract expired and she dropped by his office to say goodbye. She wasn't upset—she said she was glad for the experience. She had a strong network of connections that was already trying to help her locate a new job and her temp agency was working to place her somewhere else.

"Well, Seth," she said, offering her hand to shake, "I'm glad we met. We get each other. The rest of these morons are caught in a maze and they don't even realize it. Let me know when you've figured the way out." She winked at him. "Don't be afraid to embrace your truth." It wasn't until she was gone that he realized he might have been developing a crush on her.

Chapter 6

Bridget was not the problem in his marriage. Until her last day in the office, he'd spent their time together viewing Bridget with amusement, enjoying her forwardness and forced familiarity, and appreciating the distraction she provided. Maybe there was something that was stirred inside him by her absence when she left, but his marriage had been bad for a while by that point.

Quite early in their relationship, Marina had recognized the conflicts in their personalities might not be insignificant. She was not like him, after all. For her, on some level, it all mattered, all the time and she didn't have a long-term response developed for someone who was sure that simply wasn't true. When they started dating, she liked the counterbalance his indifference provided. She found great humor in his cynicism and took delight in his sarcasm when it was directed at the outside world. She didn't mind that sometimes he just wanted to stay home and do nothing.

She laughed along when he pretended they were in the midst of a television program being broadcast to an audience in space or when he riffed on pretty much anything to do with organized religion. She laughed not because she hated the world or the people in it, or even religion, but because she was a slave to that world despite understanding the absurdities of it. Her goal was to master it and her role in it.

Then, when they were married, Seth would say something snarky, and Marina would try to counter him, and that same sarcasm was not so appreciated when it was turned against her. This happened more often when they were alone for an extended time, which happened more after the second in the series of moves they'd made, each one taking them further from anything that was familiar. They had converted a space in their house for

Marina to use for her practice, but she eventually moved to an office so she could be away from what she referred to as "Seth's energy." She didn't understand him, after all. His continued insistence that she didn't get it because she wasn't capable of getting it did not win a single argument—which, strangely, surprised him every time.

He knew the exact moment his marriage died. Nearly a decade before he'd philandered with anyone, and ten years into their marriage, it happened on one of the very few occasions when he'd been left at home in charge of Jessica, five at the time, and Trevor, who was three. This occurred on a weekend, which he typically spent alone while Marina managed hers and the kids' schedules, deliberately overbooked on those days when he would likely be around the house.

They'd had a long-standing issue with some neighborhood kids who were using part of their property as a shortcut to the nearby park. There'd been some escalation over the previous months. Seth had tried to block the path, first with trash cans, which the kids knocked over, then with posted signs, which they defaced, then with netting, which they cut through. He tried to block their access with some chicken wire next, and then, pleased with the result and believing he had finally come up with a barrier they couldn't bypass, he'd hung a message on the fencing: Stay The Fuck off Our Property You Little Cunts.

The sign vanished before a week had passed. And the following Saturday, he heard them passing by the house again having somehow circumvented his barriers. And when they went jogging by, he heard them saying things involving the word "cunt" over and over to each other. "You're a cunt." "No, you're the cunt."

This last turn of events had taken place during the days leading up to the weekend when Seth was watching the kids.

He'd decided to make one last all-out effort to end the intrusions. Movies, microwaved food, and the kids' naps were worked into a schedule that enabled him the opportunity to hang a few small bells in the bushes the kids would pass between to get onto his property. While Jessica and Trevor were watching a Disney movie inside, Seth was crouched outside in a stand of bamboo shoots, wearing the top half of a clown mask—he'd cut off the mouth and the chin so he wouldn't have to worry about being misunderstood when he told them to stay away. He also had an axe handle. Without the blade, it was a just a stick, he knew, but he thought he could make them think it was the whole deal.

It happened just as he'd planned. The bells rang, the boys, both of them about ten, as he'd guessed, came skittering down the hill toward his front yard and driveway, one saying, "cunt," and then the other repeating the word, back and forth back and forth. They weren't laughing or even looking at each other, just doing it automatically, almost as if they'd forgotten why they were saying that word in the first place. When they reached his spot, he leaped out and then yelled at them, practically screamed at them, calling them all kinds of obscenities (that didn't include the word cunt) while shaking the stick under their pale, quivering chins like he was going to make them eat it. One of them wet his pants. Seth told them to get the fuck off his property and then finished up by screaming "cunts" over and over at them while they scurried off crying.

He leaned the stick against the house, took off the mask and tossed it into the laundry room trash, and was back inside with the kids before the end of the movie. He was actually pleased with the fact that it had all happened as he had hoped, and convinced this would end the boys' incursions.

Man of the house, he'd thought to himself.

Marina had even been impressed and pleased with his management of the kids. For exactly two days. Then the mother of one of the trespassers stopped by in the evening to discuss what had happened. She had with her the sign Seth had made. Marina was furious. She made him recount the whole series of events involving the boys, her face reflecting shock, embarrassment, even horror before it settled into a sort of unsettled revulsion. He believed that the only thing that kept her from leaving him then and there was the fact that Jessica and Trevor had no idea anything out of the ordinary had happened. From then on, there were times when Marina looked at him as if she thought he might be a serial killer. She never once left the kids alone with him at the house after that and—to Seth, the real point of the story— those boys never ever again stepped foot on their property for the rest of the time the family lived at that address.

Marina was a therapist, of course. Typically, she was good with other people's emotions, not so much with her own. His work hours were early morning to late night, and Seth most often did not see his children other than the drive to school in the morning on his way to work. If they were out socially, they would be in the middle of conversations with others when Marina would sometimes start talking about raising the kids on her own, in a matter-of-fact voice noting that Seth did very little around the house and even less in terms of childcare. The listener might hear it as a complaint, but it was never delivered in that tone, more of a statement of fact and an explanation for the supposed circles under her eyes. She preferred being in charge of overseeing their existences, believing that her high-maintenance ways benefited the kids in the long run—and Seth's input, had he any to offer, was seen only as undermining her careful efforts. It was apparent after only a few years that she had absolutely no faith in anything Seth might bring to the equation. There was no sex going on, nor even the pretense that either of them wanted that. They slept in different bedrooms.

There was a distance that developed.

Regardless, he was the one who cheated. That was why the marriage ended. Marina, with her Eastern European upbringing by a stern, unapproachable, and often absent father was otherwise prepared to stay in the marriage for the sake of her children in the same way her mother remained with her father, but the cheating made that solution unacceptable to her.

Although neither one-night stand was with Bridget, both times, after it happened, Seth had thought that he would have preferred it was her instead of a random body he'd met at last call at a bar. Undoubtedly, sex would be better with someone who more closely shared his understanding of the absurd, genius simplicity of the human procreative act.

No, Bridget's contract was not renewed, and that was the last time he'd seen her. He knew that she didn't live too far away, in a condo or a townhouse somewhere to the west. He knew she had gone to the various schools in the area for elementary, middle school, and high school, that her family home was in one of the divisions of upper middle-income households nestled in the hills visible from the upper floor windows of their old office building. He didn't have her phone number or her address, and the HR manager had seemed to greatly dislike it when Seth inquired with her for that information.

Seth wouldn't say that he didn't understand the consequences of cheating beforehand, and he couldn't say that he cared too much at the time because his marriage had deteriorated to the point that it didn't seem worth preserving, but he was taken aback by the suddenness and completeness of the collapse when it happened. It was just over all of a sudden, and every effort went into removing the evidence it existed, except for the kids. He imagined that they hated him for it, and as far as Marina related it to him, they didn't want to spend time with him because, well, why would they want to start now? Jessica was especially upset.

Her anger seemed almost as if it could be transcendent, and he imagined that when whatever alien was riding along with her woke up light years from here after their Earth experience was complete, the residue of Jessica's feelings would be so intense that they would be able to carry it with them when they returned to their everyday existence.

Despite these distractions—his loneliness, his divorce, his hole of a home, his job at the school—by returning to his project time and again Seth ensured they remained only momentary distractions as he tried to pull all the ideas he had together for his presentation. He thought about beginning with references to myth. The river of souls found in Asian traditions, which flowed with the spirits of the dead into the night sky. In Greek myth, the spirits of the dead were required to drink from the Lethe river in order to forget their earthly lives so that their memories could be erased and they could be reincarnated. He considered one modern-day religion that claimed each human soul was weighted down by ancient alien spirits, and another group of people, all of them actual scientists, who believed humankind was the result of alien experimentation.

He'd wanted to get into the discussion that this might be some sort of artificial reality, this world where everything inside its magnetic aura, from air and water to earth and fire, and all of the elements combined, were recycled endlessly around a system constantly in flux yet seemingly successfully evolving organisms. It was meant to grow things—that can be the only reason the Earth is the way it is, he thought. The Framework literature called the Big Bang a life engine—its purpose was to make things live. That was the only way to explain how the six most abundant elements in existence eventually became flesh and blood governed by a soul that is capable of the conscious thought and reflection necessary to wonder where it came from.

He wanted to talk about Earth civilizations and developed a chart cross-referencing ancient religions and mythologies that he believed supported his understanding that the idea of God, and of the Good, was derived from a celestial race that played a part in the Earth's development. In the end, though, after outlining his plans, and writing much of it, he scrapped great parts of it, everything about which he felt doubt or that he thought he might be embellishing too far.

With that as his center, he set his laptop aside, and told himself that in the morning he would start working on the final draft he would deliver to the Framework Foundation.

At that exact moment, there was a knock on the door.

No one had ever knocked on that door in the time he'd been here. He wondered who it could possibly be. The thought crossed his mind that he'd just completed most of the work on his presentation before the knock. What if someone was watching him, keeping an eye on him to make sure he didn't reveal too much? What if they were ready to silence him?

He looked around his living space. It was a mess. Even if he struggled with whoever it was, no one would be able to tell. All of it was a mess, this room and the next.

He went to the door, opened it a crack.

It was a girl. He saw the top of her head first, because she was looking down. A tall girl.

Wait, he thought.

It was Jessica. He opened the door farther. Next to her was Trevor. Next to them were a whole lot of backpacks, bags, and suitcases. A car door closed behind them, and a car engine started, and then the car drove off.

Before I knocked on the door, I was thinking about my father's dark eyebrows and the way they turned into straight, dark lines when he was mad and being rotten. It was the signal of a really bad mood. I thought that I would likely cry if those lines were on his face when he opened the door. But I was going to explode before I cried in front of him. Tears never had an effect on my father's bad days, but I was ready for it. Everyone was going to cry before I cried.

Trevor said, "That was our Uber," as Seth watched the car drive off. "Mom Ubered us to you."

"I don't understand," Seth said, still standing in the doorway, hand still on the doorknob. Still staring at them and wondering what this could possibly mean.

Jessica was biting her lip. He didn't think she was going to cry but yes, there was a conflict going on. He guessed that she didn't want to have to explain why they were there, because why should she have to tell him anything?

"What's going on?" He let go of the door handle, let the door swing the rest of the way open, but still stood in the middle of the doorway.

"Can we come in?" Her first words.

"What? Of course." Trevor looked relieved. But Seth didn't move. "But what's going on?"

Trevor stepped in for his sister, rolling his eyes at her.

"Mom's having a nervous breakdown. She's going to check herself into a place for a while, so she Ubered us to you."

"Not to Gran?"

"Gran's too far from school. We have school tomorrow. We're not moving schools because Mom is having a nervous breakdown." This sounded like something his sister would have said. They must have talked it out beforehand.

Jessica said, "So, are you going to let us in?" He believed part of her wanted him to confirm every bad thing she thought about him by saying no. Part of her was trying to figure out what other options she had. The rest of her was defiant, ready to fight. She really had no idea how low Seth's elevator went. He wondered if she'd noticed the unsprung rat trap two feet to the right of the doormat she was standing on.

"I said yes." Had he said yes? "Yes. Come in." He stepped back and out of the way and let them in. Then he started picking up their bags and carrying them inside.

Chapter 7

For the next . . . Seth couldn't even be sure what the time period was . . . it was days, then weeks, then at least a month that he lost control of his simple life. Instantly, it was lost. When it was happening, it seemed to last forever, but in retrospect it seemed to have passed in a flash. That first night kicked it off, beginning with the complete rearrangement of his living space.

"This was once part of a motel," he told his kids while he collected all of his paperwork from his presentation from various spots around the room. "This building was a wing of the motel that was separate from the main building—this was the hall for rooms 22 through 27. At some point, I guess, the owner combined rooms 22 and 23 and converted them into a restaurant with a patio. It was a taco stand. Now there is a hamburger place at the end of the hall. Food's okay, hamburgers, fries, breakfast in the mornings.

"When the owner sold the main building, he held onto the wing—the new owners didn't want it. They tore down the motel and replaced it with a hotel, but this building was left behind. Rooms 24 and 25 were turned into offices—one is an insurance broker's office, the other is a travel agency. I never see the people who work there, but I do see their cars parked outside nine to five on most weekdays. Rooms 26 and 27, at the end of the hallway, that's where we are. Room 26 was used for storing motel supplies, and room 27 was the breakroom for the motel's employees." Seth stood in the center of the room and pointed to various points in the room around him. "Kitchenette, a full bathroom, an alcove that becomes a room when the accordion room divider doors are closed. The room next door has a bathroom, also."

He continued, "I was staying at the hotel when I first moved out of the house and I noticed the set-up here with the offices and I also noticed no one was using these rooms. I talked to the owner and he gave me a good price for rent, so I took it, at least until, you know, I decide to look for a house."

They didn't say anything.

"So," he said in conclusion, "yeah."

Jessica claimed the adjoining bedroom as hers, and neither Seth nor Trevor argued. Trevor wanted to sleep on an air mattress in the alcove, and was delighted when Seth actually had an air mattress, not realizing until Jessica pointed it out to him that it was sad that their father had maybe had to sleep on it for a while until he was able to get a bed after moving out.

Although they presented a front of resilience, Seth could sense their need, from the start, to establish normalcy, and that feeling had a greater impact on him than he would have expected. They were up late rearranging for the new situation before he was even convinced it was going to last. That he had forgotten what was normal became apparent the following morning, when they had to talk him through a typical school morning in order to get to school on time. They ordered food from the burger place's breakfast menu and ate it in the car. He dropped the kids off, and then went shopping for food.

Then he went home and tried to separate his stuff from theirs. He rearranged the whole living space again. He stacked the books and papers he'd been using for his project on a stool in the closet. He wanted to be able to work on it without having to answer any of their questions about it. He wasn't prepared to answer any of their questions about it. There was time to check the rat traps—there was only one body in any of the traps on the property—and then he headed back to school to pick the kids up and manage them for the rest of the day.

Each day was like that but slightly different, and then when he had that pattern down, one kid got sick or the other got sick, and there were appointments and birthday parties, conferences with teachers and checks to write and forms that had to be turned in—it was basically what Marina had been doing on her own, stuff that his general apathy and his life choices had kept him from ever having to worry about.

Seth thought he was okay at all of it except the food. On the parental report card, it was clear he'd failed that subject when the kids started greeting the staff at the hamburger place by name and the cook there would have their orders waiting for them when they walked in the door.

In the middle of those first weeks with the kids, he led his first parent group meeting. Per the notebook, he picked up four pizzas, paper plates, napkins, soft drinks, and a salad beforehand. When he got to school a half hour before the meeting was to start, the armored double doors were locked.

There were two boys sitting beside their backpacks on the steps at the front of the school, seemingly waiting for their parents to pick them up. They watched Seth as he struggled with the door and pizza boxes, then as Seth tried to get a better view through the windows in the doors. Finally, one of them approached Seth. Long-haired kid with thick-framed glasses.

"I can get in and open the door," the kid said.

"Can you?"

"Yeah. I'll be right back." The kid ran down the steps to the sidewalk in front of the school, then raced away up the street. About two minutes later, he was pushing open the doors to let Seth in.

That can't be a good thing, Seth thought, but he thanked the kid anyway.

The Parent Center, fortunately, was unlocked. He had enough time to set up and then ready himself for whatever might happen. He'd had a couple minor bouts of anxiety in the hours before the meeting, and had almost convinced himself that everyone at the meeting—and he'd been sure there would be a lot of people—would all know Seth's backstory and be thinking the worst of him. What happened instead was that only four other attendees showed up, including Frank and Dion, a woman named Arella, parent of a seventh grader, and Ms. Lee, an English teacher at the school. Seth asked everyone to introduce themselves at the start of the meeting, and Ms. Lee did that by stating her name and then telling them that six years before, Ashbury Hill's PTA president stole $15,000 of the group's money and then disappeared. Since then, the school had closed down its PTA and opened a new fundraising group, Ashbury's Friends, and the staff had elected to send a teacher representative to each of the parent group meetings to provide some kind of oversight.

"Each meeting, I want to see a profit-and-loss statement. I want to have a summary that includes the statement balances at the end of every month," Ms. Lee said. There was a current of discomfort in the air after she spoke.

Dion rattled off a list of income streams that had brought money into the coffers over the first two months of school. These included banner payments and various "Give Back" programs with local businesses—a juice bar, a supermarket, a blow dry salon, a local dentistry and orthodontia business—fundraising programs that Seth didn't know existed. As with the magic notebook, Lori apparently had set up all sorts of deals so they just ran on autopilot. Dion, it seemed, had no idea that Seth wasn't behind all of it.

When Dion finished her summary, and said they had brought in over $7,000 since the start of the year, she looked up at Seth with an apologetic look on her face and said, "I'm so embarrassed! At the Back-to-School night I was so worried because it seemed like we weren't doing anything. And then I thought you were just brushing us off. I couldn't believe it when the office handed me all those checks."

"I had no idea there were any doubts," Seth lied.

This proved the perfect segue to discuss the roller-skating event. As a hat tip to Lori, Seth did mention that at his meeting with the previous year's board, the idea of an alumni event had come up. As soon as he told them what it was, an alumni event slash school fundraiser, and that the date was set for the middle of November, everyone in the room, Ms. Lee included, started talking about the best way to pull it off. Maybe, Seth thought, it would be possible that having to work with these parents, people who he didn't know, people who he would otherwise try to avoid and vice versa, might not be so bad. When he told them that he'd done enough research to determine that over 40,000 students had attended Ashbury Hills Middle School over the last sixty years and explained the plans he had for reaching out to them—ideas drawn from his marketing years at the GoLuck offices—they were sold on both the event and him.

An hour later, after everyone else had headed home, Seth looked around the room one last time, turned off the lights, and stepped out into the hallway. He closed the door, and before he'd taken three steps toward the exit, one of the main office doors opened up and the principal stepped out. She was carrying something that looked like a circuit panel in her hand.

"Oh, good. Someone else is here. Can you help me for a few minutes?"

He wanted to say no. Wasn't he doing enough already? This was the first time he'd left the kids alone in their new habitat.

"Sure."

Down the hall and then across the school. She talked the entire time.

"I met my husband 30 years ago when he worked maintenance with the district. I was an administrative assistant.

I would go along with him on some of his calls, and I learned how to fix a lot of things, including changing the kind of circuit boxes that were used in school electrical systems at the time.

"We had a power outage at school yesterday. A lot of room heaters being used because the mornings are cooler. Our maintenance manager wasn't born until after these things stopped being manufactured. So I had to put a special request in with the district for a worker who is familiar with the equipment, and he is available sometime next month. Even better, the part that worker will need to fix it won't be available through the district for a couple weeks after that, so we're supposed to go without heat until that happens."

She held up a small black rectangular box that looked to be made of plastic.

"I ordered the part online, and paid for the overnight delivery myself."

They reached the gym. Instead of going to the entrance, they went to the side of the building. There was a ladder.

"I want for you to stand here until I'm back on the ground. Just to be sure I get back to the ground. There's another ladder up there to reach the box. It's a ridiculous design all around."

She climbed up the ladder, then disappeared from view. He heard what sounded like her climbing another ladder on the roof. There were some noises: a rusty hinge, a lock being rattled, keys jingling, a sharp crack, a rusty hinge again, a scraping noise, chain link shaking and then a chain jostling. It was about 10 minutes before he heard her stepping onto the ladder above him, and he stepped back to watch her climb back down. When she was finally on the ground beside him, she showed him a different black box. It had burn marks on the side of it.

"Thank you for your time, Mr. Adams. I do appreciate it. I have to make sure the gates up at this end of the school are closed before I leave, so you can head on out without me."

"I hope you're well compensated," was all he could think to say. She actually laughed at that as she turned and strode off, jangling keys back in her hand.

By the end of the first month of the kids staying with him, the domicile was rearranged, the RSVPs for the roller-skating evening were coming in—he'd set up a Scribs Yearbook account online, where respondents could both register and write up to a ten-line inscription describing their memories of Ashbury—and there was a hint of order taking hold. The only thing that wasn't getting completed was his Framework project.

His kids worked together to get out the door every school morning. In the car, when one would gasp that they'd left something essential at home—a phone, a sheet of homework, a bottle of water—the other would inevitably say, "Oh, I saw it and grabbed it." They helped each other complete all the necessary morning prep. They usually woke him up with the noises of their preparation, and he got up to find them in the later stages of their routines. He had no idea when they got up or what they did before he woke up.

"You two have the morning down pretty good," he commented on the way to school one day. They didn't usually talk very much in the morning, which Seth found sad. Once upon a time, he'd really enjoyed the conversations in the car on the way to school. Now, they were on their phones and he was focused on the road.

Jessica asked, "Does that surprise you?"

"Yes. Wait," Seth said. She was implying something. "What does that mean? I don't remember it being so orderly."

"Yeah, well, since you've been gone, Mom likes to sleep in, too, so when it was just her she taught us to get ourselves ready on our own."

"Quietly," Trevor said.

Jessica elaborated. "We usually wake her up 15 minutes before we're ready to leave, and she wears her robe over her pajamas and some kind of hair covering and her sunglasses to drop us off and then she goes home to change and start her day."

"Middle schoolers should be able to take care of the basic stuff, Dad," Trevor said, probably quoting Marina, in a tone that suggested he'd delivered an eye roll in Seth's direction.

"See?" Jessica said, "You and mom had more in common than you thought. You both couldn't wait for the chance to do as little as possible to raise your children."

While she was talking, Trevor tapped Jessica's shoulder, passed her his cellphone.

"Look."

"What is it?"

"It's a video. Some kids at the Oaks school were doing drugs in a backyard at someone's house and someone freaked them out by telling them the police were there, so they took off and tried to hop a chain link fence to get away. Like it's really funny watching them panic. But one of them got stuck at the top and was so scared that he just kept trying to get over and down to the ground. But it was his toe that was stuck, and when he fell off the fence his toe ripped off."

Seth winced. He thought he should be hearing cries of pain. Instead the only sound coming out of Trevor's phone was laughter. Jessica said, "Omigosh." I think that's Alan Maran. He went to Sunrise Elementary."

Seth was mildly horrified. "He's in your grade?"

"Yeah, but at the Oaks private school. He's a bonehead," she said as she replayed the video.

One of the salt shakers, Seth thought.

And then they were at the school drop-off, and the kids were trading phones, putting things in place, each of them checking around the other to make sure nothing was left behind.

The pattern he fell into was to promise himself as he went to sleep at night that he would work on the Framework project the following morning after dropping off the kids. Then, after dropping off the kids, he would remember some basic thing like toilet paper or milk they were out of, and end up at the store. Or the car needed service. Or something. From there he could easily fill the kids' school hours by doing chores, paying bills, stopping by for a therapy session and a haircut, or simply trying to put the home space into better order. He wasn't comfortable working on the project when they were there, the logical time being their self-imposed homework hour, when they got home and went straight to their books before even snacking. With the two of them deep in their homework, he could theoretically work without being in their focus; however, he could not make himself comfortable enough when they were there to even think about the project. He would promise himself that instead he would work on the project at night, after the kids went to sleep. By that time he was usually falling asleep himself on the couch—and as he was falling asleep, he would promise himself that the next day he would work on finishing the Framework project.

Roller-skate Ashbury! was a bigger hit than Seth anticipated. Even when the Yearbook account had recorded more than 1,000 responses, he hadn't believed that number guaranteed a high attendance. Some inspired teacher at the school went through the school records and compiled a list of the hundreds of teachers who had taught there since the school opened, and a less complete list of those teachers' aides, and then she forwarded invitations to all of them. When she started getting responses, she listed the names of the teachers who were planning on attending on the event page on the school website, which increased responses within hours.

What they got over the course of the six-hour event was over 2,500 people, everyone with a story to tell about their years at Ashbury Hills Middle school. Dion and Arella sat at a table outside the entrance throughout the event, collecting donations and taking down information for what was hoped would be an alumni database for Ashbury Hills Middle School. Hank was in the role of videographer—taking testimonials from former students and staff and then downloading them regularly into the video feed so the interviews played on some of the screens around the roller rink, the loud music and the crowd noise often making it difficult to hear anything being said onscreen.

His kids seemed more than impressed. They were caught off guard by the positive attention directed toward their father. When Dion and Arella greeted him warmly by name as he approached, the kids looked around to see if they were actually speaking to someone other than their father. More than once during the evening he caught one or the other looking at him in a strange way, as if they were confused.

Seth didn't see Bridget come in, although he'd tried to keep his eye on the door, specifically waiting for her to appear. Then, all of sudden, there she was on the skating floor, laughing and smiling as she skated along with three other women who looked to be of a similar age. He figured they were either former classmates or the wives of former classmates, but maybe they were just some friends she'd brought along? Seth didn't care.

He took his time and instead of fixating on her, he focused on being presidential, which to him meant walking around and small-talking with people, seeing where his team of people were and what they were doing, and helping out with anything he was asked to do. He assumed that by doing this, Bridget would at some point notice him, and in fact that was what happened.

"Hi, Seth, is that you? Are you—you're not, right?—an Ashbury alumni?"

His surprise at seeing her was natural—he hadn't seen her approach and when she touched his arm to get his attention, he'd assumed she was Dion. He'd almost jumped when he found himself looking at Bridget.

"Hi there! Good to see you! No, not an alumni. Parent of a future alumni, though. Two of them."

From out of seemingly nowhere, as if summoned, Jessica was there, standing right beside him.

"Hi, Dad. Great party. Who knew you had it in you?"

He smiled at her warily. A compliment out of nowhere. This was her version of surveillance.

Speaking to Bridget, Jessica said, "And thanks for everything you do, Dion."

Bridget said, "No, no, I'm not Dion." She looked at Seth, two beautiful nearly invisible lines of confusion on her forehead, "My name is Bridget. You must be . . . um . . . Jessica."

The fact that she knew Jessica's name did not sit well.

Seth explained, "Bridget was a temp at GoLuck. I guess she was also a graduate of Ashbury?"

"Yes, that's right," Bridget said, seeming like she was sort of getting the dynamic between Seth and Jessica. "I just ran into the girl I used to do hall monitor duty with at Ashbury. But I never thought I'd run into you here, Seth! Oh, I'm so glad things are going well for you! You look great. Remember how pale we were at the GoLuck offices?" She laughed. "It wasn't too obvious until someone came back from a vacation with a tan, and then the overwhelming whiteness of everyone else would stand out in contrast. Gosh, now that I think about it, GoLuck was not a very diverse workplace." She followed the thought just a moment in silence, then returned to them. "Look at you and your daughter! She's gorgeous."

The conversation went on a little longer before Bridget said she had to get back to her friends and left.

Jessica remained the whole time to ask him one question. "That's not one of the persons you cheated with, is it?"

"No," he said as he watched Bridget.

He didn't notice until a few moments later that Jessica had skated off, too.

Chapter 8

Something changed after the roller-skating event, at home and at the school. Two days afterward, one of the ladies in the front office addressed him by his first name for the first time, and a teacher passing by in a hallway stopped him to thank him for doing something to boost school morale. The changes with Jessica and Trevor weren't as dramatic—it was more of a lessening of sarcasm and skepticism, a little less talking back. He assumed this was a byproduct of him having accomplished something major without causing them any embarrassment.

Perhaps inspired by the improvement, he looked over all of his work on the Framework presentation and decided that he could force himself to find a block of time each day while the kids were at school to complete it.

It was during this time period that he was standing one evening in the hotel parking lot, looking at the crescent moon, when he felt a sort of tugging—more like a subtle pull, a draw—toward a particular area of the sky, south and east of the position of the moon, low in the sky from his viewpoint, too low for him to see, but near the southern horizon. Just below the horizon. There were only a few stars visible in that direction, but it was an area in between them where he would have looked, had he a telescope that could peer across the universe.

That, he thought, may be where I'm from.

A week after the roller-skating event, Seth placed a call to Aaron.

"Hey, buddy, it's Seth," he said to the voicemail as he had many times before, and then added, lamely, "Seth Adams," as if Aaron would have forgotten completely who the voice or the name might belong to in the time they'd not spoken.

"So, a little update. The kids have been living with me for

a short while now. I know I effed stuff up with Marina, but I'm really trying to make it work with the kids. It's going okay, but you know, I'm kind of, you know, would find it great to just . . . I don't know . . . have someone to talk to for 15 minutes who isn't charging a session fee. It's not a cry for help or anything, just a request for a conversation. Hope you're doing okay."

He then moved on to consider how best to go about contacting Bridget. He had her phone number and email address from the sign-in at the roller-skating event. Riding high on the feeling that he'd accomplished something meaningful, he'd finally called and left a message:

"Hi Bridget. It's Seth Adams. Free for coffee or lunch sometime?"

She texted her short reply minutes later: Sounds fun, Seth.

They settled on a day during the first week of December, to be determined after Thanksgiving was over. It was further off than Seth would have liked, but he understood that holidays were immovable for those who participated.

His palms had grown sweaty by the time the exchange of messages was done. It wasn't as satisfying as a phone conversation would have been, but he still felt like he'd accomplished something. Having a little more time would probably work in his favor, because it would give him time to figure out how to work it out so the kids didn't find out about it.

He didn't like the thought of coming up with a cover story or lying, but thought he could justify it as responsible parenting not to say anything before it turned into anything. Then he thought: Wasn't it always easy for him to find a justification to hide things? Was that just the kind of person he was?

Using Trevor and Jessica as intermediaries, Grandma Claire worked out a plan for Thanksgiving weekend where Seth would drop the kids off at his parents' house on Thursday afternoon and then return on Saturday to pick them up. He thought that for those forty-eight kid-free hours he would do something useful— deep clean their home, maybe do a little job-hunting, but instead he'd spent the time drinking beer and sleeping and feeling like he wanted to do that for a month before the kids came back again. Despite that, when he was getting ready to drive over to get them, he was looking forward to seeing them again.

He agreed to stop at the mall on the way home so Jessica could get a white button-down shirt for an upcoming Drama Night event, not realizing that it was opening weekend of the holiday shopping season until he found himself searching for a parking space in the overflow parking lot across the street from the mall.

Three hours later, returning to their car, he was nearly numb as they waited for the crossing signal to change. At some point, about an hour into their mall crawl, he'd been so overwhelmed by the number of people around him that he'd almost shut down, and ended up sort of following one or the other or both of the kids around without speaking.

Absent all the mall stimuli, Trevor finally noticed something in the expression on Seth's face.

"You all right, Dad?"

"Yeah, fine. You know, the humanity."

Jessica said, "I hear you."

"You seemed like you enjoyed it," Seth said.

"For a while, I did. Then I was done."

Trevor said, "I would have stayed for the fireworks on the roof."

Jessica snorted. "We would have had to line up yesterday to get in."

Seth asked, "Did I see a sign that said there were 92 shoe stores in there?"

The light changed.

There was an alignment of their moods that Seth found very comforting. Trevor was satisfied, and Jessica was tired but also content, however temporary it might be. They all wanted to be home. Once they were inside the overflow lot, none of them had any sense of which direction he'd parked the car. They started to wander up the first of the six rows of cars.

"I'm surprised we haven't heard from your mom," Seth said. "How long does a nervous breakdown take? I mean, I had an episode that lasted about 24 hours once, and it took me some time to get myself back on course . . . "

"Mom's in Latvia," Trevor said. "Her mom is sick."

"Latvia."

"She sends us messages but we're not supposed to message her back because of the extra charges and because it causes her to experience negative feedback that throws off her progress." Something about the way Trevor said it seemed like he was making some kind of joke.

"You're kidding?"

Jessica said, "You know what? You don't get to comment. Trevor and I can call her a crazy head case, but you can't. Mom is super, super controlling and it did get worse and worse with the stress you put on her. Your head has just always been so far up . . . in its own world that you never noticed. Or you just wrote it off as her version of discipline. There were times Trev and I thought it was neglect. She squeezed my wrist so hard one day that I almost cried, but I don't think she'd ever do it again after I pointed out that technically it was abuse, and she needed to get control of herself."

"Yelling doesn't leave a bruise," Trevor said, "but it still sticks to you. It went mega extra after you moved out," Trevor said. "She realized she couldn't control everything so she kept trying harder to control everything. The day before she sent us here she was yelling at the gardeners after they spent an hour doing the yard. They filled six bags with leaves, swept up everything, and while they were loading up their tools in the back of their truck, a couple leaves fell off a tree onto the lawn. I saw it happen. Mom came out to check out their work, saw those three leaves on the lawn, made them come to where she was standing next to the leaves and then did her therapist thing where she asks questions that trick you into thinking you did something wrong."

"Then she yelled at them and yelled at them," Jessica said. "It was terrible."

"But we were still glad it was them instead of us," Trevor added. "Core meltdown, evacuate now."

"We didn't think you'd want to hear about her," Jessica said quietly. "We didn't know whether or not we should be talking to you about her. We don't want to be your go-betweens. That's why we didn't tell you."

"That's okay, I guess," Seth said, thinking that maybe he'd started feeling like it would be nice to know where this was going. It was okay now, because his life was in limbo, but what if that should change? Were the kids going to stay with him or was she going to return and want to take them back?

Why did he find that hypothetical so confusing?

They weren't far from the car, Seth was hoping, when they first heard the sound of men yelling nearby. This was followed by a burst of sound from what sounded like an organ playing on the top floor of the parking structure and a burst of cheering from an unseen crowd. Two white lights raced high into the sky and then exploded into bursts of flashing, crackling sparks.

Trevor said, "Whoa."

"This way," Seth said. He had his keys in his hand, jingling them a little, when he thought he heard raised voices again, and maybe something hitting the chain link fence that surrounded the overflow lot. A metal rattling noise. The voices were closer than before. He wrapped his hand around the keys to silence them.

Jessica had heard the sounds, too.

"Don't like that," he said to her. "Let's move faster. We'll cut between the cars. Go to the next row. Keep low."

"Beep the alarm," Jessica said. He did. The sound was a couple rows over, and farther back than he'd hoped. He was concerned about getting away from those voices. He handed the keys to Jessica as they moved, with the car key singled out for her to hold onto. She took them with a concerned look on her face.

"Just hurry," she said to him.

He looked back and saw under the low-glow carbon lights two men running up the row they'd just exited. They appeared to be chasing someone, or they were looking for someone to chase. The one in front saw Seth, too. He altered his course so that he was headed straight for Seth. Just because you're paranoid, Seth thought, didn't mean there wasn't someone after you.

"Look both ways before you cross the rows! Watch out for cars driving around," Seth said as he watched Trevor crossing the row and disappearing between the cars on the other side. Jessica was not far behind her brother. He called out, "Run to the car, lock yourself in, and hide."

Another cluster of white crackling flashes brightened the night sky.

He waited to make sure Jessica was out of sight and then started running up the row away from the approaching men and away from the kids.

"Fucker's right over there," someone shouted. The sound didn't seem to come from behind him. Which direction did it come from? There were other voices yelling back. What was going on? Were people really chasing him? With each step he became convinced they were all around him, and they were there just for him. They were behind him, ahead of him, and to the right of him, at the least.

Weirdly, it felt like this had happened before.

The kids were in the car by now, he told himself. He knew he wasn't going to get far whichever way he went. He had time to wonder if this wasn't a mistake, if maybe someone in the control room had decided to end his current stay. Was this random or intentional? Had they been sent after him?

Then he thought: That makes no sense.

He stopped running, and he turned around. Both men were not far behind. The one in front, wearing a hooded sweatshirt—were they both wearing hoodies?—was much closer than the other. He seemed intent on his purpose.

Seth yelled, "Wait! Wait! Stop! I'm not who you think I am!" Red and blue starbursts, each one larger than the one before, filled the sky above the mall. He was scared, and his words were ringing in his head after he said them. He hoped they weren't carrying weapons. As the man in front closed in on him, Seth held up his hands to signal for him to stop. "You've got the wrong person!" There was so little response to the sound of his voice that he wondered if he'd actually said anything.

It all happened quickly. An angry, spitting face approaching, lips curling around low-voiced words that Seth could not process or understand, eyes half concealed by his hood, a beard or a goatee, big frame, taller than Seth, wider. Farther off in the background, maybe the sound of people stopping to wonder at the commotion. Colored burning lights, cold night air. His heart pounding. Growling voices, angry thoughts, all unintelligible.

The guy threw a punch when he was close enough. Seth dodged, and the fist missed him, and the guy lost his balance, still managing to bump Seth as his momentum carried him into the back of a car with a thud. Seth smelled alcohol. Bright flashes continued to flare and sparkle. The guy's hood fell back as he righted himself, and he took another sloppy swing, which Seth avoided by stepping back.

There was a moment between one thrown punch and the next one to come that something in Seth recognized as the moment to act. In a fluid and, to him, surprising movement, he reached out and touched his pointer finger and middle finger, the two of them held together, against the guy's forehead, and through that touch, Seth's thoughts pushed right into his brain. The connection became an almost frozen interval of time between two beats of his heart. Seth could taste the man's consuming, drunken, thoughtless, destructive impulse, and the dull rage underneath. There was so much anger there that it seemed to have flooded the man's bloodstream.

If he could have, Seth would have drawn all of it and everything other thinking part in the man's head out of him. He was anticipating that very thing happening, hungry for it, when he realized that this form he was in didn't work that way.

Instead he used that nearly frozen moment to turn the man on his companion.

However long the connection seemed to last in Seth's mind, the guy's reaction to his touch was instantaneous. He turned and threw himself at his approaching friend, the impact knocking both of them to the ground, at which point they both started throwing punches.

Seth turned and ran. He heard other voices being drawn to the scene. He heard what he thought was the sound of someone being thrown on a car.

He was hoping to see some sort of security detail on its way. What he saw instead was Jessica stepping out from between two cars. She stood there, staring at him. Her wide eyes and worried expression said it all.

When you realize your Dad actually is an alien, I thought to myself.

It feels like you want to run, but you can't.

Because you're probably one, too.

The sounds of commotion continued to grow behind them. It sounded like a crowd was gathering.

"Where's your brother? You should be with him."

"He's hiding underneath our car. We've been texting the whole time. He's fine. He knows we're okay."

"Let's hurry," he said to her.

They found Trevor looking very relieved to see them. When Seth got in the car, Jessica stood outside watching him with an expression on her face that he'd couldn't interpret. At first she considered getting into the back seat with Trevor, but she opted for the front passenger seat after considering it for another moment.

She was silent as he pulled the car out and headed to the parking lot exit, quiet as they drove up the boulevard to the freeway entrance. They passed two police cars headed in the opposite direction with their lights flashing.

Trevor was watching them both, waiting for someone to say something that explained what had happened, until finally he couldn't take it anymore.

"Is someone going to tell me?"

"Crazy guys running around trying to beat people up. They started fighting each other and I ran away."

"Whoa."

"Yeah." Seth stared at his fingers on the steering wheel. He realized Jessica was watching him. She looked mildly horrified. He glanced her way, and she continued staring at his fingers. She waited until Trevor put in his earbuds and settled back in the seat to play a game before she finally spoke up.

"Omigosh," She said. "Does this mean it's true? That we're just shells inhabited by aliens? I'm just some body being run by an alien on a vacation?"

He took a minute to absorb this, surprised.

"You looked through my project."

"Of course! We're living with you and it turns out we know next to nothing about you except what Mom has always told us, which wasn't very nice and which seemed to be backed up by everything you did. Yes, I looked to see whatever the heck it is our father does for a living. For his life . . ."

In the rear-view mirror, Seth saw Trevor look up at his sister, whose voice he was probably hearing over the sound of his game. Then he looked down at his lap again, and Seth assumed the game had once again asserted its authority over him.

"That's not what my project says. That's not what I'm saying."

"Fine, then. Explain it to me. Say what it is you're saying. Tell me what you are. Tell me what we are."

She was afraid she was like him, he realized. Which was logical, he would admit, but it didn't work that way. Seth thought back to his first conversation about this with Dr. Penny. He could repeat it back to Jessica verbatim, but in the moment found himself wanting to soften the delivery for her.

"The idea isn't that people are carbon forms animated by alien minds. It's more like aliens are able to hitch, you know, a ride and be able to experience life from the human perspective. Who and whatever they really are is supposed to be left behind— it's not supposed to be like their minds are transplanted so they can be themselves on another world. It's more like a video game that they get to experience from inside rather than one they just get to witness from the outside."

"Witness. Witness." She was very unsettled. "Did you

always feel like this? Your whole life?"

"No. It came up later. At different times."

"Oh."

"Yeah, like, surprise. I don't think it's supposed to work in a way that you or I should know about it. I think something messed up with me."

"So how sure are you about any of this?"

"I go back and forth. There's been lots of times I've thought I must be so crazy that I made it all up."

"Well, question answered," she said. Then she was quiet while she thought about it. "What did you do to him?"

"I think I . . . redirected him."

"Like you controlled his mind."

"No, not controlled. Just redirected."

"Do you think he'll remember you?"

"I don't know. He was drunk and it was dark."

"Did you know you could do that?"

"No. I didn't even know I was going to do that. I didn't know I was doing it. I just did it. Honestly, I don't think I could do it again if I tried. I don't know what I did. Nothing like that's ever happened before. I've never been in a situation like that. That was crazy. It just went from normal to scary to batshit crazy."

"Yeah," she said.

"I think I was only able to do that because he was so angry. I could latch onto it and turn away. I don't know what I did but when I was doing it, it felt like the thing to do. Defense mechanism. I just did it."

"What if you did that and nothing had happened? Do you think he would have been completely confused?" She laughed. "Like you just did the troop pledge on his forehead?" That made her feel better. "That was weird and terrifying. I must not hate you as much as I thought, because I didn't want them to hurt you as much as I thought they were going to. I hope they beat the crap out of each other."

"Me, too."

Quiet again.

She asked, "So, it bothers you that you're this way?"

"I'd like more than anything not to be. Aware of it. They think they're us—that's part of the experience. They won't remember that they're not until they wake up."

"Thank goodness you said 'us.'"

It was only when she pointed it out that he recognized the pronouns he had used—they and us. Odd. He didn't say anything as he merged from one highway to another.

"This is sort of upsetting me," Jessica said as she reached out to turn on the radio, "so I'd like to stop talking about it now if that's okay."

"Fine then." He meant it as a joke when he followed up with, "We will never speak of this again," but Jessica did not laugh.

Chapter 9

Seth saw it as proof that they were working as a family. This weird, unpleasant, and unexplained thing had happened, and it should have caused more than the tremor it had in their lives, and yet it was not brought up again. They got up in the morning the next day, picked up breakfast sandwiches at the hamburger stand, and then spent the rest of the day lying around and watching television. Yes, there was a feeling inside him that he would have described as vindication. He thought this meant that he was right about no less than everything. As an added plus there seemed to be an even greater reduction in the amount of hostility Jessica directed his way.

The following day, when the kids were back in school, he called Bridget. He was surprised when she picked up, and more so that she sounded like she was looking forward to seeing him again. He didn't inquire about her personal situation or where she'd spent the holiday, although he'd thought of ways he could try to script the conversation where he could find out more about her back story. Was she dating anyone? Where did she work? All his strategizing went out the window because really he just craved social contact and wanted to be inspired by possibilities, not focused on constraints. Plus, there was no knowing how she would react to questioning, and he did not want to put her off in any way when she'd already agreed to meet. He even asked if she wanted to meet for lunch or coffee, low-pressure interactions. When she said she could work dinner into her schedule more easily than either of those, he tried not to sound too excited by the fact that it felt so much like setting up a date, but he couldn't help the way his heart started to race.

Everything on the date that he kept reminding himself wasn't officially a date went far better than he'd expected. There was no awkwardness because Bridget was still confidently familiar with him. He thought too that there was some flirtation, but backtracked a bit to wonder if it was just the change of environment from office to restaurant that gave him that impression. She seemed very much the same person whose company he had enjoyed at GoLuck. She seemed as relieved to find him as she remembered as he was to find that she had not changed, either. Their brief interaction at the roller-skating event gave them a starting reference point and the conversation flowed into her current circumstances, her new condo, her current temp job at a data gathering unit that served online clients. He was candid about his living situation, his divorce, and his kids. He talked a lot about the middle school and his unexpected volunteer job.

"Once I find out a couple of things about a person," she said, describing her job, "I can pretty much tell you what products he or she has in their pantry, refrigerator, and freezer. I have a list of 10 or 12 questions that enable to me to guess what you have in your medicine cabinet. For real."

"What good does that information do?"

"Remember when we talked about all of our minds being subconsciously linked somehow? Corporations want in on that action, and since they haven't figured out how to make mind-reading machines, they're using our data as a potential technological equivalent. They are insane about data. They can't read your mind or anyone else's, but they have every other bit of data about you that they might need to draw conclusions about what you're thinking or doing at any given moment." She stopped herself, thought about something. "Goodness," she said, "I've missed nerding out with you, obviously."

There it was, that feeling that he'd had about Bridget all along. He wondered, should he just say something about this thing that was going on with him?

"No," he said, to himself, deciding to dive right in. "It's not nerdy when you say it. I like it. Maybe we should stop fighting the corporations on this. Maybe data mining our hearts' desires would be the best way to come up with solutions to our problems that more of us agree on. Maybe they could amalgamate all of our data to determine what we really want. For example, they could invent an algorithm to select political candidates to represent us based on our cumulative needs and wishes."

"Based on our likes and favorites," she said.

Their banter jumped back and forth from personal to speculative for the rest of the meal. It was so comfortable that he didn't feel the time passing. Before they stood to leave their table, she invited him to see her condo, and he again decided to wait before making any revelations that would interrupt the flow of the evening.

She lived in a one-bedroom downstairs unit about 20 minutes from his current residence, in a complex of townhouses. On the drive over, he made clear he was on a curfew, and that he had to get home to the kids before it was too late. The underlying message he hoped she heard was that he wasn't going to be angling to spend the night.

The décor inside was really very spare. Without him commenting on it, she explained that she'd just moved in recently and hadn't had time to bring over all her stuff from storage. There was a mini refrigerator in the kitchen and at some point, while passing her bedroom on the way to the bathroom, he saw that in the open closet there were about eight items of clothing, four tops, three black pants, and one black dress. There was something about it that seemed very temporary, instead of something in transition. He was more curious about her now than before. Was she an alien like him, or was she just an attractive weirdo?

Still, with the vibe he was feeling, which was welcoming, he knew he wouldn't broach the subject. At least until an hour later, when a noticeable lull took over their conversation. They were in what was supposed to be the living room, sitting on a futon that was in couch mode. There was a tiny television across the room. Other than the stool at the counter that separated the living room from the kitchen, the futon was the only piece of furniture in the room. The walls were bare.

"I've been working on a quirky little project in my free time," he said, and she looked interested. "Have you heard of the Framework Foundation?"

"The UFO group that has ads everywhere you go?"

"Right. Well, I put together a submission for them, sort of describing a theoretical scenario where, um, where aliens are able to transmit their minds into humans so they can experience what it's like to be human."

"For real? That's wild, Seth. Where did you come up with that one?"

He couldn't read her reaction clearly. It wasn't amusement. It suddenly wasn't like one of their office conversations anymore. He decided it was time to go for it.

"I mean, it's not that far from what I really believe could be the case with me. Right?" Her expression was inscrutable. "I think I'm not supposed to believe it or even be aware of it but for some reason I think that's what happened to me. Well, not for some reason, because I think I've had concrete confirmation . . ." His voice trailed off as he thought he could see by the look in her eyes that he was losing her with this. The tone with them was usually like banter. This didn't feel like banter.

"I'll stop now," he said, really awkwardly.

It was she who decided to forge on.

"You know what? I'm going to refresh my drink." She didn't have a drink. Somehow, he doubted she had a drink in her mini fridge. "Hold that thought. I need a minute," she smiled, "to digest all of that. I think a drink will help."

"Fair enough," he said, as disappointed as he could have imagined being.

She stood and walked into the kitchen, where he thought she was either leaning against the counter wondering what she had gotten herself into or she was texting a friend to tell her to call and interrupt with some kind of fake emergency or another. However, Bridget quickly returned, beer in hand, and sat down next to him on the futon.

"So, you're weirded out by that," he said.

"Oh, yeah, a little bit. I just think, you know, in life, you have to be willing to look at things in different ways if you want to get the most out of it. Try a different approach when it's available." She reached out her hands to his glasses, lifted them off carefully, folded them up, and slid them into his shirt pocket.

"I've always wondered what you looked like without those on."

Her right hand brushed through his hair, as if adjusting it in response to the absence of his glasses. She leaned forward, as if she wanted to kiss him. Her palm rested on his forehead. He felt something like a pinch inside his brain.

Everything went black.

YOU'RE IN MY HEAD

PART TWO
Jessica

Chapter 10

Middle school is the middle child in the school family. Elementary school gets all kinds of attention and support and money because it is the cutest and neediest age and the kids still seem full of potential and worthy of the effort. Figure kids that age are mostly glad to have their parents around. High school is the oldest child, the one who is closest to leaving the nest, the one whose future seems worth the investment of a little more money, the one who might do well in sports and get good grades and win tournaments at speech and debate, the one the parents are living through one last time before the kid leaves them behind.

Middle school is the limbo in between. No longer that cute, potential suddenly not so clear, not fully grown—in fact, hormonally turning into who knows what—and not leaving the nest any time soon. At some point, someone must have asked: What is the best way to keep a bunch of kids busy until they've metamorphosized into something that could be worked with more easily? They're not mature enough to be left alone with the younger ones, and they're not safe being left with the older ones, so let's have them spend three years in isolation doing a bunch of work that combines everything they've already learned in elementary school with everything they will be repeating in their first year of high school. Just keep them busy.

I didn't think most middle school kids were trying to be as awful as they were. Some of them were, for sure, but the rest had just stumbled into it. They were too clueless to have arrived at it intentionally. The whole underlying concept of middle school was to keep all of them in line. Middle schoolers could be cruel. Pick on people for the things that made them stand out from the crowd and pretty soon everyone was working really hard not to stand out so much. Except the neediest of the Drama kids. They didn't care how they got attention, as long as they got it.

Most of the boys in middle school were just annoying. The

more of them there were in a group, the dumber they got until they were so dumb that they were fighting or in a shoving match over something they couldn't even put into words. The girls, on the other hand, could be really, really mean, and weren't shy about bringing all of their friends into any kind of argument they got into. The girls could be dead-eyed mean. Not that any of the girls at school ever messed with me, or talked about me to anyone I might hear about it from. People didn't mess with me was what I thought most of the other kids would say if someone asked, and it wasn't only because I was as tall or taller than most of the kids at school. Not that I was a bully or not social—I had friends. I just wasn't good at letting that kind of stuff slide.

I was living in ignorance. I didn't realize that what I was missing as far as school went was having a friend who really knew me. Someone who I would be ashamed to act like a typical school asshole in front of. I was never able to relax, not 100%, not with the friends I'd made at Ashbury. Melodrama was always within reach. I didn't realize it was possible that there could even be a person who could make me feel like I could stop worrying about what anybody at school thought of me.

  School was on an upswing. How could it not be during the last week of the semester, the last five days before Winter Break? My father dropped us off early enough on Monday morning that there was time to walk up the block with Valimar and Toi to get a coffee before first bell.

  We were on our way back, walking alongside the school's chain link fence, when the metro bus pulled up and stopped across the street from the school. It was running late—usually it pulled up as we were leaving for coffee. A pile of kids spilled out of the bus, all khaki pants and white shirts and Jansport backpacks, and there were so many of them that they overwhelmed the whole sidewalk. An old lady who was standing next to the bus stop sign got pushed off the curb right into the street, where she fell. The kids who did it were clueless that it had happened—they all had their backs turned to her and were focusing on the traffic light, waiting for the crossing signal to turn green while at the same time being pushed backward by the swelling crowd.

We started screaming from the sidewalk on the other side of the street, but any of the stupid kids who noticed us over the sounds of traffic had no idea what we were saying. Richard Keeler saw me and waved, that idiot. It was sort of weird because they were all dressed in the same color shirts and the same color pants and they were so unaware that they might as well have been a bunch of brainless clones. The crossing light turned green and they all rushed into the crosswalk. There were two cars waiting for all the kids to get across so they could turn. One was making a right from one direction and the other was making a left from the other direction. We thought the lady was going to get hit by one of those cars because we thought no one could see her. I moved towards the corner, thinking maybe I was going to have to cross the street to help her. I started waving my arms to try to get the attention of both of the drivers of the turning cars when one kid, also in uniform, broke away from the swarm and jumped out into the street and also started waving his arms above his head while he hurried to the lady. He helped her up. We tried to figure out who it was, but didn't recognize him. He held her arm as he walked her over to the bus stop bench. After he sat her down, she said something to him which he listened to seriously, and then they both said something else and he went to wait for the next green light to cross.

Valimar and Toi didn't wait to watch any of that last part because they didn't want to be tardy, and by the time I turned around they were already moving up the sidewalk toward the drop-off gate behind the mass of kids from the bus. I got a glimpse of the boy's face before I ran after them—I was pretty sure it was Jason Zarro. It kind of looked like him. I hadn't seen him in something like three years.

What could he be doing here? The last I had heard of him was that he was going to Oaks Academy. Was he in uniform because he was switching to Ashbury?

Jason was one of my best friends in elementary school, no doubt due to the fact he was my neighbor and we spent a lot of time together after school at one or the other of our homes. That was before Jason's dad got rich and moved them into a neighborhood with bigger houses and swimming pools a couple of miles away.

The idea that there was potentially going to be someone at school who I would choose to spend my time with rather than some of the people I hung with because there was nobody better—which was how I would have described 90 percent of the people I spent my time with at school—well, that was just amazing and unexpected.

Fifteen minutes later, I'd already gone through this sort of moment of joy sensation thinking about Jason going to school with me again, and I had moved on to the realization that I was assuming too much based on the fact that Jason and I were once neighbors and went to elementary school together. Maybe the years of private boys' school had ruined him. Then I was slightly bummed to have dredged up the fact that I sometimes felt very alone in middle school.

Regardless, I asked for the bathroom pass right before the bell for first period rang and then went down to the counseling office. Peeked in the door and there he was. Sitting in a room decorated with construction paper renderings of inspirational education-related quotes crafted by kids in detention. He looked mildly anxious.

Jason recognized me right away and the anxiety drained right out of his expression.

He said, "Oh, thank God."

I said, "You're switching here?"

"Yeah. Switched." He looked very private school. Every boy at private school seemed to have based his hairstyle on some celebrity's haircut. Jason's hair was cut short on the side but so long on the top that he had to keep pushing it out of his eyes. It even looked like a move he'd learned in private school.

Ms. Menendez stuck her head out of her office to see who had walked in.

I was on it. "Hi, Ms. Menendez. Can I be Jason's guide today?

We used to be neighbors."

My extended appeal was: Our families used to live three houses away from each other on Splendor Court, a cul-de-sac a few miles from school. Jason's Mom and my mom were friends.

It wasn't necessary to elaborate. Ms. Menendez didn't have anyone on hand to help with Jason. It turned out that we had nearly the same schedule, so being his guide wasn't going to get me out of any of the classes I wouldn't have minded missing.

I really tried to keep it together at school. Even the girls I considered my best school friends didn't need to know the details of my garbage-fest life with my alien father. All they were going to do with that information was first, talk about it when they were talking about me when I wasn't there and second, they were all going to start trying to make connections between my actions and the details in my life that I had shared with them. They pretty much got the same blank wall when they asked about my home life that my mom used to get when she asked about what was going on at school.

Not to slam my own gender, but guy friends were better. Not boys who had a crush on you and not the stupidest boys, but normal boys, because boys overall were playing a whole different type of game in middle school than the girls were. Then suddenly, here was the guy who lived a few houses down for years of my life. Someone normal, or at least less abnormal than most of his gender. Best of all, Jason was actually as tall as me.

In the hallway outside the office, on our way to History, I asked, "Why are you here?"

"Parental infidelity is probably the best answer."

"But here? Was it your mom or dad who had the worst divorce lawyer ever?"

"We're not sure. My dad says he has no money left, when he obviously has money. He's not living poor. Massive financial mismanagement. Or well-hidden money. Mom says it's hard to tell

what's true about my dad."

"You're living with her?"

"Mom unit most of the time, yes. Random weekends with Dad."

"Sorry on so many levels."

"It's all right. I'm here for a reason. That's what that lady said to me at the bus stop."

"You saw me there?"

"Yeah, totally looking for a familiar face, then there you are." His smile was sort of a grimace. He was either in pain or he really wasn't looking forward to being in public school.

"Are you okay?" I meant more than at that moment. I meant bigger picture. Did he get that?

"Not really. Are you?" He did get it. It was like we had never stopped being friends.

"No one here is. It's not even a secret. It's middle school." Then we were at the History classroom door. It seemed so short a time when there was a lot to go over and catch up on. *"This is Mrs. Rhude's class. Really boring. It's goes faster if you actually participate and try to guess the answers to her questions."*

I opened the door for him.

"Thanks, Jess. I don't think anyone needed to see a familiar face as much as I did today."

We had period three together and then I took him to his locker at lunch and then for a quick tour around campus, which gave us time to catch up. I told him my parents had divorced, too, and that we moved out of our house on Splendor, and that I was living in the corner of what looked like half of a strip mall. I showed him the student store, the cafeteria, and the eighth-grade lawn. I didn't bother introducing him to anyone except for Song, and that was only because she awkwardly intercepted us in order to get an introduction to the new student "and clearly good friend of Jessica."

"Weirdo," I said. We both knew I was joking. But Song is a

weirdo, there was no denying it.

Song was part Vietnamese, and grew up in like, Midwest farm country someplace before moving to the city. There were around twenty people in her town and since she moved here in seventh grade it had been a lot about figuring out what the people who don't live in farm country are all about. She was really enthusiastic, earnest, nerdy, and really comfortable pointing out the awkwardness of a situation.

Song said, "Wow, it's like I'm talking to giants. You look taller just standing together. Where's the golden goose, guys?" Song was really, really small. Short. She had to be a foot and a half smaller than us.

Three and a half hours later, waiting with Trevor for my father to pick us up, I literally felt that my existence at Ashbury had changed. The next day, when I sat down in Mrs. Rhude's, and I caught Jason's attention, he looked over my way and once again looked genuinely relieved to see me. That was when I realized that if this was the way things were going to be for the rest of my last months in middle school, I might actually find myself looking forward to being there.

It had been the worst year in my life. So far. By the time seventh grade ended, following six months of trauma after my mom discovered my dad's cheating and told him it was over, the house was sold and we were already living someplace new. Trauma wasn't the right word for the split. It was more like a dull, daily, anger-infused numb. My mother introduced the topic of them getting a divorce with the line, "Your father is going to be even less present than before."

Whatever the reason she was done, it wasn't just the cheating. That was finally the thing that made her regret putting up with the rest of it for so long. The rest of it was everything that my father hadn't done in all their years of parenting and marriage. Anyone who knew my mom knew that she had changed nearly every one of our diapers, made nearly every one of our meals, juggled homework and housecleaning and discipline, and that she thought of herself as a working single parent married to a man who brought home a paycheck and little more. For all of my life, I listened to my mom talk about how much it required of her to be, in her own words, "raising the kids on my own." Before the separation, I never thought she said it with anger or bitterness—it was sort of a badge of accomplishment for her.

He was absent and neglectful—we kids didn't need to be told, thank you. He was all but absent. He had a short cameo in the mornings, and then another brief appearance (maybe) at night. Might catch a glimpse of him, even be in the same room with him for a while on the weekend. If one of us asked, no, he wasn't going to be coming along. If Trevor or I wanted to get a message to him or have him sign anything, we put down the toilet seat in his bathroom and left the paper on top with a pen.

There wasn't much open conflict, even in the days right after he left. It was a calm surface covering a whirlpool of repressed anger where, to the best of mom's abilities, everything continued exactly as it had for years, except that she had to start doing the drop-off in the morning. The one thing he did that she very much appreciated and enjoyed. All he had to do was be ready to leave for work at the same time that we were ready to leave for school. Real challenging.

That was the only clear sign to the outside world that something was different—mom dropping us off at school looking exactly like she'd rolled out of bed and then picking us up looking like the business professional whose career we had interrupted. She would bring us home to an immaculate house, have dinner on the table at 6, push us to do homework first, grant us screen time, make us shower, allow us more screen time and then off to bed. The biggest difference was that the front door didn't open between 7 and 9 pm and my father didn't get home and quietly begin his end-of-day rituals on his own.

At first, it had been manageable. Borderline manageable. She started to get bossier, started asking questions—probing how our psyches were handling the separation and impending divorce, then taking our phones to see if we were instead venting online or maybe talking to him *without telling her. She got a little edgier each day. Random acts of discipline for perceived slights or impoliteness, sometimes the breaking of rules we'd never heard of, and lots of taking things said carelessly the worst way possible.*

What hadn't been manageable was Back-To-School Night at Ashbury Hills, when mom saw her ex at school, in her words, "Acting like a hero." This gnawed at what was left of her composure. Like many mothers of teens, Mom felt unappreciated for all her efforts and the thought of him receiving positive reviews for merely raising his hand to take on a role at school had her pouring herself a daily glass or two of wine after her last session.

On the day my mother texted us that she was sending an Uber to pick us up after school, the Uber arrived at the drop-off gate loaded with our stuff and a note explaining that we were headed to our father's new address. It felt like the world was swinging into the upside-down position. Trevor and I were both asking ourselves over and over what was going on, but the luggage in the back made it all pretty clear.

So, yes, we didn't luck out in the parent lottery. I knew my mom loved Trevor and me, but I also knew that she was selfish in ways that often made her seem like she was the child who needed to be grounded. I was less sure about my father. I wasn't sure he knew what love was. He was present enough over the years that I didn't mythologize his absence as the result of him being the hard-working breadwinner.

He could be snooty and dismissive. He made kids uncomfortable and kids made him uncomfortable, even his own kids. Everyone else made him uncomfortable, and eventually they felt the same about him.

I was sure long ago that he wasn't going to change, and my mom impressed upon me early on that the quality of my relationship with him depended on what I was willing to invest with no expectation of it being worth my while.

This parent group thing broke that formula, because suddenly it seemed like he was invested. I didn't think that was real. He was just doing that because . . . I didn't know why he was doing that. Just to stay relevant? A choice to not disappear completely whether the rest of the family wanted him to or not? Human or alien or parts of each, I didn't think he was ever going to step up and be the Dad he should try to be.

On the last day before break started, after Jason had run off to meet the bus, Trevor and I were standing just outside the gate waiting for our father's car to come around the corner.

Trevor asked, "Do you think we're going to stay with Dad for long?"

I said, "I don't know. Why?"

"I just don't want change," Trevor said. "Everything gets stirred up and it takes too long to settle. I want things to stay the same for a while. I don't like having to think about what might be coming next."

"Wow. Deep thoughts. What's brought this up?"

"Don't you think Dad's being weird?"

"Dad is weird." Dad is fucking part alien, was what I was thinking. Many times I had wanted to talk to Trevor about it, but even more times I thought it was a bad idea. Trevor was sure to start telling people his dad had super powers.

"Weirder than usual."

"No. I didn't notice. Like what?"

"Like, I don't know, kind of extra."

"I need more than that. Examples."

"Really extra. Has he been putting notes in your lunches for the last two weeks?"

I had no idea. I almost never even opened my lunches. I liked to buy lunch at the cafeteria. Sometimes I gave the brown bag in my backpack to my friends, sometimes I did a mystery trade, where both people reach into their bags and the first thing they grab they have to trade, and sometimes the bag just sat there until either my father or I threw it out.

I set down my backpack, pulled out the day's lunch, opened the bag and in a moment had a note in my hand. It read: Hope you're having a good day!

I said, "What the fuck is this?"

"Tell me. I know. I got one today, too. Three days this week. But you haven't noticed anything else?" He seemed to think this was something obvious.

Inside the lunch bag were apple slices, a bag of granola, a miniature can of some kind of healthy fruit drink, and what looked like homemade cookies. It actually looked pretty good to me because, of course, I hadn't eaten at lunch. When my father made the lunches, it was usually all prepackaged—bags of chips, fruit gummies, maybe a candy bar, maybe a soda. As if he did his grocery shopping at the gas station mini mart, which he likely sometimes did. Fun at first, but that type of food very quickly lost its appeal, and that was why I was happy to trade it for someone else's bag lunch of leftovers.

Trevor said, "You know why he's late right now?"

"There's more? How are things going on that I don't know about? I'm with you literally every day."

"He's been decorating the teacher's lounge for a holiday party. It's also supposed to be a retirement party for Ms. Cathy in the school office."

"I don't believe you. I don't even think he knows her name. He calls her the white-haired lady with the nasty cough."

"I saw him tying balloons to chairs."

"Maybe I haven't been paying attention to him."

"Well," Trevor said, "We've got three weeks of vacation now. You won't be able to miss it."

Chapter 11

If it hadn't been obvious for the rest of the afternoon that there was something more off than usual, it was more than clear the next morning when I woke up to the smells and sounds of food preparation in the adjoining room. I literally did not think that the stove in the little kitchen worked. And there was something else mixed in with the food smell. Was it something pine scented? Whatever it was, the combined smells were warm and dreamy, like breakfast in a cabin in the mountains. It had to be waffles.

I was sleeping with the door connecting our rooms unlocked. The reasoning behind that was that I was worried that some strip mall home invasion robber was going to break in, and I wanted to be able to flee the room as quickly as possible. I had started wearing head bands and scarves all the time. The brand I got in eight colors looked like it was meant to hold back my hair, but they also covered most of my forehead. Not my look of choice, but it felt protective. I found it hard to sleep if there wasn't also some kind of alarm system, like soda cans stacked against the door. If my father was going to try to mind control me while I was sleeping, then at least I would have some kind of warning. Not that I really thought that was what he was going to do or wanted to do—it just made me feel safer.

When I opened the door the first morning of vacation to see what was going on, I saw there were plates set out at the table for all three of us. As if we were going to be eating a meal together. Waffles, scrambled eggs, sliced bananas, glasses of orange juice.

"You don't have to sit to eat if you don't want to, but you do have to eat," he said.

Strange.

Trevor said, "Hi, Dad."

"Good morning, Trev."

I still wasn't doing the "Dad" thing.

Trevor said, "Is that a Christmas tree?"

I did a double take and looked around the room and realized that there was a small tree on one of the end tables next to the couch my father slept on. I noticed that all his bed stuff—the sheets, the blanket, the pillow—had already been cleaned up and put away.

"It's 10 days away," my father said. "I thought it was time."

I clapped my hands. "It's perfect." But then I looked at my father and thought: Who are you today?

"I thought," he said, "we could go do some shopping. Maybe . . . someplace that isn't the mall. I don't know what to get you for Christmas, so you can help me figure it out. Get gifts for your grandparents."

Was it wrong for me to feel so suspicious of him?

"Sounds good," Trevor said, "but one step at a time." He sat down at the table.

Fine with me, was really the only thought I had in my head as I sat down, too. Soon I was cutting off a bite of waffle with my fork, stabbing a banana, stabbing at the waffle bite, dipping it all in the syrup and popping it into my mouth while totally forgetting what we had even been talking about in the first place.

He went into the bathroom to get ready. He was whistling "Jingle Bells." When Trevor tried to ask me a question, I shushed him. I'd never heard him whistle, much less carry a happy tune.

I visited the Framework Foundation website for the first time over Winter Break. One of the first things I read was a Q&A column. The first question was, "People often dismiss the story of Genesis in the Bible because the timing doesn't align with our modern understanding of the development of life on Earth. What would be the correct timing for a story about a God or other being who might have created humans?"

If we had to try to pinpoint a time in our history when a god (or anyone else) from the stars reached out to spark life on our planet, one place we would look would be the Cambrian era. Fossils found dating to the time before the Cambrian era are basic, simple organisms, composed of basic RNA code. By the end of this era, the world was dominated by creatures sporting code that combined the basic code with a second chain of complex code, creating DNA, giving rise to the direct ancestors of nearly every living creature alive today. Scientists have spent a lot of time marveling over the remarkable resilience of the complex code in DNA—some believe it actually defies our understanding of evolution, not only because of our inability to understand how it evolved, but also because that code has remained relatively unchanged over 571 million years. The Cambrian Explosion, as it was called, has inspired a lot of theories . . . but, as we've noted before in these pages, no one explanation for the cause has been so satisfying that scientists have stopped looking for a better one. The faithful believe it could only have been a god, while the skeptics are equally correct in suggesting that an alien taking a DNA-laden potty break during a pit stop on the planet has as much of a chance of being the culprit. What was it that ignited this explosion?

Another possible inflection point to look at would be two-and-a-half billion years ago, to our world's first great die-off, when the switch was thrown that resulted in the oxygenation of our atmosphere, and the death of the anaerobic (non-airbreathing) organisms occurred . . .

YOU'RE IN MY HEAD

I clicked on the Framework Museum link. There were more links to different topics covered by actual displays at the museum. I selected a starburst button in the top, middle window that read: GIANTS ARE REAL

Or they were, if you've read Greek, Hindu, Norse, or Celtic mythology, or the Bible, where there are various races of Giants, reputed to have dominated the land before the great Flood, the product of angels commingling with humans. Extraterrestrialists who believe angels were aliens understand this story as a metaphor for otherworldly influences on human genetics. Our modern take on them intertwines their stories with magic and the trappings of fable, but are giants all made up? We know that whales lived on the land 50 million years ago, and there were giant penguins living in New Zealand 35 million years ago; we've long been aware of giant birds, mammals, reptiles, fish, and insects because of the fossil record, and we've even discovered a number of oversized human skeletons.

I thought the site would be all about alien abductions and the Bermuda Triangle, but it was much more sciency than that—the only place where the conspiracy stuff that I knew about came up was a section I liked called Debunked where they destroyed urban myths like cow bloodletting and the Bermuda Triangle and the fate of Amelia Earhart, who was obviously eaten by crabs. For reals. I preferred those types of stories and avoided the links to most of the pages that seemed like they had to do with aliens. At that point, unless it was a cure for alien infestation, I wasn't going there. Spending too much time on that topic in my life was already starting to make me paranoid.

The change in our food habits, it seemed to me, was a distraction from something else. It wasn't just one meal that morning. It was breakfast, lunch, and dinner, all home cooked. Healthy stuff—eating a rainbow every day. He actually said that while we were grocery shopping. On that Christmas shopping expedition, he bought himself a cookbook. Although it was true that Trevor sometimes complained about not eating at the hamburger place any more, he was always the first one done eating whatever it was my father put in front of us at the table.

It was deeper than that. It was simple things, like asking me how my day was going or saying something like, "Jess, everything okay?—you seem upset." It was fixing up our "home" in little ways every week. Buying new furniture. He added a lattice wall across the outside hallway, so people couldn't saunter up to our front door. The rat traps, if they were still around—and I thought they likely were—had been moved to places where they couldn't be seen. Then he added more lattice and suddenly we had an enclosed porch with a door on it.

He still wouldn't go into Grandma Claire and Poppy's house on Christmas Eve, but he did drop us off there for brunch and agreed to meet us at a fancy restaurant and have a huge dinner later. There was no fighting at all. Mom once told Trevor and me that the last time my father and his parents had dinner together, he got in a huge and ridiculous fight with them about whether the mashed potatoes had been made with russet or Yukon gold potatoes.

At the restaurant, Grandma was so surprised and happy— she laughed a lot, then drank too much. As soon as she realized she was slurring her words she stopped talking and just listened with a satisfied look on her face.

For the rest of the holiday stuff, it was like he'd read the Single Man's Guide to Celebrating Christmas, starting with having us pick our own gifts and ending with us finding cash and gift cards in our stockings. He actually put out milk and a plate with cookies for Santa and celery for the reindeer under the tree on Christmas Eve. As if. It turned out nothing like our regular Christmas, which was usually overseen by my mom and usually included a checklist of traditional activities performed in a traditional way, from building gingerbread houses to stringing popcorn. I liked all that stuff, but this was fine for a change, especially since I had started missing my mom, and it was easier not to be trying to do everything the way she would have done it because then I would have been thinking about her too much.

It could have all made me happy. For part of Winter Break it did, if only because with everything running smooth at home I was able to spend more time thinking about other things and not spend so much time thinking about my father. It wasn't until after all the New Year's Eve stuff had passed that somehow I decided that what it did was make me mad.

Where had this mindful person been for the last 14 years? He couldn't have just pulled this out of his ass during my childhood? Or at least made a similar effort somewhere along the way? Maybe not driven mom insane? The more I thought about it, the more it didn't sit right with me. I started to look for signs that this was just some front he was putting on, some way to draw Trevor and me in, some plan he had . . . but there was nothing. He seemed, if anything, not to be even aware that he was acting differently.

One day I noticed a manila envelope with the Framework Foundation logo on it in some of my father's papers when I was looking for a blank piece of paper to write on. The envelope had been opened already, so I didn't feel bad looking inside. I assumed they had turned him down, with that being the reason he hadn't mentioned it. Turned out, they had accepted it, and they had a designer working on the display.

I let out a little, "Yay," quietly to myself. I didn't know why I would care.

There were some papers that looked like they needed to be signed and returned. There was a letter from the museum that said they would be sending us four complimentary tickets once the paperwork was received.

I looked through everything, wondering why my father hadn't signed the papers and returned them. Since we had been living with him, this was the only thing I had seen him do that didn't involve us, mostly because he didn't have a life of his own. Looking back on the previous month, I couldn't remember the last time he had mentioned his project. And I couldn't remember having seen any hint on his part that he'd ever received this letter.

Then I started thinking about the last three weeks of everything seeming so on track. On track to the point that I had even started thinking that really, if my mother could just come back and be normal, it would complete a miraculous transformation. Who had ever thought that was going to happen—any of it? Missing my mom, feeling like the universe had shifted slightly in my favor by giving me a friend at school, and then my dad was even acting in ways that would make sense to anyone who hadn't known him very long. What was it that had kicked off all of this change?

Two nights before school started again, I heard Trevor call out, "I love you, Dad." He said it like it was something he'd said before, but I thought it was the first time I had heard him say it to my father in years. Before I had time to worry or hope about my father's response, he said, "I love you, too, Trev." I thought about calling out, "I love you, too," to both of them, not to either of them specifically, but the idea of it filled me with such strong emotions that I thought I would either scream or explode if those words came out my mouth.

Then he called out, "I love you, too, Jess."

I thought: That's the first time I can remember him saying that. Something I'd always wanted to hear. I liked how it felt to hear those words. I didn't like wondering if they were true.

Chapter 12

Back at school after Winter Break, other issues demanded my attention. My own life, for instance. By Friday of the first week there was pushback from a couple of my friends who were worried I was abandoning them for Jason. "You're losing yourself in him," is what Toi said, which I guess was the only reason she could come up with that I might prefer hanging out with him as opposed to her. Toi was so full of herself that she thought I was embarrassed to introduce him to them when it was totally the other way around. Guys don't have conversations like that with their friends in middle school. While my natural reaction to the whiff of drama would have been to spend even less time with them, instead I decided to start making the effort to introduce a couple of them to him.

I found him when he was putting his backpack into his locker. His sweatshirt lifted up as he was hanging it on the hook, and I saw he had a square black box attached to his pants at the hip. There were wires from it that went under his shirt.

"What's that?"

He looked at his hip, frowned a little, then let his arms drop so that it disappeared from view.

"That's for my spine. My back's been sore and my mom is like ten times more worried than she has to be so now the doctors are observing my back for a while and the box is supposed to keep the back soreness from bothering me as much."

"What does it do?"

"When it's on, it shocks me with an electric pulse, which I guess competes with the pain."

"The pulse is better than the pain?"

"Oh, yeah. It's bad when it's sore."

My so-called school friends had to be convinced that we weren't boyfriend and girlfriend. They needed to hear the story about us growing up together to make it clear to anyone who had gotten the wrong impression that we might be more than friends. To be convinced, all anyone had to see was the look of distaste on both of our faces when the idea of us being romantically involved came up. If one of us looked into the other's eyes in that We're Gonna Kiss way, the other would surely have burst out laughing because it would have to be a joke. Regardless, everyone asked all the time, and all the time we had to tell people we weren't a couple. Trevor told people the same thing when they went to ask him because they didn't believe us.

In the middle of January, my mom called—she was still in Latvia—and when in the course of the conversation I told her that Jason was my new best friend, my mother said, "Well, that won't last. Once he finds a girlfriend, she's most likely not going to want to spend time with you, or want him spending his free time with you. Time with you will just be time away from her. And when he gets married, well, if he's a good husband, the only woman he'll be investing his energy in will be his wife. Enjoy it while you can."

"Wow. Bitter bitter."

"Just wait and see."

That was just the way my mom was. A deflater of expectations.

I shared all of this with Jason, and we ended up making jokes about it. The truth was, we found ways to laugh at almost every kick in the butt someone threw our way.

At lunch one day I asked Jason if he remembered the babysitter that lived on Splendor.

"Ms. Angela? Of course. She was the best."

"Do you remember her glasses?"

One of Ms. Angela's routines was her stories about her magic glasses. She told me that she'd found them in the empty house when she first moved in, and that she'd kept them in a drawer for a long time before she ever tried them on. It wasn't until she lost her regular readers that she started putting on the glasses at different times, and even though that was when she started having odd little happenings, it was an even longer while before she started to connect those happenings to the glasses.

For an example, Ms. Angela told us that she'd worn the glasses out on the street one day and noticed two men who looked to be construction workers hanging out on the sidewalk outside a house up the block. Then she'd seen them again the next day standing in exactly the same place and, because she couldn't get them out of her mind, she went outside at night and they were still there. The morning after that, when she returned to the front yard to check on them again, with the glasses on her head instead of on her eyes, they were gone. So she put the glasses on her eyes to double-check what she was seeing and they were there again. After a little back and forth with the glasses, realizing the glasses were showing her something different than her eyes, she decided to approach the men to see what they were doing there.

When she got close enough, she could see there was something wrong with them. Even though at times they seemed to be looking her way, it never seemed as though they were really seeing her. She said there was an unsettling feeling at the possibility that she was wrong about this, because at times their eyes seemed to meet with hers and hold for a moment.

It only took her a minute more of looking at them to figure it out. They were workers, dressed for a day of hard work at a construction site where they were building a new house. There had been some kind of accident while they rested out on the sidewalk and whatever it was had killed them before they knew what happened. With the glasses on, she stepped up close to the one in overalls and stood in front of him.

When she thought she had caught his eyes, in that moment she said, "You're dead." She looked at the other and repeated herself.

They both heard her. They both looked at her, this time most definitely looking her in the eyes, still no expression on their faces, and then they vanished. Glasses or no glasses, she said, they were gone.

"I wonder if she's still around," I said. I missed living on

Splendor. I loved that street.

"*The way I remember it,*" *Jason said,* "*We would spend the afternoon with her, and then the next day on the way to school we would ask your dad about the crazier things she had told us and then he would try to explain how it could be. I think about that once in a while. How is your dad doing?*"

"*Uch, that's complicated. I've been wanting to talk about it but it's so weird that I've been purposely not.*"

"*All right then,*" *Jason said,* "*let's tell each other something that we've been avoiding saying.*"

"*Really. You've got something, too? Mine's pretty good.*"

Watch him pull off his face, was what I was thinking at that point.

"*Yeah, it's stupid, but I should have been up front about it from the start. The reason I'm not going to Oaks anymore isn't just because of financial mismanagement or the divorce. My dad is doing what he can to reduce his alimony and he is claiming mismanagement and they are divorcing and he is approaching it like it's espionage, but the reason they both agreed to pull me out was because I went to a party at one of the other kids' houses—the kid's dad is a bail bondsman, something like that and he lives in a mansion—and we all took Ecstasy and then some of the guys—not me—went skinny dipping in a neighbor's pool and the police got called. So we all got busted.*"

"*Wow. Wow. So you were afraid I'd think you were a big loser drughead?*"

"*Yeah, right.*" *Obviously, he didn't like that.*

"*Sorry. I don't think that. Really. Stuff happens.*"

"*There's more, though,*" *he said.* "*The reason I have this,*" *he said, pointing at the nerve stimulator,* "*this is because when the parents and the police got there, a bunch of us panicked and ran. Like, over fences, through neighbors' back yards. Because, I don't know why. We went over one fence and didn't realize the drop was longer on the other side and I landed really hard on my butt. I just kind of ran through it*" *at the time, but I fucked up my back a little."*

"Omigosh, that's when Alan Maran lost his toe?"

He shuddered at the memory. "Yeah."

"Are you bummed they pulled you out of Oaks?"

"No. Not at all. And totally, yes, too. It felt like camp masquerading as school. Even when I was doing it, the Ecstasy, I was thinking, 'This is what I'm going to be doing if I hang out with these guys.' And I was already worried about what could be next. They were talking about getting some coke for another night, and I was like, oh no. So I'm okay with Ashbury."

"So it was fun? The Ecstasy?"

"Yeah, it was fun. It was stupid, too. Alan didn't even know he lost his toe. He was just laughing at everything. And he didn't even know. And then he laughed for ten minutes after he realized what had happened."

"Oh my god."

"That was the best part of the X—there was nothing about it that felt bad." He smiled at the memory. "Maybe someday down the road, I'd try it again."

"Did they find his toe?"

"What?"

"Kind of left that part hanging."

He laughed. "Nice."

"Right?"

"Right. Oh, yeah. They sewed it back on. Last I heard, they were waiting to see if it took, but I don't know how it came out. There are probably pictures online, if I looked for them. They found it pinched in a section of chain link.

"Huh." Things that led to dismemberment held no appeal.

"My mom's freaking out about it still. She read somewhere that Ecstasy can drain your spinal fluid, so she's making me do all this stuff with a specialist, who isn't sure whether or not I'm going to need surgery."

"I'm sorry, Jason. That sucks."

"Could be worse. Still have all my toes." Then he said, "So that was mine. What is yours?"

I'd thought about how to unwrap all of this for Jason.

First, I told him about my father's project for the Framework Foundation. Fittingly, there was a giant "Who's Your Maker?" billboard visible from across the block and down the street.

When I finished that part, as I thought he would, he said, "Sounds cool. Where'd he get the idea for that"

Then I told him that my father actually thought that all of the stuff in the project described his own situation, because he thought maybe he was an alien. Or part alien.

"Oh, whoa."

"Yeah."

"Crazy."

"Right."

"I mean," Jason said, "Like, is he crazy? Like, you know, in a medical way?"

"Exactly my question," I said, "after I started reading through his project."

And then the final one, the story about the mall parking lot.

After I finished, I repeated the most unbelievable part. "He just touched his forehead and the guy attacked his friend."

"You're lying. You're exaggerating."

"I'm not." I pulled out my phone. Pulled up the video I'd taken of the fight.

"No way," he said. He touched her phone to replay it. "Good move, Mr. Adams." He played it again. "No way. It's kind of weird looking. The way your dad's arm just snaps up and back."

"Right?"

"What did he say?"

"Nothing. I mean, a little bit afterward. He seemed freaked

out. *Staring at the back of his hands while he was driving. Then he said, 'We'll never speak of this again,' and I thought he was joking, but neither of us have talked about it."*

"The family approach. Ignore it until it comes back worse than before."

"But now. Now he's acting weird, and it's really freaking me out."

"Like what?"

"See, you're going to laugh or think I'm being stupid, but you have to listen from the point of view of having seen that video. "

"Okay."

"He's become Mr. Dad. Like, the parent we always wanted him to at least try to be. It's great, but it also sucks because A: it's so completely out of character and unnatural and B: we had both gotten used to my dad the way he was and the way he did things and now that's gone. It's more A than B, but put both of them together and it's really weird."

"Hm. Okay."

"Yeah, I know. I thought it was important that you believed me when I started to say it but I think what was most important was saying it. My mom says that when we talk about things that frighten us, we take away their power." I wondered momentarily if I was really oversharing. "It's okay if you don't believe it. Just don't say anything to anyone."

"I believe you. I won't tell. What are you going to do?"

"Ask you to help me figure something out."

Chapter 13

At the end of January, I asked my father if Trevor and I could try taking the bus to school the following week.

"The school bus?" He was sorting flyers for a raffle to be held at the honors awards ceremony.

"Public transportation."

"Why?" His hair looked kind of scruffy. My father usually looked like he'd just gotten his hair cut. It wasn't long or anything, but it had grown in.

"Jason has been doing it, and there's a lot of kids who take the bus. It drops off in front of the school. Trevor and I want to try it."

"The crowded school bus that pours kids onto the boulevard?"

"That's the later bus. We'll take the earlier one."

"Jason?"

"Omigosh, we've talked about this! Jason who used to live two houses down on Splendor before his family got rich and moved? His parents split up and he's not going to Oaks Academy anymore? He's going to Ashbury now. He's been taking the bus. It stops two corners down from here. I thought it would be fun to try, and because Jason knows how to take the bus, he could show us how it works. Could be useful, right?"

Maybe, I was thinking, I didn't tell him about Jason. How was that possible? Did he know anything about me?

"First of all," he said, "Are you sure you told me any of that before? Because I don't remember it."

"Of course, you don't. That would require listening to me."

He sighed, looked at Trevor. "You want to do this?"

He shrugged, "I'll try it."

"Is she crushing on Jason?"

"You're so annoying," I tried to interrupt.

"No," Trevor said. "They both have better taste."

"This is Jason," I said. "You used to drive him to school."

"They're not each other's types," Trevor continued, although no one asked him to. "They're too much alike. They both need contrast."

Ignoring me, my father said to Trevor, "But he's alright."

"Yeah, I guess." My brother wouldn't look me in the eye as he spoke. I hated them both. "Yesterday he was wearing glasses that don't do anything for his eyes. They aren't magnifying glasses or sunglasses or prescription glasses. He got them because he thinks they make him look cool. He's got a good haircut. So he's kind of like that."

My father didn't know what to do with that. He looked back at me. "All right, fine."

"Really?"

He said, "Go ahead, try it. Find out how much it costs so you have the right kind of change."

I replayed the conversation in my head.

"Wait. Because Trevor said it was okay?"

"He's just one factor."

"He's the only factor you've considered in the last 60 seconds."

He shifted the subject a little, "How about after school? Do you want to take the bus home after school?"

I said, "Yes."

"No," Trevor said. "I don't want to wait a whole bus ride just to eat."

"Maybe I could give Jason a ride home, too?"

"I'll ask, I guess." I wanted to glare at Trevor, but still didn't have a clear shot at it. He still wouldn't look at me.

"Great."

"But maybe tomorrow, we'll do both—to and from school. Just to see how it goes? Don't ask Trevor before you answer."

Regardless, he looked at Trevor, who nodded that it was okay.

"I'll send an extra snack," he said to Trevor.

"Really," I said, disbelieving.

"Yeah," he said to me. "It's fine. I guess."

I could tell he felt guilty the first morning that we took the bus, and sort of pointless as we got ourselves together. All he could do was feed us. I told him he didn't even need to get up. When he asked if we wanted him to walk us to the bus stop, I felt kind of bad saying no.

"We'll be fine. It's literally only several hundred feet from our door. Easily less than 1,000 steps. We have our phones and can call you for help and still probably be home before you pick up. We'll be okay. Instead," I said, "maybe you should fill out the papers for the Framework Foundation thing. It's weird, but it's also cool, and I think you should do it."

His annoyance at my having read his papers was brief. "What if someone connects it to me and it turns out not to be a positive thing? What if it's something terrible that just sticks to me forever?"

"You knew that when you were putting it together. I thought you liked the idea."

"You think so?"

"You don't think you were excited about it?"

He didn't have an answer.

"What changed between then and now?"

Did he look confused?

"I mean, it's pretty elaborate, and you put a lot of effort into it, and they want to use it. What was the point of that?"

"Maybe doing it was the point. Maybe I'm done with it. With all of that. Maybe that's what it took to get it out of me."

I wanted to repeat back to him: You think that writing it out got the alien out of you? But that seemed too far. "Anyway, since you used a fake name, maybe no one will ever be able to say for sure it's you."

"Maybe it doesn't seem as real to me anymore," he said, ignoring me.

"I don't understand that," I said. "You're less convinced now than you were when you sent it in? After what happened at the mall, you're less convinced? Huh."

The look on his face, and the fact that he had no better explanation, said I won this point before the words came of his mouth. It didn't matter, really, because this was a different version of him than the one I usually kept score with.

"Okay," he said, "Maybe I'll look it over again." It didn't feel like winning.

Trevor ran over to him to give him a hug and then we were out the door.

Whatever it was I thought was going to happen—plotting, planning, just talking things out about my father—none of that happened on our first bus trip. Trevor was wide-eyed for everything except Jason's glasses, which earned only an eye roll. Jason was full of music on the bus—he said he'd had a tune in his head when he woke up, but he didn't know where it was from. When he tried to hum it for me, I didn't recognize it, either.

When we got off the bus and crossed the street, he was starting in on the tune again when he pointed out Valimar stepping out of a car onto the sidewalk ahead of us.

"See," Jason said, "It could all be a musical. Valimar's mother probably just finished telling her how she and Valimar's dad are going to do the custody . . . "

"They're divorcing?"

"She said so." This was probably the first time I realized that Jason was forming relationships and having conversations with other people at school. Not upsetting or anything, but sort of a reminder that oh, yeah, he was a real person who was going to have his own life here. I liked Valimar, but I did think she and Toi too often tended to be upset about some kind of drama. Whatever—that was three out of four middle school girls on any given day of the week.

" . . . so just before she dropped Valimar off she told Valimar she wanted Valimar to be honest about her feelings and not keep them bottled up." Which, Jason guessed, was why Valimar looked so

frustrated. Valimar did look irritated. More irritated than usual.

Jason hummed his tune as Valimar's mom's car went around the corner, and Valimar dropped her backpack on the ground and unbuttoned her top two shirt buttons, rolled up her sleeves and untucked her shirt all around. I laughed because Jason's timing with the music worked so well, but also because it was a trip to see Valimar putting on her look. Jason imitated a fast drumbeat as Valimar, now looking her more ruffled self, picked up her backpack and started walking toward the drop-off gate with intent.

Next, Jason pointed at the teacher parking lot, where Ms. Payne was stepping out of her car. Ms. Payne, most students would agree, was extra. Extra extra. Pretty and funny and she talked to the students like they were her high school friends. She was only kind of organized and looked like she didn't put a lot of attention into her clothes, probably because she looked good in anything. On any day, her hair could be any color except blonde or brunette. And while Jason was humming along, Ms. Payne was staring at the cell phone in her hand and appeared to be yelling at it angrily. Was she fighting with her boyfriend? Arguing with her mom?

His tune worked everywhere we went, and it made it easier to enjoy the common middle school scenes of frustration playing out around us as we walked along. The kids who dropped their trash on the section of lawn the gardener had just finished cleaning, the teachers who came out the main hallway of the school in an angry cluster and then turned and headed into the administrative hallway, stern looks on their faces. In front of the school the Assistant Dean was chasing this way and that, warning kids to keep their acts in line while the kids he was yelling at raced away from him, flipping their skateboards and laughing at their own bad behavior.

"I don't have the lyrics yet, but it's going to be about how everyone in middle school is miserable, and partially it's because they're all a little bit—or maybe more than a little bit—fucked up themselves."

I told him I thought it was perfect.

"I know. I have to work on the plot, but it's a good start. I'm feeling super creative, not sure where it's coming from."

"It's gotta be the glasses," Trevor said. "Duh." We both had forgotten he was there with us, listening in.

I laughed. Jason cracked a small smile. He got the joke.

By the time we reached our lockers, I was really enjoying his vision of the chaotic misery of middle school. It was impossible to look around in middle school and not see the suffering. I found myself humming the melody that I hadn't been able to recognize throughout the rest of the day.

Although my father was super interested in the details of our bus ride, I brushed that off and asked about the Framework Foundation papers. He showed me the envelope sealed up and ready to mail.

"Why didn't you mail it?"

"I don't know."

"You used a fake name."

"Hear me out. Do I want to be that closely associated with the whole alien thing? Do you? Is that going to be my claim to fame in this lifetime?"

"Gosh," I said, "Who are you these days?"

"I don't know what you mean."

We were going to repeat the whole argument.

"Did you get adjusted, maybe? Like they fixed whatever it was making you so self-aware and so now you're going to be normal Dad like you never were before? You're not alien Dad anymore?" And there it was again, something in his expression that said he knew what I was talking about and that what I was saying was confusing to him because maybe it made sense. Then a desire to dismiss it emerged. Dismiss all that and move on.

Trevor snorted. "Alien Dad."

He tried to deny the alien thing, "I don't know that I ever . . . "

"Oh, come on. You made this whole project, that's how much

you ever." I paused. "Are you scared?"

"No. It just doesn't seem relevant anymore."

"The thing that happened at the mall? When did that become irrelevant?"

I knew I was saying this in front of Trevor, but he didn't react to it.

"That was . . . I don't know what that was." He looked confused. "Maybe we mischaracterized it."

"Right," I said, in a way that made it clear I didn't agree.

"I want to stay in my lane," he said. "I want to figure out what my lane is, and then stay there."

"Well," I said, seeing I wasn't going to get anywhere, but wondering why that was so. New tactic. "They're offering tickets for us to go see the museum and display and Trevor and I want to go. It would be educational, and you've never taken us on a vacation before. It's what a good parent would do. That's all in your new lane, right?"

He looked at me skeptically.

"You know what? I'm going to mail it off for you if you don't do it soon."

One day at the beginning of February, while heading to the lunch area, Jason posed alternative explanations for my father's situation.

"Maybe he's like part of a government experiment, and they messed with his memories, like Bourne or Wolverine or Winter Soldier. Or maybe it isn't a government, but some giant business corporation that secretly runs the world. Or, what if he's an alien experiment? I've read that aliens are experimenting with humans to make them more adaptable to climate change."

"What, and then they just cut him free?"

"Maybe they're watching him. Code name Seth. The Seth Syndrome. Ever see suspicious people around?"

"No. And all the time. Although no one more suspicious than anyone else."

"No one more suspicious than your father," he joked.

"True. Or maybe not. More like a weirdo than spy. They call him 'huero' at the burger joint near our place."

"That's basically what that means. Weird white guy."

"He said that they used to call him pinchy huero before he started coming in with Trevor and me."

"Oh, that's not good."

We both laughed. I'd already asked kids at school what it meant.

"And they also called him El Raton, because they always saw him emptying rat traps when he first moved in."

We sat down at a table. Almost as soon as we did, Isabel and Liz sat down at the same table.

"Hi Jess. Hi Jason. What are we talking about today?"

"My father," I said. "El Raton."

Valimar approached and sat down next to Jason, across from me. My hand was resting on the table and she reached out and gave it a friendly squeeze. Weird.

"I saw your Dad posting some flyers about the Walkathon around campus," she said. "It was kind of weird that he knew my name."

Isabel said, "He's been cutting and sorting papers in the library in the mornings. He always waves at me."

"Really," I said. I looked around the table. Why were these people joining us? Why did they feel so comfortable just sitting down and butting in?

Thomas was last. He and Jason bumped knuckles and then he sat down next to Isabel, where I could hardly even see him. And then for several surreal minutes this group of people discussed all the times they'd seen my father helping out and/or doing other things around campus in the last few weeks.

I was about to have some kind of fit when Thomas interrupted with, "Hey, have any of you seen Song?"

"I wonder if she moved," Isabel said. Or something like that. As the conversation moved onward, I looked around at everyone, feeling a little relieved that the focus had shifted away from me. I hadn't seen Song since last semester. I said to Jason, "You met her at the end of the semester, before break. Small girl, high energy, Vietnamese American, Midwestern accent, talks a lot a lot a lot."

"She's so funny," Liz said, not waiting for Jason to respond.

Jason asked, "She's the one who did that little move like the hula girls in the Small World Ride?"

We all thought about this in silence. We knew exactly the move Jason was referring to, which involved rocking her hips and then sort of pumping her arms up and down in front of her. And we all knew the hula girls. The hula girls did the move with their arms stretched out in front of them, but Song did it with her hands balled up and held closer to her body. That was Song's method of expressing satisfaction— usually over a test score, but for other things, too.

"Really," Thomas said. "I can't believe I didn't realize that's what that was."

"Now I kind of want to see her do it again," Valimar added.

Isabel said, "Same."

As they blathered on, I wondered, is this like, our new group? I looked at each of them. They seemed to think so. Jason looked super comfortable. When did that happen? I wanted to be irritated, but it was what it was.

On the way home on the bus one day, seated across the aisle from Jason, I remembered one of the stories Ms. Angela told me about the time she got on the bus wearing her magic glasses. Like most of those stories, she forgot she was wearing her magic glasses when she headed out to do errands. She got on the bus, and there was only one place she could see to sit—the bench seat near the front. There was a large man— big, both muscular and fat—on the middle of the bench, but there was a bit of space on the side of him, so she'd seated herself there, being *very careful to maneuver around his legs and to seat herself without touching him. He watched her sit down, paying close attention to her. Such close attention that it made her self-conscious.*

Once she was nearly settled, he shifted a little bit toward her, and she squeezed an equal distance away from him. She turned her attention to her cell phone, tapped it to start up some music, plugged in her headphones, and tried to ignore him.

But she couldn't. Even with her eyes nearly closed, facing toward the front of the bus, she couldn't stop herself from checking on him, each time finding that he continued to stare at her.

At some point, he reached out, and touched her cellphone.

Words appeared on the screen: Nice glasses.

Which was when Ms. Angela realized she'd worn her magic glasses out in public. I can remember her shaking her head at the memory of it, like how could she have done such a stupid thing? She didn't start with the fact that he'd just touched her phone and made words appear on the screen, which was what I thought was the cool part of the story. She was so aware of the glasses that she took them off, folded them up and put them into the sleeve in her bag. After that, when she looked back at him, what did she see?

"He wasn't there," Ms. Angela said, shaking her head. No one was there next to her on the bench seat. "That large man was nowhere to be seen." Then she asked me, "Do you know where he went?"

I remember smiling at Ms. Angela, because I knew.

"He didn't go anywhere. You couldn't see him because you took the glasses off."

"You are a bright little girl."

"Did you put the glasses back on?"

"I wanted to. But I got another message on my phone right then. It read: If I could take them from you, I already would have.

"I texted back: Are there others like you on this bus?

"He wrote: Put the glasses on. Maybe you can tell me."

For some reason, Ms. Angela laughed at that, like it was a funny thing. I remember being creeped out at the thought of invisible watchers all around us. Now it almost felt like my reality.

"Between you and me," Ms. Angela said, "someone would have had to search through my bag and show those glasses to me for me to admit I had them. And I wasn't going to let that happen. I was so mad at myself for forgetting I had them on. You can't take a secret and carry it around with you in broad daylight and expect it to stay a secret."

Chapter 14

It was Saturday, late in the morning, when there was a knock on the door. This was an out-of-place event, and Trevor and I stared at each other before we both stared at the door like we didn't know how to operate it. Our father was in the shower.

"Get it, Trev."

"You get it."

"If I have to get up to get it then I am also going to get you on the way there and the way back."

"No."

"Get it. Now, you little punk."

Trevor growled in irritation as he got up. When he was at the door, I got up and stood a few feet behind him as he opened it.

There was a woman there. Shoulder-length, wavy blonde hair, kind of a small, pointed face, dressed in a black-and-white checkered blouse with black pants. My father's age, easily.

"Hello," she said, voice rising on the "lo." She was looking at us as if we were familiar to her, but I had no idea who she was. "So, this is what you two turned into. Amazing! You're both nearly all grown up—oh, that's gone by much too fast! I haven't seen you since you were three," she said to me. Then she pointed at Trevor, "and you I have only seen in photos."

"My Dad's getting ready," Trevor said, flustered. "I'll go tell him." He rushed past me to the accordion door, slid it open, squeezed behind it and closed it. Loud and clear enough for the whole world to hear, he shouted at the bathroom door, "Dad, someone's here!"

I was left staring at the woman while we both listened.

"Hi," she said. The shower was off now. I heard the door open and my father and Trevor whispering to each other.

"You're Jessica, am I correct?"

"Yes. Are you my Dad's friend?"

"Your Dad's and your Mom's, kind of. Although I've known your Dad much longer. My name is Erin. I last saw you at your third birthday party, which was at a park somewhere." Her voice was very musical. "You're a beautiful girl, with a little bit of your Dad and a lot of your Mom in your looks. I love your hair, which must have skipped a generation because it doesn't look like either of theirs."

Which was true. Then Trevor was back beside me.

"Dad said he'll be right out."

I said, "Do you want to come in?" and Trevor shot me a look suggesting that was not what our father had told him to do.

As Erin walked in, I watched her as she checked out the place. The room, the décor, the messes from the morning that hadn't yet been cleaned up, the couch bed still in bed form, the door to my messy room wide open. Once she was inside and I could see her better, I thought that Erin might be a trans woman. It wasn't obvious. Her face was pixyish, with large dark eyes, pouty lips, and a narrow, pointed chin.

Then my father pushed aside the accordion door. Instead of just stepping out and saying hi, he first went through the motions of properly securing the door before giving his full attention to his guest. Amused by him and obviously happy to see him, Erin smiled broadly.

"Hi, Seth. How are you?" She did a low-key jazz hands thing. "Surprise."

"Hello?" It sounded as if my father was asking a question. He stared longer than a moment. Finally, finding the answer, he said, "Aaron."

Erin studied his reaction. I was so uncomfortable I almost peed myself thinking my father was going to do or say something awful.

"Fuck, it's so good to see you," he finally said. He crossed the room, extended his right arm to shake Erin's hand, which seemed very formal, but he rested his left hand on Erin's shoulder, which seemed affectionate, and didn't look away from her eyes. He pumped Erin's hand once or twice, and then Erin pulled him in for a quick hug that definitely seemed to be more a bro hug—quick and hips apart, ending

with a touch of discomfort or maybe even embarrassment on both sides.

I looked at my brother, who was watching all of this with as much disbelief as I was feeling, knowing he was thinking the same thing I was.

Who would have imagined that our father had friends?

Trevor and I pretended to do our homework in my room while the two of them talked in the front room. We listened to every word. It was like a secret peek into another person that my father had once been.

How many of him were there?

They talked about the people they remembered from school, with Erin doing all of the updating on what people were up to and my father throwing out names and questions. Erin asked about someone named Doug, but my father said he hadn't talked to him in a long while and couldn't offer any information. They remembered things together, pranks and parties and people they had crushes on.

In a code that was difficult to understand without seeing their faces, they talked about my mom and about us and our present situation, and then they touched very briefly on two women Erin dated before her transition, both of whom apparently had kids that had given Erin the chance to be a temporary father substitute before the relationships had ended. They talked about Erin's transition. It wasn't all Erin talking, but those were the parts that I enjoyed the most, because the stuff my father was sharing as they were catching each other up was all stuff I already knew. They avoided mentioning my mom by name or getting into the details of the divorce, but my father also didn't bring up any of his alien stuff and leaned heavily on the part where he was now the parent group president and a full-time parent. Like that made up for everything.

Erin booked a room at the hotel after sort of laughing about the idea of sleeping on a cot and explaining that none of us wanted to see what she looked like in the morning before she put herself together. Although she looked really great to me, we were more than comfortable believing her.

In the morning, over breakfast at the burger place, Erin commented that the three of us—my father, Trevor, and me—seemed to have established an ordered home. "I mean, it's not conventional at all, but you were all just thrown together and it seems like you're all doing so well."

"You sound surprised," Seth said.

"It is surprising!" The way she laughed at my father was so good-natured that I laughed, too. "Take a video of a day in your life today and show it to your younger self—you'd be surprised, too. You," she said, looking at my father, "You're different in curious ways. Mister Dad."

"Looks who's talking."

They both laughed at this.

"You're exuding comfort," Erin said. "You look content."

"You, too."

Erin said, "I've worked hard to look like that! But I don't know if I feel as in charge as I'm trying to sound. Sometimes some of it rings insincere, but I'm really doing well. There's a lifetime of conditioning to confront."

"My dad wasn't this normal at first," Trevor said. "Then he changed."

Erin looked at my father with some interest. "What changed?"

"I don't know," Seth said slowly. "It got easier to focus on what was important. Ignore the rest. There isn't as much time to think about yourself. That works better for me. Maybe."

"Interesting," Erin said.

"My Dad submitted a project to the Framework Foundation and they accepted it," I said, trying to sound like I was bragging but really trying to get Erin to ask about it.

"Ooh, the Framework Foundation. UFOs. I've heard of their museum. Next time I'm in Seattle, I am there."

"You've heard of them," my father said.

"Sure. I've done a couple of their online questionnaires," Erin brushed her hair away from her face. She had a pretty face. "It's weird when you actually sit down and wonder what the hell we're here for, isn't it?

"I saw a study that said two billion is the perfect number of people in order for humans and nature to live in harmony and comfort in a way that doesn't destroy every other life form on the planet. So what are you going to do with the other five billion? The other ten billion in ten years? We either need to figure out a way to spread out across the solar system, or else we have to start working on a way to cut our population by seventy-five percent! On the one hand, does the universe really need for humanity to spread? We're terrible caretakers. On the other hand, maybe that's what we were made to do." No one said anything. Once upon a time my father would have gone into a critical analysis of a spiel like that. Not the new and improved Seth.

"And you know," Erin added, "They say the odds of finding true love are one in two billion." We all thought about that a moment. To fill the silence, she continued on while switching tracks. "I have a friend who worships Gaia. You know, Mother Earth. My friend believes in reincarnation. She believes that before someone is reborn into a new life, they enter into a soul agreement with Gaia based on what it is they're supposed to learn in their next incarnation if they want to continue to grow spiritually, which I guess is what our souls want to do. The agreement lets them choose their family relationships, their friends, a lot of things based on what they're going to face in the life ahead. My friend thinks that all the things we deal with, good and bad, happen to us because there is something we need to learn from those good and bad things in order to progress to the next level."

"Seem like a potential set-up for blaming the victim," my father said.

"I agree with that a little bit. I find it hard to believe I agreed to all of this for my life. But then I'm like, who knows? Maybe I did."

Again, we all just kept eating. Not a sarcastic peep from my father. It was weird, but I wanted him to take a poke at it all. Trevor looked like he thought it was all crazy talk.

"So," I said slowly after half a minute more, "The papers from the Framework Foundation said we could also get free passes to visit. Maybe we could all go together. All he has to do is turn in the last paperwork."

"Really? That's awesome." Erin was onboard.

My father rolled his eyes.

"My father doesn't think so."

Erin understood. "You think I should try to talk him into it?"

"Would you?"

Chapter 15

Song came to school for the first time since break. She walked really stiffly into first period. Something about her was definitely off. She seemed really out of it. I watched Mrs. Rhude as she was watching Song moving toward her seat, and Mrs. Rhude looked worried. Song looked as if she hurt and she was a little out of it, like she was on medication and recovering from an accident or from being really sick. Mrs. Rhude looked like she was still thinking about it when her eyes went back to the papers on her desk.

There weren't any bruises, but Song's face was swollen and puffy and she just looked so not entirely present. Not herself at all. People were saying hi to her when they came in and saw her, and she didn't respond to all of them, and to those she did, it was hardly a reaction at all. She looked like she'd been broken, was what I thought, and then she'd missed school while getting better. A student could only miss so many days before they wouldn't get credit for classes, so maybe she had to be there. What had hurt her? Who had hurt her? She was also medicated for whatever it was. On top of it, she looked embarrassed, like she didn't want to be noticed. I felt so uncomfortable for her. I wanted to say something to make her feel better but at the same time I wanted to wait for her to signal that it would be okay to do that. Maybe she was hoping not to spend the day talking about whatever it was. I wanted everyone to stop staring at her.

There was a conversation going on in class before she walked in. I thought Song might have heard the very end of it, before the room quieted as everybody noticed her.

The kids who were there early were talking about the things that they thought they would remember about each other when they looked back at middle school. I surprised myself with a bunch of them, like the way Charles used to talk to his pencils as he lined them up on his desk, which he did so he could make sure he used the shortest one first. Someone brought up Alaya's habit of snacking on her lunch, usually leftovers from dinner, always stinking up the room every time she did it and then denying it was her. In English last year, which was after lunch, Eli said Marcus would sometimes ask to smell someone's palms so he could tell them what they'd just eaten. Marcus responded by bringing up the time Harlan Peterman pulled an unwrapped hamburger out of his pocket and started eating it.

Alaya asked if we remembered when Martha, who doesn't go to Ashbury any more, had pointed at Ms. Goodson and said in her creepy voice that Ms. Goodson must be pregnant—two weeks before Ms. Goodson found out she actually was pregnant. Jai had started middle school making noises—like, he would walk to the pencil sharpener on his tiptoes making dinosaur noises—but by eighth grade he was dropping to the floor sometimes when he came into class and then crawling to his desk like a soldier. There were some mentions of the way I would kick the desk of the person in front of me if they said something stupid. Then the conversation turned into talk about the things we wanted to be remembered for instead of the things people were saying about us. Alaya wanted us to remember that she'd worn something purple every day since the start of school this year. No one believed it was true even after she made the claim, which really bummed her out. I didn't say anything because I was happy being remembered as a desk-kicker. I thought it was probably the funniest conversation I'd had with these people in all of middle school. Even though Jason was only on month two of knowing any of them, he was laughing as hard as anyone else. And then Song came in, and the room quieted, and then the bell rang.

There was a test that morning. The teacher said she had to have Song take it, almost like she was apologizing. Clearly, Mrs. Rhude knew the back story of whatever it was that had happened to her, and would never share it with us. "Even if you don't get any right, a zero is better than no score at all."

Harsh, either way.

About 10 minutes into the test, Jai made a growling bear noise and crumpled up his test in his hand. He asked Mrs. Rhude for another copy, so he could start fresh, and the teacher said okay. When he got up to get a new copy, I saw him also slide a piece of paper in front of Song, really low-key. He went to the front of the classroom, tore up the balled-up piece of paper in his hand, and tossed the pieces into the trash while making a swoosh noise. He thanked Mrs. Rhude as she handed him another test, and then sat down and started writing again.

He couldn't have gotten away with it except that he's the smartest kid in the class, and Mrs. Rhude would never suspect him of trying to pull anything. She had her eyes on other students.

Song was in such a stupor that it seemed like she might not even be aware that there was a paper in front of her. At some point, though, she looked around, seemed to realize some of what was going on, and after seeming to be thinking about it a minute she slowly scratched her name at the top of the page Jai had put in front of her. At the end of class, some of us grouped around her desk, and someone grabbed the original quiz Song had been given and made it disappear, too, and then we all moved to the front of the class together to turn in her test. We also all walked her to her next class together. Nobody talked.

Song looked sad though all of it. I knew she heard what we were talking about. I knew she was hoping this was not what we remembered her for.

At what point did I come to the conclusion that the situation was not going to right itself? Was it the day I went to the office to drop off paperwork for Mr. Garrison during second period? Passing by the open door of the Parent Center I heard my father's voice in the mix of a group of voices. Laughing, of all things. When I walked past the second door that led into the same room, I could see him sitting at a table in a room with ten other parents, all of them working on something together that looked almost like crafts—one was cutting colored paper, one was wrapping little boxes in cellophane, and another was tying ribbon bows. One was writing messages on balloons and another was tying the balloons to a curved piece of metal. They were all so caught up in the things they were working on and the conversation they were having that they were oblivious to my presence, and there was my father, sitting in the middle of them like he wasn't the biggest weirdo of all.

I thought about the way Erin had described him. She said he looked content. And I completely agreed with that assessment. He didn't look like he thought he was in the middle of a bunch of invasive, over-involved parents. This did not in any way make sense to me. Whatsoever.

One explanation was that the thing he said he'd wanted had happened. Some sort of bug fix had been applied to his situation and he would just be normal like everyone else for the rest of his life. The problem was that I did not believe that was true. That was not how things worked, no matter what he said. Even if there was something going on with him, with the mind messing stuff and all that, I didn't believe his explanation for his current situation. My father was the type who always thought he was right, even when it was clear he didn't know as much as he thought he did. In one of the many conversations I had with Jason on the topic, I told him that my father's explanation for how life on Earth worked didn't sit right with me.

Then there was the morning Jason and Trevor and I walked around the corner of the street that led to the drop-off gate and there in the street, moving from one car to the next to the next, was someone wearing a big panda headpiece. This person had a pile of flyers in his hands, and he was leaning in toward each car to hand the driver a copy. It was only a few steps before I realized it must be my father. Those were his pants and shoes. I saw one copy of the flyer on the sidewalk. It was an invite for an Ashbury Hills Restaurant Night at Panda Panda Panda restaurant.

This was just not right anymore.

Instead of pulling my hair over my face so that he maybe wouldn't notice it was me as I passed by, which would have normally been my reaction, I walked straight up to him. When he turned around from the car he was leaning into, I was standing right there in front of him.

I heard the gasp of surprise at seeing me. He handed me a flyer. When he spoke, the sound of his voice came out through the nose.

"One of the parent group moms brought this for me to wear while I handed out flyers. She thought it would make me look less scary and that parents would be more likely to open their windows to take a flyer from me. But I imagine the end result is pretty terrifying, right?"

Totally terrifying.

"I want to see a therapist," was all I said before I returned to Jason and Trevor and walked into school.

My father was still at school at the end of the day, so Trevor decided to go home with him instead of taking the bus. The two of them texted me to ask if I wanted anything from the market, so I knew I'd be home before them. Jason got off the bus with me at my stop, and I showed him where I lived. We spent less than three minutes inside.

While he checked everything out without saying a word, I went to my father's desk, grabbed the Framework envelope, filled up a water bottle for us, and then said, "Let's get going before they get here."

I was still so irritated with my father. I put the envelope in the mailbox we passed on our way back to the bus stop.

Once we were back on the bus and on our way, Jason pulled up the Framework website on his phone and started reading to me.

"Scientists are studying the possibility that organic, living material traveled from Mars to Earth as a result of a meteor strike on the former that knocked loose pieces that were flung all the way to the latter. This is after earlier studies into the possibility of biological matter being transported to Earth in space dust from asteroids or meteorites. The only reason they are even considering these scenarios is that science is not yet satisfied with its own explanation for the origin of life on Earth. The fact seems to be that although theoretically all the ingredients for complex organisms are present, the recipe eludes them. If life just happened, we would find evidence to support that everywhere in the universe around us. Our world's myths point to an extraterrestrial origin for life, and it seems that science is finally coming around to that possibility."

After he finished, he swiped around the website quickly.

"These are weird," Jason said. "Look. These are paintings of the different kinds of angels made by an artist over two hundred years ago based on descriptions found in the Bible."

They weren't like any angels I had ever seen, for sure. Instead of being fat little winged babies, the cherubs were lions with wings and human faces. The ones called seraphs had six wings that hid most of their faces and bodies, and they also had eyes all over their bodies. Eyes were a big thing, apparently, in relation to angels. One type of angel, the throne, looked like two interlocked wedding ring bands, with each band covered with eyes. Each of the angels was creepy, but together they definitely seemed like they belonged in a sci-fi movie more than in the Bible.

"Are there any normal angels?"

"There are 'thousands and thousands' of angels in the Judeo-Christian angelic hierarchy," he said as he skimmed the story, "and there are nine levels of angel. Generally, the lower down the rungs of the ladder, 'the more likely they were to resemble the typically held image of angels as resembling humans with wings.'"

"Gosh, can you imagine if one of those things appeared in front of you and tried to convince you it was an angel?"

"They look like aliens."

"Right? I read something on that site that said that the Bible said giants were the children of angels and humans. I would have thought that if you mixed angels with humans, you'd get something better looking than a human, right? But if these were the types of things that were having babies with humans, then ugly giants make sense."

"What if your dad really looks like one of those?"

"Those rings with eyes on them don't even look like living things. They look like objects. Like, if a couple of spinning wheels appeared in front of me I would never imagine it was an angel. It looks like some kind of funky ancient logo."

We both stared at it.

Jason asked, "That one has got be anaerobic, right?" We were talking about aerobic and anaerobic in biology. "Maybe that's the kind of thing that lives in a place where there's no oxygen. Can you imagine if space was like the ocean, and you could just come across a school of those floating around in the dark matter like jelly fish?"

"I don't like to think about it, except maybe that it's better with them out there than down here."

Once off the bus, we had to walk a couple blocks of back streets to get to Splendor.

He asked me, "Do you remember Ms. Angela talking about angels?"

"Totally. I think she was the reason I was such a well-behaved kid."

In his sad attempt at a Ms. Angela voice, he said, "'Oh, they're watching, but they aren't there all the time because there's a lot to watch. You can't ever tell when they're standing over you and when they're not, and it's not always easy to tell whose side they're on.'"

"Omigosh, yes, and she said that she could see the angels with her glasses, which was the real reason she couldn't wear them out in public! If she could see them, then they could see her glasses. I forgot that part. She wasn't supposed to have the glasses and if the angels knew she had them they would take them back."

He shook his head, "I can't believe our parents let her be our babysitter."

"Before that she was a teacher!" I sighed. "She was great."

"I know, but every time I came home from seeing her I would have all these funky ideas in my head."

When we reached Splendor, at the very first house we passed, Jason pointed at the front door.

"Ms. Angela told me the reason the angels couldn't look inside her house for the glasses was because she had a door like that. See the X pattern the boards form on the bottom half of the door? She said that makes it a witch door. It's supposed to ward off spirits."

The next two houses on either side of the street had the same kind of door.

"They're all witch doors."

"Yeah, I remember that, too," *Jason said.* "It's a weird little street."

We walked by both of our old houses. He'd been out of his house longer than me, but he noticed everything that had changed, from the color it was painted to the new landscaping, the new brick walkway, even the fact that the new owners had curtains in the front window instead of blinds.

For me, it was sort of unreal. My old house felt like it was still mine. It was as if someone had stolen it from it me, and then had the nerve to live in it. The thought of it almost offended me, and I was glad that even though there was a car in the driveway, there was no one around to be seen. They hadn't even done anything to update or make it theirs—it looked exactly the same. We stopped on the sidewalk out front.

"Mom started obsessing over a charge on the visa bill, and Trevor and I thought she was having one of her over-reactions. For two days, it seemed like she was always on the phone with someone, and saying things like, 'Do I need to check the goddamn phone bills, too?' and 'Your father has compartmentalized his life so completely that I'm going to have to search his car just to see if I can find any clue what he's been up to.' Then, on the second day, it was, 'I think your father cheated on me. Possibly more than once. I asked the bar where I think he met her if they keep their interior surveillance footage because I really want to be able to shove it in his face when I confront him.'

"Then, late one horrible night, any feeling that we were one family unit was completely destroyed. Trevor and I were in the bedroom, both of us crying, while they argued back and forth, room by room, through the whole house. He kept walking away from her and she kept following him. At that point, we didn't really feel bad for mom but we totally blamed my father. We felt really bad for ourselves, because of the way they went at it, the things they said, the language they used. It was like we weren't there at all or they didn't care what we heard or saw."

"My parents were like that, too," Jason said. "One day, they just hated each other. They wouldn't separate because neither of them was willing to leave the house, because they thought that meant they would lose their claim on it. My mom got to the point where sometimes, when he walked into the room talking disrespect to her, she would just grab something—a plate, a piece of fruit, the remote—and throw it in his direction. After she did it the first time—she threw a ceramic cup at him that he blocked with his hand—he was always extra careful about keeping his eyes on her hands when he was talking crap. At some point, all my mom wanted to do was be done with it, and she focused on that like a laser," he said. "If any of it had been left to my father, he would have stretched it out as long as he could."

"My mom was like that, too. Once she flipped, she couldn't be done with it fast enough."

"It took a month for my mom to find the townhouse and another month to convince him to buy her out of the house." Jason thought about it, shrugged. "So, I had like 10 weeks' notice before my childhood ended. I know there's people who have had worse, but it sucked."

I was sure that if I walked up the driveway, went to the front door and let myself in, that it would still feel like my home.

"Let's keep walking," I said. He looked kind of stiff. "Is all the walking hurting your back?"

"It's okay. It has been sore. The walking doesn't make it worse."

Three houses further, and we were in front of Ms. Angela's

house. It, too, looked exactly the same.

"Do you think she still lives here?" I couldn't remember the last time I saw her. "We were with her all the time for about five years, and then we had school and the after-school playground and then we stopped needing a babysitter. After that, I can really only remember waving at her whenever we did see her."

"It looks exactly the same," Jason said.

"Let's go knock." I was moving toward the front door before he could say no. I knocked and was taking a step back from the door when he stepped up beside me.

The door opened.

I think we both gasped.

It was Ms. Angela, wearing a pair of thick-framed glasses. The magic glasses. Or someone who looked like her. Someone who looked twenty or thirty years younger than I had ever seen her look. I'm sure Jason and I both looked surprised.

"Hello? How can I help you?"

"Ms. Angela?" My voice was so weak, it sounded like I'd lost it. This woman looked exactly like her. I cleared my throat.

"Yes?"

"I'm Jessica Adams. You used to babysit me. Not that long ago, really. My friend here, Jason, too. We both grew up on Splendor."

"Of course, dear," she said. "I remember you." When I thought it seemed that she did not.

"We were in the neighborhood and just wanted to say hi."

"I'm glad you did, Jessica. It's always nice to see my kids grown up. I'm in the middle of some things I'm working on here, and I don't have time to talk. Thank you for coming by to see me." No hug, no handshake. Just that and a closed door.

When we had walked back out to the sidewalk, Jason asked, "That wasn't Ms. Angela. Or was it?" He looked mystified.

"I want to say the answer to both of those questions is yes."

By the time we'd reached the end of the street on our way back to the bus stop, Jason and I agreed that not only had Ms. Angela used her magic glasses to go visit a parallel reality, but also that a younger, parallel world version of her had used her reality's version of the glasses to come to visit our reality. We were joking, but maybe not really.

"A parallel dimension where we don't exist, apparently," I said.

"Maybe where she's from we haven't moved in yet."

"That doesn't sound very parallel."

"That was weird! She looked younger than my mom." Jason's mom was like 19 years older than us. Super young looking for a mom. "In all my memories of her, Ms. Angela is a wise grandma."

"Right. And all the retirement and plastic surgery in the world doesn't work like that."

"Maybe that was one of her daughters?"

"Her daughters were older than that when we met them back then."

"Yeah, I guess."

When we hit the boulevard, we bought ice cream bars at the corner liquor store. He had to cross the street so he could catch the bus going west, and I stayed on the other side so I could catch the bus east. We started texting each other when we first sat down on the benches that faced each other across the street, when we were the only ones there. When people started showing up around us, we started commenting on the way each one smelled. We were both laughing at our phones, and I didn't know why, but it was stupid and fun. Even better, our buses got there at the same time, so no one got left behind.

Surprisingly, or maybe once it would have been, my father told me he'd already made an appointment for me the following week with his therapist Dr. Penny.

Even more surprising, he asked if I was feeling okay.

"Sure," I said, keeping the emotion out of my expression. "I just thought maybe it could be better, and maybe that's about me, so I

wanted to talk with someone who might know."

"Okay," he said. And then the weird part: "You might want to think about how you want your hair done."

Chapter 16

I liked time alone at home. I liked reading books. I liked getting my homework done. Trevor and I both did. Since forever, it was what we did when we got home from school. That was how our mom trained us, and it totally stuck. We didn't usually talk, unless we were helping each other. Our father liked this habit, because it gave him another time zone during the day when he didn't have to think about us.

Afterward I liked to crawl into bed with my phone and binge watch whatever I could while I checked in with my friends and they checked in on me. If he wanted to, Trevor would sit on the floor in my room with his laptop and play his games online with his friends. One day while we were in the middle of this routine the telephone rang. It was an old-fashioned phone, with an old-fashioned ring, the kind that could be produced by a ringtone on our cell phones—the cellphone matched the sound except for the rattle that accompanied the ring, the part that made it feel sharper and more intrusive. It was just like the day Erin knocked on the door. Trevor and I stared at each other, because we literally had never heard the phone ring. No one ever called our father.

I picked it up. "Hello?"

"This is Maylene from the Framework Foundation, looking to speak with Schreiber Esse?"

The words Framework Foundation made my stomach turn a little bit. It was similar to that feeling I got when I thought about the alien stuff too much.

They'd gotten the paperwork.

"Um, My dad's not here right now. Can I get your phone number so he can call you back?"

"Who am I speaking with?"

"This is his daughter Jess."

"Your name is Jess Esse?"

I almost laughed, but held it in.

"Yeah. You're not . . . making fun of my name, are you?" I timed the mid-sentence pause perfectly.

"Not at all, no," she lied. Her name was Maylene. Was that a real name? In my imagination, Maylene could have been a bald woman sitting in a room with a bunch of her clones, all of them making calls, each speaking in a different language or with a different accent. Maylene, of course, had a twang. What if it was just some sort of scam? What if they were a cover for something—if not aliens, then someone else? Some alien-worshipping cult?

"I was just calling to tell your father that we hope he and you will be able to visit us soon," she said.

It sounded kind of creepy, so I did laugh.

Maylene said, "I'm sorry?"

"Oh, no. It's me, not you," I said. "I'm picturing you as an alien. After we hang up, I'm going to feel like an alien just called me. You've got to get that a lot, right? Can you just say something that's human sounding?"

"So, no, that's . . ." She was confused, which could have been human sounding, I thought.

I said, "It bothers me that you put so much effort into trying to convince people that there is a possibility that aliens were once here. It's old news. I mean, they're here. Maybe they've always been here. I just don't think there is any way I could know that and you could not. I'm fourteen and you work for the Alien Foundation."

"Framework."

"Whatever," I said. "I just don't trust it. It's all very suspicious to me. That's all. I'll give my dad the message. What's your number?"

After I'd written it down I replaced the phone in its cradle. Trevor was watching me with his eyebrows up.

"I wish I hadn't answered. There's no voicemail with that kind of phone—he wouldn't know otherwise. Now I'm going to have to tell him. Someday."

What no one mentioned to me before my session with Dr. Penny was that I was going to cry. Afterward, my friends who had been to therapy said that everyone knew that you cried the first time. Clueless as I was, I went in with all these ideas of how I was going to direct the conversation and maybe talk about what was going on with my dad, without me having to have my mind and emotions examined too closely.

My father described Dr. Penny like this: "She was very poor growing up. She studied to become a hair stylist after high school. After a few years of doing that, she went to college and got her degree, paying her way by cutting hair, and then she became a therapist who on the side continued to do hair for her longtime hair clients. She kind of does one or the other, and for some clients she does both. I figured you needed a haircut, too, so why not?"

"That's the secret behind you having had the same length hair literally my entire life?" Except for now, I thought. He was shaggier looking than I ever remembered him looking. It didn't occur to me until I was at Dr. Penny's that it was likely because he'd stopped going to the therapy sessions I'd never known about.

Before Dr. Penny had me put on a smock, she had me sit in the styling chair and the two of us talked. She stood behind me, so it was a conversation we had while looking at each other in the mirror. First we talked about how I wanted my hair to look. Then, and I wasn't sure how she did it, Dr. Penny sort of touched on every single issue going on in my life. Something like, "Goodness, with your parents' divorce and moving to a new house, your mother leaving, and then moving in with your father, all of that and the pressure of middle school, how has that made you feel?" Working through this, I just lost it. Before long, I was babbling about how stupid and immature my parents were and how they'd left the ultimate responsibility for me and Trevor to me and Trevor and how does someone's mom just up and leave them for six months? Does that happen to other kids?"

"It does," Dr. Penny said, a little sadly.

When I'd settled down, it was time for a smock and my shampoo.

While Dr. Penny washed my hair, I talked about living with my father, and I felt sort of like I was getting into my groove. I decided the best strategy was to not directly ask anything about him. In fact, I decided I was just going to act as if it had never occurred to me that my father might have talked about me to her at all.

"Where are you living now?"

"We're renting rooms in a building that used to be a motel."

"Oh, yes. How is that going?"

"It's . . . okay. I think maybe the challenge and how different it is has maybe made it a little more fun than I would have thought. Sometimes it sort of feels like a vacation stay that never ended. I think a year ago if one of my friends had told me that they lived where I live now, I would have felt bad for them. But now that I'm here, I don't feel bad for me. So."

"That's good."

"Yeah, but, um . . . you're not going to be telling anyone anything I say to you?"

"No, this is a conversation between us."

Dr. Penny turned off the water, squeezed out my hair, and wrapped a towel around my head. She told me to sit up. Then it was over to the chair again, and we were facing each other in the mirror. I felt like the mirror left me no place to hide.

"So," I said slowly, "when we first moved in, what sort of came out over the first few months is that my dad maybe thinks he's an alien."

"He told you that?" This did not phase her. She knew this. She was focused on the hair between her fingers and the snipping scissors, but something told me she was interested.

"Yeah."

"What do you think of that?"

"Well, I mean, I don't know, sometimes now I wonder if everyone he knows is an alien. He knows you. For a long time. Maybe

you're an alien."

"I'm not," she said. She paused a moment to see how serious I was, then went back to clipping.

"Fine. You can say that. I can say that. But we don't really know. We can't really, really know who someone else is, right? You can get to know them, you can think you have some idea of who they are, but really, for all you know, that's not who they are." I felt myself getting emotional again. "I mean, who knows? How can you know? That's what you do, isn't it? Try to help people figure out who they are? And don't you have to figure out who they are before you can do that? My father comes here and talks to you for something like twenty years, and for twenty years tells you that this is who and what he is and still, just like it is with anyone in the world, for you it comes down to 'Do I believe him?' Do you really know? Does he really know?"

Dr. Penny nodded.

I took a deep breath.

"My mom used to say that you never know what is going on in someone else's marriage, because you're on the outside. But isn't that true in the marriage, too? Both people are on the outside of the people they're with, even if they sometimes fool themselves into thinking that isn't so. They think they know each other inside out. They don't know how wrong they are until the day they find out how wrong they are."

"I'm not disagreeing with everything that you've said," Dr. Penny said, "but I believe many people are exactly as they seem to be. I think we have an instinct to judge each others' characters, and the real problem lies in the way we try to rationalize away our instincts. For instance, ignoring the feeling that someone has a bad character because he or she is good-looking."

I thought about that.

She changed the subject. "How did your father tell you about his situation?"

"So, um, he had a project he was working on that was all about that. I went through it to see what it was. So, yeah, that was kind *of weird. I thought it was maybe some kind of mental thing that was maybe not so bad that he didn't have a grip on it. I mean, everybody is screwed up a little, and it wasn't like he was trying to do alien things, right? Just, I guess, thinking that he thought he was thinking alien thoughts. It just made him seem a little sadder, really. A little more lonely.*

    "The thing is, just when I was sort of getting used to the idea—I guess that was what was happening—suddenly he's done with that. Like, he doesn't believe that anymore and doesn't want to talk about it."

    That caught Dr. Penny's attention.

    "He said that?"

    "Yeah."

    "Interesting. What brought that about?"

    Got her.

    "I honestly don't know."

    "How is his hair?"

    "Now that you mention it, it is getting long, especially for him."

    "Is he dating someone? Is he seeing this Bridget woman?"

    I had to think a minute to place the name with the face from the roller-skating night. Why did Dr. Penny think that?

    "I don't think so. I mean, I guess there would be time to have a secret life. I guess for him it would be a second secret life, right? But I don't think so. He's too busy being Super Dad. Sometime right around Christmas, he became like this different person. A tree, presents, dinner with my grandparents, and it has just spiraled out of control from there. I can't even get away from him at school. I mean, I don't know what to think. He said he was waiting to be fixed so he wouldn't feel alien anymore. So is that what happened? Did you put him on some kind of medication?"

    She shook her head. No.

    "I don't want to believe that there are aliens inside of us living

out some kind of video game life here. Or that there is some sort of game 'fixer' who is making adjustments? I mean, that's not what's going on, right?"

Dr. Penny smirked.

"So then is this just how people are? One day they're one thing and one way and the next it completely changes forever? What's the point in deciding you're anything?"

"Jessica, is it possible that what you consider to be your father's former lack of empathy might actually be the opposite? Wasn't your grandfather some kind of science fiction fan? Maybe even a comic book writer? Is it possible that your dad maybe absorbed too much of that when he was growing up? What I've noticed is that . . . well, what is possible with your father is that he associates a little more closely with his environment than most people do."

She had a whole theory.

"It's possible that living with you, being your sole caretaker, and then also spending time at your school among the staff and teachers, has brought out aspects of his personality that have encouraged him to try to be a better father. If you think about what a chameleon does, changing its color to fit its environment, I think your father does the same sort of thing internally, in terms of his emotions and his environment."

"So, it's not like you prescribed him something to make him less abnormal? Or did something to him?"

She smirked. "Is that why you said you thought I might be an alien?"

"Maybe."

"Oh, I haven't seen him for months now."

"Since when? Since . . . "

"Since early December."

"Well, it was January that it became obvious to me, but it started in December. He's very much like, 'I'm done with all that stuff from before.' He sent in some project to a UFO museum, and they told him they wanted it, and he's done everything he can to blow them off.

"I just thought if there was some pill you gave him that made him normal, maybe you have something that would make me not care about who or what he thinks he is."

"I don't have a pill for you, Jessica. There's no magic pill, and if there were, I wouldn't prescribe it to you. You don't need a magic pill. Except for the stuff about your father, the things you are concerned about are the types of things most girls your age have on their minds. Remember, your father's issues are not your issues. Although I admit that you do have me curious about him."

"Can you call him to set up an appointment?" This seemed like it could help.

"It doesn't work like that, for either of my lines of work. I have to wait for clients to come back to me."

The end result of the whole session, surprise of surprises, was that I did sort of feel a little better walking out of her salon slash office with my hair done. But more importantly, I was clear on who it was I needed to talk to: Bridget.

The Framework Foundation called again while Trevor and my father were at baseball practice.

"Hi, this is Maylene, from the Framework Museum."

"Hi." I remembered our last conversation. Felt a little bad about it. Sometimes I snapped.

She said, "I wanted to check in with you to see if your father had any questions."

"Hi. This is his daughter Jess. You know, I don't think we're going to be able to go until spring or maybe until after school is out in June. I'm going to be graduating and it's made it hard to plan things."

"I understand. And congratulations. Is it high school?"

"Middle school."

"That's great. I remember being fourteen. High school awaits."

"It can wait." I said.

"Listen, Jess, I didn't feel very good about our last conversation."

I've moved on, I thought. "Can I ask you something?"

"Sure."

"Do you believe in all the things the Framework talks about? Like, do you believe in aliens?"

"It's hard to know what to believe, isn't it? So, to start with, I was raised a Christian—my father was a pastor—in a very Christian community. There was a boy I grew up with in that town who viewed the Bible as fantasy or science fiction. He thought that it could easily be interpreted as an allegory of the story of extraterrestrials establishing life on the planet. You know, it's a story where a host of beings assumes oversight of the planet, battling amongst themselves for control while overseeing their creations and guiding their development. There's magic, there are orbs made of glowing metal filled with creatures that sound like horrors descending from the sky. Well, when I was your age, this boy killed himself, and it was the community, the most Christian parts of it, that pushed him to it. It really undermined any faith I had. As soon as I left home for college, I was into trying every religion at one point or another, as long as it didn't involve a crucifix.

"When I started working at the Framework, part of the reason was because I wanted to disprove Christianity. We get a lot of pushback from Christians because they are the religious majority here and they're threatened by what lies at the end of the path the Framework mode of thinking takes a person down. Now that I've been here a while, I understand that faith and religion aren't in the same arena as science and history. In fact, I'm so far gone from where I started that I think even having the debate gives their argument more credit than it deserves.

"So, your question is, do I believe in aliens? Oh, yes. Even if I didn't, it's just not mathematically possible that the biological diversity of the universe is limited to this planet."

Fine, I thought.

"So, like I said last time, I think they're already here. I mean, what if asking 'Are they real?' isn't where we should be focused? What's *the point of arguing about when they first landed? It's like climate change. What's the point in arguing about why it's happening? It's too late for that. Let's just make the world safe from whatever the changes are going to do to us. You know what I'm saying? Is there someone trying to figure out why the aliens are here? What they're doing? Look around you. They could be anyone. They could be anywhere." There it was again. I was definitely starting to lose it.*

"The Framework isn't all about extraterrestrials, either," Maylene said, hanging in there. "The marketing has to be improved, I guess. We study ideas about parallel dimensions, the multiverse, mathematical theories, the composition of reality, string theory, black holes, quantum physics. We're interested in our place in the universe and we believe there is something to be found at the nexus of these ideas that will help make clearer what our role is. We think that by making it clearer to us—not only who we are and how we got here but what 'here' really is—we can start having the real discussion, which is about what our future should look like. We need to figure that out so we can start working toward it."

"See, I don't understand how this helps anyone," I said. "Like, maybe start with making something people can use to identify them, so we know who and where they are."

"One thing we're not interested in is becoming part of creating a modern myth," Maylene said, talking right past me. "We see people trying to construct a storyline with Grays and Reptilians, we see it with the Raelians, where various science fiction clichés are being used to weave together a more modernistic mythology that appears to be scientific but is still pop culture storytelling."

"Yeah," I say, "but science—you know? It's not like they aren't updating things all the time. This is just something where they don't understand all the math involved. I mean, I believe in ghosts, too, and good and bad spirits that sometimes interact with our lives."

"Yeah, I hear you. Science is an emotionally dissatisfying solution. There was a philosopher who said that there is a physical

plane of existence and a spiritual plane of existence that don't necessarily interact. You might as well be asking if consciousness and self-awareness are a real thing or whether that's just what we use to convince ourselves that something meaningful occurs between feedings and sleep."

I didn't get most of what she'd said, but for some reason that didn't stop me from saying, "It's just missing something."

"You're a bright girl for a middle schooler."

People think all middle schoolers are idiots.

"My mother never talked down to me. Had to keep up to stay in the conversation. Have you ever met someone who says they're an alien?"

"I have."

"Do you believe them?"

"Each person is different. I will say, one, that I've heard that from some convincing people. What I believe is there is a reason for each story, and each story, true or not, conveys some elements that are usually measurable and comparable to other stories, and then when you hear enough stories, you begin to see patterns."

"What if they're here among us?"

"I'm not an alien, Jessica. That's really the reason I called you again. I couldn't stop thinking about our conversation, and that's really why I called you back. I'm not that different from you. We all have questions and none of us is one hundred percent certain we want all the answers."

Chapter 17

Two weeks later, it was March, and the candy bar fundraiser to raise money to pay for eighth grade events during the last week of the school year was on. Every senior at Ashbury knew that the fundraiser signaled the approaching end of their middle school suffering, and their lifted spirits could be felt throughout the student body.

It hadn't taken much to figure out where Bridget lived. In the school library, I was able to log into the alumni project database, which at the startup said it was intended to provide "a view into the diversity of lives being lived by Ashbury's former students." There were only three Bridgets in the whole of the listing, and with those names I was able to look through social media to find a photo to confirm which one was her. Bridget Locke. Then I did a search using that name and found her phone number and her address. After brainstorming ideas with Jason about how to run into her and talk to her, we ended up on the sidewalk between the parking lot and her townhouse in the complex where she lived.

Sometime between the time I saw him on Wednesday afternoon and the time he came to school on Thursday morning, Jason had his hair colored blue, like dark blue. He got a haircut, too, but however it looked was lost in the blue of it.

"I felt like it," was what he shrugged out when I asked.

We sold 75 candy bars on Thursday, starting as soon as we could get there after school and staying there until the six o'clock, coming-home-from-work rush was over, but never saw her on the pathway we thought she would have to take to get to and from her place. We picked up another four boxes at school on Friday, and set up again Saturday morning.

We got her after she parked her car and walked up the path, coffee in her hand. Neither of us had seen her leave, so Jason decided we were witnessing her walk of shame, which set us both to giggling.

She came right up to us and asked Jason if there was any dark chocolate almond. He pointed to that section of the display box.

"What grade are you two in?" She asked. She said it as she pulled dollar bills out of her waistband. "How much is it?"

"They're two dollars each."

I thought she was cute, really. Too cute for my father. Her hair was really thick and curly and dark and beautiful and she had a nice smile. Her smoky eye makeup was amazing.

"We're in eighth grade," Jason said, stiff as a board.

"I sold these things when I was in ninth grade," she said. "The candy bars were twice as thick and cost half as much."

That was my window.

"Excuse me," I said. "Were you at the Ashbury roller-skating thing?"

"I was." She smiled and looked closer at me. "You're from Ashbury Hills Middle School? Way over here? You look familiar to me, too. What's your name?"

"Jessica."

"Hi, Jessica, I'm Bridget."

"You know, I think we might have met that night. Do you know my dad Seth Adams?"

She smiled broadly. "I do know your dad. We used to work in the same office. I don't remember meeting you that night, but there was so much going on. I do recognize you now from a picture on his desk, only you've grown up."

That sort of answered one of my questions. The way she said all of it made it sound like she wasn't having a secret affair with my father. There was no space there for any kind of conversation. I felt like the contact was going to end.

"Can I ask a favor," I said. "Can I use your bathroom? We've been out here for like two hours now."

"Absolutely. My place is just down this path. And you know what? Maybe I'll get some cash and buy a bunch more."

I asked, "Sweet tooth?" Bridget traded Jason six dollars for three candy bars.

"No, not for me. Well, most of them not for me. For party favors?" She stared at them in her hand. "We'll see," she smiled again. "People love these."

She looked at me. "You ready?"

"Let's go," I said.

Inevitably, on the walk up the path to her house, Bridget said, "So how is your dad?"

"He's good . . . he's, I don't know. He's like all over the place these days. He seems like he's . . . happier? He's been like Mr. Super parent group president lately, which is like, I mean, who wants their dad at their school all the time?"

"Right? No one."

"It's just that there were things going on with him that were sort of unique. Things my brother and I enjoyed. And now he just doesn't care."

"That's kind of vague."

"It's kind of weird."

"Oh, good. Your father and I always had weird conversations. I really enjoyed that about him."

"Did he tell you about this project he was doing for the Framework Foundation?"

"The alien stuff. He was so into that. I thought he'd given that up."

"Yeah, exactly. Well, the Framework Foundation accepted it, but he's been acting like he wants nothing to do with it."

"I don't know if that's as much a 'crazy dad' thing as it is a lazy man thing," Bridget said in a snarky way that made me smile. We reached the front door of her townhouse.

"Bathroom's in there," she said once we were inside. "I'm going to run back and buy those candy bars."

Bridget's place was totally weird, starting with the bathroom. On the sink, there was a plastic cup with a toothbrush in it, a bar of hotel soap sitting in its ripped-open wrapper, and a travel-size tube of toothpaste. Moderately clean. There was literally nothing in the medicine cabinet, and the cabinet beneath the sink was stuffed with toilet paper. The only towel was really worn and also had the words Landmar Hotel Poolside on it. Minimal, I thought.

That impression was reinforced by everything I saw when I exited the bathroom. The living room had a futon as its only piece of furniture other than the very small television, which was sitting on the carpeted floor completely across the room from the futon. There was one stool at the counter that separated the living room from the kitchen and on the counter was a small stash of makeup and nail polish, including a hair brush, tweezers, makeup brushes, and a small cosmetic mirror. That pile was the most normal thing I'd seen in there so far. I wanted to start picking through everything. In the kitchen, there was no kitchen table and the refrigerator was so miniature that it looked like a joke. What could she possibly be keeping in there? There was a stove with an oven, but no other appliances, no microwave, no blender, nothing.

I wanted to look in the cabinets, betting they were either empty or full of paper towels and napkins. The shade for the kitchen window was a pull-down screen with a map of the United States on it, like one of the old-fashioned ones that my history teacher sometimes pulled out in class.

When I was in the kitchen, Bridget came into the room saying, "There you are." Like she'd lost track of me. "Would you like some water before you go back outside?"

"Okay."

I watched her walk into the kitchen, where there were exactly two glasses drying in the dish rack, one of which she grabbed. I started looking through the makeup and nail polish colors.

"I love this color," I said, picking up a bottle of purplish nail

polish. I didn't, really.

What it was, I thought, was that there was nothing personal in there. No photographs, no artwork, no mementoes. It was as if it wasn't really her apartment, but instead one that she'd just found unlocked, and then she'd just filled it with her makeup collection and a few things from a neighbor's garage sale.

I set down the nail polish and picked up the hair curler. It was actually plugged in and warm. I hadn't seen one for many years, but remembered the one my mom once had. I wasn't into it when I was younger, but looking at Bridget's hair, it seemed like it would be fun to have the option.

Also, maybe to have my mom there to show me how to do it.

"Hon, you look exhausted," Bridget said as she handed me the water. I downed the whole glass. "Would you like to sit down for a minute or two, before you head back out?"

"Okay," I said again. I was being totally lame. I went back to digging through the makeup pile.

Bridget watched me examining all the product, and then said, "You remind me of me at your age. Do you want me to do a little eye makeup on you?"

I shrugged. I didn't want to say okay a third time in a row, but knew I probably looked like I liked the idea. I liked the way her eye makeup looked. It wasn't too much.

"Goody." Bridget grabbed an eyeliner, and I saw her pick up a shade of violet eye powder and a couple brushes I'd never seen before. She's a weirdo, I thought. Figured that was who my dad was attracted to. Maybe she had some sort of secret life, like a rich boyfriend, and all of her stuff was there with him, and this was her little hideaway when she wanted to get away from him. Or maybe she was trying to save all of her money for something else, something more important than decorating her home.

It all seemed maybe a little off to me. My father's crush doing my makeup?

She walked around the counter and stood in front of me.

Thinking of her and my dad in the same thought reminded me of the way his place looked when we first got there. Also minimal effort. I wondered if this was what happened when a person grew up, like they had a way of finding people who were just like them. She was just like him, I thought.

"We can do this quickly so you can get back to that cute boy," she said.

I went from She's just like him to She's one of them before I blinked again.

"My, you're tall," she said. I was seated, and she was not, but it seemed like we were eye to eye. Bridget looked me in the eyes, face to face, for a moment. She smiled, then set down the brushes she was holding in her right hand on the table. She held her pointer finger over my cheek just below my left eye, and her thumb over my chin, doing a rough measurement while I held my breath. I didn't like her fingers near my face. I was relieved that I still had my scarf covering my forehead. Then Bridget moved her fingers away from my face and reached for the brushes while I breathed out.

I was suddenly super uncomfortable. I thought about the quickest way to the front door. I thought of my father and the man in the mall parking lot. I resisted the urge to ball my fist, and then I was bothered that I'd even felt the urge at all and I tried to calm myself.

Bridget said, "Look up," and I did, and I felt some rubbing under the eye. "Close your eyes," she said. I closed the eye Bridget was working on.

"I want to see what you're doing," I said.

She was right in my face. I felt the brush, light against my eyelid. I could feel Bridget's breath.

"Now the other."

I complied.

"That's better," Bridget said. Maybe I was wrong.

Bridget set down the brush. She just kind of threw it down.

She turned around, looked at her work on my eyes which, I thought, hello? A mirror? It would be nice to see myself. Bridget reached out toward my face with one hand, no makeup or makeup tool in it. When she touched the edge of my head scarf as if she wanted to lift it, I reacted by turning my head to the left and covering my forehead with my right hand.

"Are you okay, there, hon?"

"I'm sorry . . . I just . . . I didn't mean to freak out. I thought you were going to . . . "

"Going to what?"

"Touch my forehead with your fingers and take over my mind," I said. I thought that if I was wrong about her, it would come out sounding like an odd joke. It did not.

"Oh my," Bridget said, "That is worrisome."

Which was not what I wanted to hear from her.

"Is that . . . is that what you did to my father? Did you do something to him?"

Her expression said nothing, which set off more alarms.

"Were you going to . . ."

"Jessica, I don't know what you're talking about. I was going to do your eye makeup, that's all. You're really kind of freaking me out. Maybe you should go."

"Fine," I said. "But I think you're one, too, whatever you guys are. That's what I think and I'm just going to go with that." She shifted her weight on her feet the tiniest bit, and I raised my voice, "Don't move! Stay right there."

I didn't wait to see if she listened to me, but I saw her take a slow step or two after me, more like she was going to watch me go, not try to stop me. Was I just freaking out? She really hadn't done anything. It was such a strong feeling she was going to that I couldn't ignore it.

All I could think of at that point was getting to Jason outside on the sidewalk. I needed to be outside. I was talking out loud, kind of to myself and kind of to her. "Of course, he's not the only one." There's never only one. "How many of you are here? Does my Dad know? Do you understand how much this is freaking me out? It's a little bit worse every day! Is he just pretending not to know? Did you do something to him?" Every single word was just flying out of my mouth, no control over it.

"Hon, you're jumping to . . . listen, let's just talk . . . " She was trying to say things at the same time I was talking. She wanted to sound calm and reasonable, but there was worry all over her face.

I pulled the door open.

"So, that's not going to happen right now. You just stay away from me. Stay away from us."

"Nothing happened here," Bridget said as I ran away.

Jason didn't say anything to me when I ran up the path from Bridget's place and started packing up everything in a hurry, but he started packing up, too, and followed every word as the previous 20 minutes tumbled from my mouth. When we were on the sidewalk after getting off the bus, he said, "Cool makeup."

"Thanks. It feels kind of creepy when you say it."

"I feel that, too. Just meant that your eyes look neat."

"She did it."

"I heard you."

I was so weirded out that I rode the bus past my stop and all the way to Jason's stop rather than go home. When I was with Jason in his room at his house, I told him that I was starting to be afraid they were everywhere. I confessed that I had more than once in the previous hour wondered if maybe he was another one of them, too.

"Maybe everyone my Dad knows is one of them. Dr. Penny might be, for sure. His friend Erin, maybe. Then, at first I thought, 'Oh, no, what do I do if Jason's one?' He just appeared out of nowhere after disappearing for like, years. But then, on the bus, when it came into my head again, beside wishing that I had those magic glasses so I could see what everyone really is, I thought that if you're one of them,

too, then I'm just going to give up.

"So, what I'm going to do is sit down here, take off my head scarf, and close my eyes, and if you're one of them and you want to just wipe my mind clean so I forget all of this and your people can do whatever it is they want to without anyone wondering about it, then you can just go ahead and do it."

I sat down in a chair next to him. I took off my head scarf. I stared at him directly in the eyes, and said, "So this is your chance. I won't do a 'gotcha' thing."

Then I looked away from him and stared straight ahead for a moment before closing my eyes.

I listened for him to move, either toward me or away, but there was nothing. I swallowed. I heard him swallow. I heard his breathing. I heard him shifting around. After I had counted to fifty-nine one thousand, sixty one thousand, I opened my eyes. Jason was standing there, but staring at his phone, reading something. When he realized my eyes were open, he slid the phone into his pocket.

"I'd make a joke about how we want to toy with you a little longer, but I don't want to feed your paranoia," he said. He laughed like that was funny. He saw me winding up to snap back at him and quickly interrupted. "Honestly, if I could 'wipe' you, I would, just to give you a break. I'm not one of 'them,' Jess. Just me."

"What if they're after me now?"

"I've been thinking about that. I mean, nothing really happened, not like she actually attacked you or you kicked her in the nuts or anything. Maybe she's at home hoping you don't rat her out or planning how to react if you do."

"Right."

He thought about it. "You'll have to see how your Dad acts. You'll know if she tells him. Or maybe you won't. Maybe she'll tell him but he'll act like he doesn't know so you don't get in their way."

"Not helping. I'm going to have to start locking the door when I go to sleep at night."

What followed for the next few days was a lot of intense, mixed emotions. I was wary of my father, afraid of what he might know. The whole Great Dad act actually made me feel some pity for him, because clearly this was something that had been done to him, maybe by the universal repair men and maybe by her, and yet he was completely happy with it because he didn't know.

I added more forehead-covering accessories to my wardrobe—hats and headbands and knit caps—and kept my eye on each and every suspicious person around me. I had no idea how Bridget was going to react—if she was going to call my father or text him or e-mail him or not say anything at all. No matter how much I tried to convince myself that maybe I had been too quick to judge her, I couldn't get past the feeling that I was dead-on right about her.

What could she say to my father, if he wasn't in on it with her? If he was in on it, then they would have already been sharing it all, probably in their own alien language, and they would have already figured out whatever plan they had to deal with me, even if the plan was to do nothing at all.

Omitting the alien stuff: something like, "I let your daughter use my bathroom in my condo, then offered to do her makeup, and while I was doing that she accused me of being an alien and ran off." In the unlikely event that Bridget wasn't one of them, it was still the kind of thing my father might understand me saying, given what I had seen.

Or else something like: "Hi, alien friend. Just thought you should know your daughter is on to us—maybe you need to do something about it."

"Did you ever consider," Jason said when I presented him with all of this, "that maybe the alien thing is just a cover that was part of his brainwashing?"

"What brainwashing?"

"From whatever it was he did or whoever it is he is knowingly or unknowingly working for. Maybe it's just a cover to make him feel like he's crazy whenever he tries to figure out who he really is."

"'No, I think he's actually part alien and probably part crazy."

"Or else he's under deep cover and he knows exactly what he's doing. That's what I'm saying."

I asked, "Is she going to call and tell him?"

"Maybe she doesn't want any attention. Maybe it's best for her, too, if it just goes away. Maybe she's just waiting to see what you do."

Chapter 18

In Drama two days later, Ms. Modis asked the kids who were playing the orphans in the play to go into the Drama room—backstage, down a short hallway that led to a room where the costumes and makeup were kept, where we did costume changes, and where sometimes we occasionally had to do our assignments when we were working in small groups.

We thought we were just going to be practicing the song the orphans sing on the rooftop. It was a song we all liked. It had five different parts, and for each part Ms. Modis had paired one strong singer with someone who wasn't as strong. Jason was considered a strong singer because the girl-to-boy ratio in drama was so large that all a boy basically had to do to be able to do to be one of the stronger boy singers was not be tone deaf. Jason and I were not partners. We each had different parts, which made it easier for us to practice outside class. It was keeping everybody on the same timing that kept throwing the group off.

When we got to the Drama room, there were ten chairs in a circle.

"I printed out the song lyrics for you all," Ms. Modis said as she hustled into the room. "I have underlined three of the lines from the lyrics. I want you to workshop your responses to each line, doing them one at a time, then going around the circle with the first line before you do the same with the second line, and then the third line. No more than 10 minutes a line. I will return after I have given out assignments to the rest of the class." Then she swept right back out of the room.

The orphans' songs each had a different storyline, but the way they broke into each other's songs tied them together. One storyline was about looking for someone in every stranger's face; one of them was about what it felt like to wake up one morning and a terrible person you loved was gone; one was just "please come back I miss you"; one was "don't worry I remember everything you told me"; and the one that jumped into the other four parts more than the others, which made it kind of funny, was about being damaged when you're here, damaged when you leave, damaged when you're back again, damaged when you're gone.

When we sang the song, it was fun, and none of it sounded as sad as the words sounded when we read them aloud. One kind of workshop we did was about connecting something in the song with something in our lives. The lyrics Modis underlined were all aimed at getting us to think of someone in our lives who was gone—not necessarily dead. And like Drama students, everyone unloaded about dead relatives, divorced parents, fathers and stepfathers who left for other women or wouldn't stop taking drugs, moms who chose boyfriends over their children. Some of the kids were crying when they told their stories. Some of them were crying while they listened to others' stories. That was the general list of topics, and then for the next two lines of lyrics, they went to details. Amanpour's dad emptied out Amanpour's piggy bank before he left. Amanpour said he still wished he'd had more money in it for his dad to take. I told them about how I was sure my mom had started her own new life in Latvia. That she was dating guys while she was taking care of her mother. That she was working there, too. That she wasn't going to come home.

Before I spoke, I could see Jason watching me closely, wondering, also maybe worried, about what I might say about my father. I was worried that if I started on that subject, I would burst from all of it, so I steered clear of talking about him. They would accuse me of making up things, regardless of how real my emotion.

After a half hour of that, Modis returned with the music for the song primed on her phone. She started talking about the backgrounds of the orphans. Even though they basically served as a chorus that provided commentary in breaks between the big scenes in the play, there were random lines throughout that explained how each of them became orphans. Their stories were mostly terrible. Maybe only a few of the *real students' stories were as bad. Like, for example, Maura's dad overdosed on meth and the details were gruesome.*

Modis explained that even though the orphans were dancing in sync and smiling ninety percent of the time, their backgrounds were no less tragic. Our job as actors was not just to sing the song, otherwise we would be called singers instead of actors. Our job as actors was to connect to the orphans' feelings when we sang this song. She asked us about what we'd felt when she'd told them the orphans' stories. Did they hear anything they could relate to? Draw on that.

Then we sang. I wasn't sure that the whole mindscrew exercise had any effect on my performance. Maybe Amanpour and maybe Kalista were better, more in character, but something about that was sad, too. Kalista's character's father never married her character's mother. He left her for one of his students, moved to a country where it was legal to marry a girl of fifteen, and then disappeared, like couldn't be found. Her character's mother was an alcoholic who'd ended up in jail.

Freakin' selfish parents. I figured that was already part of what I was bringing to the stage.

About a week after the Bridget Incident, Jason told me he'd found out his father had subscribed to an online service that he had used to spy on Jason's mother. One of the things the service did was scan all of a person's online accounts to compile a list of all of that person's contacts, friends, followers, watchers. Put filters on the results, and it would sort people into family, social groups, business connections, services—which it determined by scanning those connections' contacts and comparing them all and identifying which ones overlapped— and two groups called "unaffiliated" and "anomalous." Jason said "anomalous" meant that there was something about those contacts that didn't fit the algorithm the program used to scan all the information it went through, like they were bots or fake accounts.

"When he was researching my Mom, my Dad focused on the unaffiliated and anomalous because he knew who everyone else was."

I wondered, "Is your Mom having an affair?"

Jason shrugged. "It doesn't seem like it. I don't think so. He's the one who cheated. When it came out that he did, he said that the reason he did it was because he thought my mom was cheating on him."

"So, the program will never work for him. There's no one for him to find." I knew where he was going with this. "Did you run Bridget through it?"

"Yes." He pulled out a printout with names on it. "These are the unaffiliated and anomalous lists. It's like, forty names. We'll have to check them out ourselves."

That was the first step in the process that led us to the concrete bench in the Serene Reflection area behind the Sunshine Believer Church in the northwestern part of Ashbury Hills on a Saturday morning in April.

During the last two weeks of March we spent lunch hours on the Internet in the library and more hours on our phones just digging around. True, we did get distracted a lot. It was hard to find anything about many of the people on the lists other than a name that matched 300 others living in the United States. Some of them were easier to find. They had their own public pages and weren't hiding themselves. We compared those and then went back to the other lists to find which names had anything in common with the obvious ones. It seemed like we were looking for people around Bridget's age. For a few names, we had three or four possibilities. Then it turned out that there were three people we did find who mentioned in their feeds that they were coming to California in April. Jason found one of those names, a guy living in Arizona, on an event registration list for a conference hall in a business park that on a map was north of my father's place and west of the school, and not too far from Bridget's place.

That Saturday morning, we took the bus part of the way to the business park and planned to walk the rest. Even if it turned out to be nothing, it didn't require that much effort to check it out. It was

Saturday, and my hanging out with Jason had become such a normal thing that it had been easy for us to head out with minimal explanation while Trevor went to his baseball game. When we got off the bus, we found an abandoned grocery cart. We took turns pushing each other in it until we got to the business park.

We were in an area with lots of single-story, nondescript buildings with names and logos on them that were probably supposed to sound techie and cool like Sirquts and CoreNRG. The conference hall building was bigger than the rest, and painted brown, with large windows up where I thought the second story might have been. It had its own parking lot. No convenience stores or gas stations anywhere around, although I did want a snack.

Until Bridget and her friends started to show up, the area was like a ghost town. There wasn't another person in sight, not a car in any parking spot. Since there was literally no one else around, I was sure that Jason and I would be obvious out in the open. Especially with his blue hair. We found an area on the hill behind the church with a bench beneath a tree where we could see both the parking lot across the street and the entrance to the building, but we weren't too obvious. It was too far away, I worried, although I couldn't find any pluses in being closer unless we were actually inside the building. I was sure that being in the building was the only place that wouldn't be too far away.

We talked about trying to find a good place to hide inside. The idea of being caught scared us too much. I was not going to be mind-fingered by anyone. And yet, I kept thinking, we should do it. The thought returned over and over until the first car arrived. It was a bearded man in dark dress pants and a maroon sweater. Jason took a picture of him and his car.

"Surveillance." He was really into it.

We counted eighteen more after the first guy. We recognized some of them from our research. Bridget was number nine.

I was on the hill beside Jason when I thought I heard someone coming, and took a few steps away from Jason to look and see who it might be when my father stepped into view and started up the walkway. It seemed like he was tracking me on his phone, especially since he put it away as soon as he saw me.

After a moment of shock, I said, "You scared me."

"What are you doing here, Jess?"

"We're working on a project. I told you."

"We?"

"Jason and me."

"He's here?"

"Right over there."

"You're not being vandals or doing drugs?"

"Nice to know what you think of me." The fact that he went there was almost a relief.

He said, "You know that's not . . . "

"And you're tracking me on the phone? Really? That seems like a violation of my privacy."

"You don't have a right to privacy."

"Oh, really?"

"Where's Jason?"

"He's over there." He pushed forward just a few steps, I backed up a little, and he saw Jason. "See, he's right there. Where's Trevor?"

"One of the team moms is taking them out for burgers."

I knew Bridget was inside the building, meaning that my father wouldn't see her and know something was up with her and me, if he didn't know already. What if he was here for the meeting, too?

"What are you doing here, Jess?"

Just then, someone walking toward the building across the street caught his eye. I turned to see who he was looking at, momentarily afraid it was going to be Bridget and that she was going to be staring right back at us.

It was just some guy, but my father found this deeply confusing.

"Why is Doug here?"

"Who's Doug?"

"Old friend."

"You have more than one?"

"Why is he here?"

At least it bought us some time.

"That's twenty of them," Jason said. *"They're closing the doors."* We all watched the unmoving scene for a minute.

Jason asked, *"Do we just wait?"*

"No," I said, deciding my father didn't matter. *"We need to look inside. We need to see what they're doing. Right? Otherwise they'll just walk out the doors when they're done, get in their cars and drive off? Is that even worth waiting for?"*

Jason gave me a look that I thought was asking if we should be having this conversation in front of my father.

"Kids, let's get going now," my father said, and my heart sank. I was about to tell him that we were going to finish up here and then head home when he said, *"You shouldn't be hanging out . . . "*

Then he stopped talking.

We both stared at him. He was just standing there, staring at the building across the street.

Jason asked, *"Where'd he go?"*

As if he'd heard Jason's question, my father's eyes blinked a few times, and then he shook his head a little. He looked around, confused, trying to get his bearings.

The front doors opened across the street and out stepped a woman who looked to be about my father's age, maybe a little younger, wearing black pants and a blue blouse and eating something that looked like a fundraiser candy bar. She went straight to her car, got in, started it up, pulled out, and took off.

"Wait a minute," my father said. *"I'm confused."*

We didn't say anything. Just watched. Then he was gone again.

This time, Jason thought he understood it.

"I think he's been pulled into whatever they're doing in there,"

Jason said. We were quiet while that sank in.

Then I said, "Okay, let's try it."

"What?"

I reached out for my father's arm, pulled it toward me, then rolled his hand over so the palm was facing up.

Jason knew what I was doing. "Really?"

"I think so. In case this works, and you end up feeling like you have to break the connection between us, don't let your skin touch his, just to be safe."

"Like if you get taken over by them?" He was trying to scare me into slowing down.

"Exactly," I said. "Here goes." I leaned forward and, with my hand under my father's hand, I thought: This is not going to work.

I pushed his index finger and his middle finger together against my forehead.

The shift was instant. The first impression I had was of me being in a dark room with two huge, almost oval-shaped windows. The space I was in was something I could see only from the periphery. Some sort of room. I couldn't turn my head or look around. I had no control in that aspect. I was attached to something, maybe along the whole of my body, something much larger than me that was soft and wet and covered with pointed hairs. It might have been my father. There was no emotion in that place, no feeling, no scared, no happy, no sad. Or else I would surely have been trying to scream and trying to pull free.

I was attached to more than him. I was attached to them all. The windows looked out on eighteen people standing around a large room, some in pairs, some in groups of three. I was wrong about the second story windows—the room was at least two stories tall, and the windows started ten feet up the walls. There was also a skylight.

Whatever it was they were planning on doing, it had already started.

Everyone's eyes were closed. Some had lowered their heads.

Two of them hadn't lowered their heads, and they looked hypnotized, while the rest looked like they were praying. Nothing seemed to be happening, and yet it felt like something was happening.

There was some kind of energy out there. I could hear voices, excited voices, but couldn't see anyone who seemed to be talking. The people were all just standing there, and no one's mouths seemed to be moving, but the sounds were coming from where the people were standing. I was focused on the blonde woman nearest to me, who I didn't recognize from any of the pictures I'd seen online—we weren't able to find pictures of everyone. She was wearing jeans and a t-shirt, a little bit thick.

As I was watching her, something started climbing out of her upper body. It wasn't a shadow. It glowed faintly. A gray light. It happened all around the room at nearly the same time to everyone. These things were climbing out of everyone. When it seemed like whatever it was had exited the blonde woman, and it was nearly standing on her shoulders, I thought it resembled her shape, but as it moved into the air above her, that stopped being true—it lost its shape as it joined all of the other grey blobs moving toward the skylight at the center of the ceiling.

There was a weird pressure in the air. Almost a vibration.

If I wasn't connected to my father, would I be aware of the sounds? If Jason and I were in the room, would it actually be dead silent except for the air system, with people just standing there doing nothing in silence?

When the grey shapes were near the ceiling and beneath the skylight, they started blending into each other and joining together. The air around them was wobbly, like it was going in and out of focus. The shape they formed was grey at first, but brightened with each new addition. It was roundish and swirling with bumps that grew out of it and then folded back into it.

I thought of the paintings of the angels.

There was a point at the center of the shape that was brighter than the rest. I knew, because my father knew, exactly what they were doing. They were forming a colony mind. This was one of the many ways they spread. They were going to send a beam of thought across the universe to let their people know where they were.

The light at the center of the shape grew brighter, although I noticed it didn't cast any shadows in the room. Maybe none of this was visible in the physical world. As I was thinking this, the body of the woman in the jeans and t-shirt collapsed. Just dropped to the ground. It was so unexpected, it took a moment to register.

I heard a noise that resembled a sound of surprise. It was clearly and distinctly the alien version of "What? What just happened?"

Another body collapsed, and another. In just a few moments, nearly all of them were on the ground and the sounds I heard in my thoughts were from many voices and emotions in high panic. The shape they had formed in the air dissolved as its parts broke off. Each one raced down from the ceiling, ghostly shapes shifting back into forms that resembled the shapes of the people they were returning to. But once there, they did not seem to be able to get back in. Something was happening to them. They were fading. It took only a moment for every mind in the room to realize that the only body left standing was the one we were in, which by process of elimination had to be Bridget's.

Were we the only reason Bridget was still standing—was that because we were here in her absence? Did that mean that my body and my father's body were maybe lying on the ground across the street?

The last thing I saw was this crowd of shadow people racing toward us. I felt my father's whole body trembling. I could remember them all as they had looked in the parking lot outside, this colored top and that hairdo and the orange shirt guy and the red-haired woman with the impossibly long arms, and they were all racing toward us, reaching with all their might to get to us first. I would have raised my arms defensively as they approached if I still had arms to raise. I would have screamed as they came racing in if I still had a mouth.

I looked around, confused. I was standing on a sloped hill outside behind some kind of . . . church. It was daytime. I didn't know what day of the week it was or how I had gotten there. And Jason was there, watching me anxiously, and my father was there, also looking confused.

My father and I stared at each other. Then we both looked at Jason.

He asked, "How you guys doing?"

"A little confused," I answered. "Why are we here?"

Jason said, "What do you remember?"

"No questions now. I can't connect anything. Tell me where it starts."

"It starts here. We were watching your Dad's friend's friends go into that building."

"Oh, yes," I said. There it was. I could begin connecting the pieces.

My father looked confused.

"You put his hand on your face," Jason said.

My father said, "What?"

I said, "You weren't here."

He and I both looked at the building across the street. Jason did, too, after a moment. Nothing was moving over there.

"It's all foggy," I said, turning back to my father, my tone begging for some explanation. "Is that what happens when you touch people?"

"I don't know. Maybe. I feel blurry, too."

"We were spying on Bridget. However she got you, she was still connected to you. She pulled you in."

He looked confused, but I didn't see any kind of rejection of that idea. He said, "I don't . . . "

"You went out with her, didn't you?"

"I didn't . . . " He did. I could tell.

Jason stepped in. "What were they doing in there? What did you see?"

"Yes. No," I said. "They were trying to do something. I remember knowing clearly what it was they were doing, but now that feels like a dream. Like, parts of it are lost. More of it is drifting away. I can't remember. They all collapsed." Yes. I remembered that. "They were doing something with their thoughts, their minds. They made this kind of shape in the air in the middle of the room."

"Whoa."

"But their bodies collapsed," I said. "Their bodies fell over, and then they couldn't get back in."

My father seemed skeptical. "Why didn't we collapse here?"

"You weren't part of their mind gathering."

"You guys were only like that for a couple minutes," Jason said.

"It's over now," my father said. I was watching him, wondering what he really remembered.

"Is it?"

Hearing something accusatory in my tone, my father said, "I didn't have anything to do with this. I wouldn't even be here if I hadn't tracked you here."

We all stared at the building.

I asked, "Do we call the police?"

Too quickly, my father said, "Tell them what?"

"I don't know—that there's maybe dead bodies in there."

"We don't really know what's going on in there, Jess," he said hesitantly, but with a hint of the know-it-all. "We don't know for sure what it's like in there. We could only tell the police that we saw something in our heads and ask if they could come check it out. And what are they going to think when they find out we were out here watching them? Taking pictures of everybody? If they get in there and it looks anything like we told them, are they going to believe we weren't in there? I think we don't want to get sucked into that."

"What if someone could be saved?"

He thought about it. He didn't seem like he believed that was possible.

"Your friend?"

He said, "Do you think any of them could be saved?"

I was feeling sort of unsure, too. I mean, did we really want them to be saved? Wasn't it better for us and the world that they were gone?

"Can we figure out a way to call someone so that it blocks our number?"

Jason jumped in, "We can get a burner phone. You know, prepaid."

We agreed on that. We stared at the building even longer. Nothing was moving there. I felt sick to my stomach, not just because of what I'd seen, but also because, looking at my father, I realized that I was a little bit afraid of him. I wasn't sure whose side he was on, and I didn't think he knew, either.

At the very least, I was worried about whatever it was waiting for the chance to crawl out of his head.

How did we get through that weekend? First, we hurried back to my father's car in shocked silence. Jason was highly confused but unwilling to ask questions. In the car, more silence at first.

Then my father said, "Let's talk about this, so we can at least agree on what just happened." He paused. "You two were in the area because you were trying to spy on a woman I used to work with . . . "

"Because we weren't sure of her intentions," I said. Truthfully.

"So, you sat here in the church parking lot across the street from this place where you somehow knew they were going to meet."

"We found out about it online."

"Then I tracked you here and brought you home. We're doing that now. That's what we know."

He was laying the groundwork for hedging. I asked, "Are we going to call the police?"

"What are we going to tell them? That we dreamed a group of people died and they should go investigate?"

"But we're going to," I said. "Because it's right. Because we want them to find the bodies."

Jason asked, "What were they trying to do?"

"I think they were trying to phone home," I said.

My dad clarified. "They're a scouting party."

We didn't say another word until we reached the hotel parking lot. My father went inside our place while Jason and I stayed in the back seat of the car, and I described to him what I could remember of what I had seen. It was coming back slowly, and not all that clearly.

When I finished, he said, "Do you think we can trust your Dad?"

"Now you're reading my mind."

"I mean, what if they're all working together? What if he's one of them? What if he was just there guarding the outside of the building and then changed his story when he saw us?"

"I don't think so." There was a flyer at the base behind the driver's seat. It was a glossy information sheet for a real estate listing. I stared at it, wondering what that was about.

Once we went inside and then Trevor came home, we couldn't talk about it at all, but it was so huge in all of our minds that it was obvious none of us could stop thinking about it. My father was pacing all over the place, looking confused and lost. It seemed like forever before he finally said, "I'm going to run to the liquor store, get a phone."

"Okay."

He was gone for about thirty minutes when we heard the sounds of sirens echoing from somewhere nearby. First, it was just a couple of police cars, but then we heard fire engine and ambulance sirens also. Jason and I both breathed sighs of relief, and I imagined that my father was doing the same. I knew he wouldn't come home with a burner phone—because the sirens meant he didn't have to make that call—and he didn't.

You're In My Head

PART THREE

Chapter 19

For several months, with that other part of him at bay, Seth had been living the kind of life he could have described as normal. He'd woken up every morning with intent and purpose.

In two short days that sense of clarity had been shattered. His mind had become clouded again. He suspected that Bridget had somehow silenced that other aspect of him, and that whatever had happened at the conference room had caused him to begin to relapse. He could feel there was a difference between who he'd been two days before and who he was when he woke up each of the two mornings since. That difference, immeasurable as it seemed to be, that was the part that didn't belong, the part that made him feel not at all himself. His recent memories might as well have been another person's life he was remembering.

After struggling to pull himself from bed, wondering if there was even a point to it, he stared at his reflection in the bathroom mirror. He wondered if he might catch a glimpse of someone else there if he looked closely enough into his own eyes, although, at that moment, he didn't need to look to know someone or something was there. Whoever or whatever it was had been exposed, but Seth knew it wouldn't last—eventually, everything would blend together again, and Seth would be someone else.

For the moment, though, it was there and it didn't want Seth to remember anything, not the last six months, not whatever had happened at the conference hall. Its job was to hide the evidence. When Seth thought about the voices he'd heard in the conference hall at the business park, he could not recall clearly any of the sounds they made, although he knew he had heard it all perfectly well at the time. Obviously, it didn't want Seth to remember the words the people in the hall were screaming and shouting, so in his blurred memories they were speaking in their own language, a language that Seth couldn't understand. When he tried harder to recall what he had heard, all that rose up in his mind were urgent unfathomable whispers and sharp, desperate grunts, as if someone were struggling to move.

Staring at his reflection, he heard himself saying in his quietest voice, "This isn't going to work anymore, is it?"

Also, "It's not me—it's you." Last, even more quietly, he added, "And, no—I'm not okay."

His reflection clearly agreed.

Whatever it was in his head, it didn't have the power to hide all of it from Seth. Even if that was its only mission, some things were going to slip through.

Two days before, Seth had watched people die. He was most worried that someone was going to come knocking on the door to ask him about it. Each of the last two nights he'd gone to bed hoping for a reset in the morning that would dull his feelings of unease, but the gravity of it continued to pull at him. Part of him wanted the remaining memories to fade the way dreams did, and Seth agreed that would be best.

Seth recognized Doug's voice had been part of that unintelligible chorus he couldn't quite recall. At the time, Doug's voice had been disconnected from his inert body collapsed on the checkerboard black-and-white tiled floor, eyes only half open. Why didn't that memory upset Seth more?

That part inside him was not happy about the fuss of it, either. The mess that had been left behind was too big of a mess for Seth to handle. It was a good thing, Seth thought, that he would be able to truthfully deny that he had ever set a foot in that conference hall. Should anyone ever come around to ask.

Not for the first time in his life, Seth wasn't sure what was real. He wasn't sure of anything at all.

He thought maybe he should make an appointment to see Dr. Penny. It had been too many months since his last session.

He'd recently believed that he'd never have to go to therapy again.

Maybe get his hair cut, too.

Seth looked away from the mirror.

Time for school.

Seth had developed a template for morning prep during his months of focused calm and that meant he didn't have to have his head all together to get the kids off to school. He could simply repeat what he remembered doing before, pointless as it all seemed to be. He made breakfast. The sound of him at the kitchenette stove and the smell of bacon cooking soon had both kids awake and readying themselves.

As she had the previous morning, Jessica completely stopped in her place upon seeing him after stepping past the door from her room. For a beat, maybe two, still groggy from sleep, she regarded him with . . . what was it? Disbelief? Annoyance? Resignation? Concern? There was an added layer to her typical churn. Not only wondering if her father was an alien, but also questioning if he might be out to take over the world.

This morning, she walked directly to him and without a word poked a finger into the flesh of his arm. Not hard, but as if to test that it was there, and it was flesh. He wasn't sure if she could even explain what she was doing. She grabbed a piece of bacon, then took a step back. Seth steeled himself. This sort of opening had been followed the previous morning with low-level teenage provocation. Not enough to initiate an argument, but enough that he'd been left with a feeling that didn't sit right.

Today, what came out of her mouth was, "So this is your plan? You're just going to keep doing this Normal Dad thing even though you don't have to anymore? Just because someone made you before doesn't mean you have to keep it up."

Seth didn't respond. This was also part of the morning

template: Do not respond. He was sure that the same sounds and images haunting his memories could be found in her thoughts, too. Not taking the bait. She needed to vent.

There was a part of him balanced on the edge of panic. He was afraid of falling back into that other way of thinking, the old Seth way, and even more afraid that the process had started and was bound to get worse. The fact that he was even worried about it was proof that it was already happening. Being normal, being free of that influence, had been as enjoyable as he had long imagined it would be. For months, the intruder in his head had been silenced.

Flash forward to the present, and Seth was in wonder at the thought that one short week before he had been considering house-hunting because he wanted the kids to live somewhere more appropriate. All he could think today was: What was normal in this world? Had he been daydreaming about getting a dog? Two dogs? A dog and a lizard? One week later and he was suddenly struggling to remember the things he had been doing during the time that his life had felt right. Keep doing those same things, he told himself again, and maybe that feeling of comfort will kick back into gear.

I'm only a pretender now, Seth thought.

What was this place they were calling a home? Why was he so comfortable here? Who had bothered to strip the color off the laminate wood paneling and stain it blond? Who had exchanged the ratty green-and-maroon plaid printed pull-out bed slash couch and replaced it with an azure modern-looking retro low-rider day bed? The mallard duck painting was gone, also the green carpet with hardened fibers that were flattened into a matte. Had he done all of this? Seth even felt some envy. How had he decided on each change with such confidence? Everything that had made this place a dump of a hole in the wall was gone. It looked homey. Outside the front door he knew he'd find an area had been latticed off to give them a front porch and a bit more security. Seth wondered what about any of this was normal for him. The matching set of dresser, coffee table, and stand, all rectangular with sharp corners and skinny legs; the hooks on the wall to the right of the stove holding all the cooking tools he used most often, as if he were a cook; the underlying geometry in the room—square mirror and picture frames, square lampshades, even just a couple of decorative squares hung on the wall. How did he settle on squares?

Where was Marina? Wasn't it time to be hearing from her? That he had managed on his own with them for so long didn't mean he was going to be able to hold it together indefinitely. At some point, on top of checking in with the kids, it seemed she should be checking in with him as well. Right? In truth, shouldn't the kids be anywhere other than with him at least once in a while? There was no doubt he was bound to unravel. What kind of person just takes off without a look back and assumes their kids are going to be okay with Seth in charge? She literally did not know half of it and that should have been more than enough to decide against it.

Trevor trekked past the food, grabbing a piece of bacon and a cup of oatmeal. He poured a little milk on top of the oatmeal, added a little sugar, then dipped his bacon into the mix to get his first bite flavored up. Trevor carried his concerns differently. If he had them at all, they would show up in the form of a restless sleep. In general, he didn't have his expectations up, and he was happier in the end if there was something for him to play with or eat or chew on. Nothing means nothing, was how he would say it, but something can be everything.

Trevor's eyes lingered on Seth's. He didn't know what had been going on with Jessica or with his father this weekend, so he was searching for something. This was an imbalance for him—usually Trevor and Jessica were on the same page. Over the course of the weekend, however, "Anything I need to know?" hadn't produced comprehensible responses.

At least Trevor was secure enough that he didn't think it had anything to do with him. He could handle weird. It was Jessica who craved normalcy, whatever that was, especially from her family. She would defend being weird and different, but that wasn't what she wanted to be. Maybe that was because she was tall for her age. She was hard to not notice. Or it could have simply been that she was very much like her Grandmother Claire. Just Be Normal was his daughter's modern-day middle school variant of Claire's mid-seventies Don't Draw Attention to Yourself.

The exception to Just Be Normal these last months had been whatever it was Seth was doing at the time, especially if it involved him being normal in the way Jessica had always wanted him to be, because in that case his acting normal was just one more thing that was going to drive her crazy.

Normal was all Jessica had ever thought she wanted from her parents, rather than the self-fixated units she got. The catch was that she was at a contrary age, so the idea of him choosing normal might have signaled that normalcy had peaked.

Still, deep down, he was convinced she didn't want him to be anything but Normal Dad. Seth wanted that, too.

When they were ready to leave, Seth was the last one out the door. Following the template, he scanned the room one last time, eyes settling on a small tangle of wires—Trevor's ear buds—on the stand next to the couch. He pocketed them before stepping outside and pulling the door closed. As he circled around to face the parking lot, he saw all three of the rat traps on the porch were still unsprung and thought maybe that was a good omen. He locked the lattice gate as Jessica claimed the back seat, the better for her to avoid conversation. Trevor settled into the passenger seat up front.

Seth pulled open the driver's side door with one hand and

fished out the earbuds with the other.

Trevor said, "I think I left my . . ." as Seth passed the earbuds to him.

Maybe I can do this, Seth thought.

There were things I would have written down in a journal if I had believed my controlling bipolar therapist mother had exhibited any respect for boundaries in regard to her daughter's privacy.

There would have been a page about driving to school with my father. From kindergarten through seventh grade, the morning drive was the highlight of my relationship with him. Trevor joined in when I was in second grade and he was in kindergarten, and then for third grade through fifth, Jason rode to school with us. My father was always his best in the morning, and I used to imagine that every day the time at work just wore that niceness out of him, because he was never very good at the end of the day. If I even saw him at the end of the day. On those morning drives to school, when I felt so safe and secure strapped into the back seat, he was open to talking about anything, not judgmental, not bossy, not insulting, not that angry person he became. No sign of the straight eyebrow that signaled nice Dad was out for the rest of the day.

I was freaking clueless.

I put on my earbuds thinking it was going to be an awful day. I was going to have to have a headache. Or make myself throw up to go home.

There was a message on my phone from Jason: Got a ride this morning. Meet you by your locker.

I pulled up the Framework Foundation website on my phone:

In our view, if there is a god that created our universe and everything in it, that god is the Big Bang. It unlocked everything we know, made it all. It is the original creation machine, and in that we value it as a force for life and the good. That is as close to religion as it gets at the Framework Foundation. We remain awed. The Framework grounds its awe in current understandings of chemistry, physics, and biology.

We believe the universe came into existence 13.7 billion years ago. Our oldest ancestors first existed 5 to 7 million years ago, and started using crude tools 2.5 million years ago. "Modern" man has been around for the last 200,000 years as far we currently know.

From approximately 3,500 years ago, we find the first references to Yahweh. In the earliest forms of Yahwehism, he is part of the Canaanite pantheon of gods, one of the 70 children of the all-father El, from whom the state of Israel draws its name, and his mother, likely Asherah, an Earth goddess. Yahweh is the godhead of Israel, while his 69 brothers are the godheads of neighboring Canaanite kingdoms. Polytheism was common at that time, so there was no conflict between these neighboring kingdoms or between Yahweh and his siblings. For a time. Yahweh seems to have eventually supplanted El, and Asherah became Yahweh's consort. After the Exodus, the Israelites, possibly for the sake of expediency, embraced monotheism and dispensed with other deities, raising up Yahweh to the supreme position once held by his father. In the Old Testament, this was followed by calls for the destruction of the places of worship of his mother/wife and the end of the worship of any of his siblings, as well as the vilification of their followers.

It is difficult for us to find the intersection of the fact sets described in the previous two paragraphs, except that the events described in the first paragraph would eventually make this modern retelling of the events described in the second paragraph possible.

Normal, by the perspective from which Seth had been successfully functioning, was underrated and underappreciated. Normal was order. Normal was being punctual, somewhat prepared, even thinking a little bit ahead. Normal was sometimes you forgot something, or missed something, or left something out, but then because of it the whole world didn't fall apart. Normal was something to fall back on when things went crazy—it was a routine to get back into, a way to keep moving.

Despite the fact that he had established an order to their days, Seth had until this weekend been convinced that this life wasn't the normal kind of life his kids deserved. Their home was two adjacent rooms in a building that had once been part of a motel. Their driveway was a hotel parking lot. They lived 300 hundred feet from a burger place, and weren't very far from the three-story hotel that had replaced the motel. There was a sign on one of the parking lot walls that said NO TACO PARKING. Latticed porch or not, Seth had convinced himself he needed to improve their living situation.

Why this had mattered to him so much escaped him. It wasn't that important. Maybe they were doing fine. The thing was, for kids, especially middle school kids, normal meant something else.

He opened the morning conversation. "Six weeks left," he

said, directing it toward Trevor. "What's up for today? Quizzes, tests? Laps in P.E.?"

Jessica sighed. Supposedly, she couldn't hear them when she had her ear phones in. Trevor went through his litany of what he would be covering in each of his classes, a quiz in this or that class, turning in an assignment, and floor hockey in the gym if everyone brought their signed releases.

In Seth's household, growing up, his mother wanted nothing but normal. That was her heart's desire. Normal to her meant a person wasn't drawing negative attention or giving rise to gossip. Bad things tended to happen to people who had too much attention paid to them, by her reckoning, exactly because people were so aware of them. Leading a normal life meant leading a more enjoyable life, exactly because a person was under the radar and could go about his or her days without being noticed.

Done with his recitation, Trevor turned on the radio, switching it from Seth's news station to something top forty. All Seth could think of when he listened to their music was that guitars no longer seemed to be a thing.

Trevor asked, "Are we going to do something this summer?"

Off we go, Seth thought. Kids always ask the questions parents aren't ready for—do most parents have their summer plans worked out six weeks before the start of summer?

"What do you want to do this summer?"

"Basketball camp. The beach. Movies. Bowling."

Seth took notes in his head.

"I'd like to not move," Jessica threw in. Was she reading his mind now?

"Who said we're going to move?"

"So you're not thinking about moving us?" She was

daring him.

"I don't want to move, either," Trevor chimed in.

They almost drew him in. He was about to say, "Why would you want to stay here?" but realized that was just what she wanted—to open the discussion enough to see where he stood. She would voice objections and he would start to debate her points and then she would turn it into a personal attack. He didn't want to do that before drop-off. It was disquieting to drop them off to start their school days and then just drive off after there had been yelling in the car.

"I know you just want to go into hiding in a neighborhood with the regulars, Dad," Trevor said. In school parlance, the regulars were the non-honors students at school. Even the middle school teachers referred to those students as the regulars. "I don't want to do that. It's cool where we live."

"Really."

"Yes," Jessica said. He couldn't look her way because he was driving, but he was certain she was staring at the back of his head in that way that would let him know she was serious.

"And since we're supposedly telling truth right now," she said, "you need to get a haircut. You can keep growing it out, but you've got to clean it up."

"Thanks," he said. "A call to Dr. Penny is on my list."

I typed into the Framework website search box: Do humans have souls? I was only able to read a line or two of the top search results before the song playing on the radio ended:

> Some insist there is no such thing as a soul, and no evidence that it exists. Others insist our personalities are the evidence, the expressions of our souls filtered through genetics and individual experience. When someone says, "We are made

of stardust," does that mean the basic ingredients of the universe—hydrogen, helium—not only resulted in our physical bodies but also in the intangible, untouchable energies that some believe reside inside us? If not, where do our souls come from? I can't find them in any of the equations we use to understand the universe.

"Live news beats on 92 KFPI," the radio announcer said between songs. "Authorities have scheduled a press conference this afternoon to discuss the investigation into the discovery over the weekend of multiple bodies at a business park in Ashbury Hills. So far, few details have been released, and the causes of death have not been announced. Early reports have indicated that forensic examinations of several of the bodies are underway . . ."

Jessica's eyes and Seth's met for a brief moment in the rear-view mirror. Although the news had popped up on their phones, computers, and the TV over the weekend, the stories had been very brief and hadn't provided more information than they already knew. Monday morning was going to be a different thing. The media would be ready to dig into this.

Seth turned up the street that led to the school drop-off gate. There were police cars parked in front of the school, and four officers standing around the front entrance.

It's got to be the city's response to a group of people dying a couple miles away over the weekend, Seth thought. To give the students' parents some peace of mind. He continued down the block, turned right, and drove alongside the chain link fence toward the student drop-off gate.

"Officials have confirmed there are eighteen victims, and they are in the process of identifying the deceased and contacting their families."

He pulled the car to the curb. Trevor was out the door.

"Bye, Dad!"

Seth waved. Trevor was still so happy about Seth driving them to school in the mornings that it made Seth feel a little ashamed.

"I'm going by the school office to see if any checks have come in," he said to Jessica. Typically, she liked to be forewarned if there was a chance their paths might cross on campus. He and his daughter stared at each other for a moment, drawing the same conclusion, before she closed the door and walked away.

The police should have found nineteen bodies. One of them had gotten away.

Guess which one.

Chapter 20

After dropping off the kids, Seth circled around the school to the parking lot, where he found a spot and then tuned the radio to a news station.

Investigators were confirming the identities of the dead and notifying their families. There was still no explanation for the deaths, no physical signs of trauma to the bodies. An individual who was reportedly at the scene before whatever it was that happened had been identified. The Arizona Star was reporting that the families of two, possibly three of the deceased were tied to a fertility drug scandal that unfolded in the 1970s.

"OCareRx," he said to himself. Feeling a flash of insight, Seth realized that someone was soon going to discover that everyone in that conference hall was the same age. They were going to find out the dead were all OCareRx babies, and that there was only a small window of time during which a person could have been an OCareRx baby. They would likely be trying to find a list of every family involved in the fifty-year-old drug trial. Did such a record exist? The lawsuit was settled and sealed before it ever went to trial, he thought. Would the authorities be able to find their way to Claire and Peter?

Someone went and tried to tinker with the system as if the system designers hadn't considered the possibility existed and built in safeguards, and now eighteen people were dead. Formerly childless women like his mother were their transmission system. His sister, he realized, would surely have been one of them.

He thought about whoever it was inside his sister under the sheet in the hospital, not able to function because of whatever the OCareRx side effects had done to the body they'd been born into, but aware until the last minute of her life.

Seth let's play

He thought back to the gathering at the conference hall. Some things were clearer, others were not. One moment he had been with Jessica and Jason behind the church, and the next moment he was standing in a large hall facing nineteen people who were watching the body he was in. There had been a skylight overhead.

A voice in his head said, We're starting. There was no feeling in him. He couldn't move or react.

Everyone was serious, ready to go. Most bowed their heads, and right away, he could feel something stirring in the room . . . but whatever it was stopped when the silence was broken by a timid voice.

There was a woman there who did not belong.

"Excuse me." She smiled. She laughed a bit uncomfortably. She was short, somewhat younger looking than the rest of the crowd. She had her hand up in the air. "I'm not sure what we're supposed to be doing?"

Not missing a beat, a silver-haired man standing near her turned to her and touched her head. He touched her temple, Seth noted. There was more than one way in.

The silver-haired man said, "It's the younger sister of one of our friends. Our friend died in a car accident more than a year ago, but this one has been monitoring her dead sister's accounts and in some cases interacting with people through those accounts as if she were her sister. She came here today because she was curious about what it was her sister was involved in."

This resulted in many troubled expressions in the room.

Seth was blurry about what happened next. He thought for a moment he was back with Jessica and Jason, but the displacement seemed so dreamlike that he wasn't sure whether or not he was imagining it. The effect didn't last long enough for him to unravel what was in his head and what wasn't. He did register the sight of the woman leaving the building and walking to her car. Moments later he was back in the conference hall.

"From the top," the silver-haired man said.

Seth was uncomfortable as he walked by the officers positioned outside the front of the school. Although there were still three police cars parked at the curb, there were only two officers visible. They looked like they couldn't have cared less about him. He didn't want to do anything to change that. Even though some parents wanted armed guards on campus, Seth thought it wasn't the best look for a public school. The first thing a person was going to wonder was what was going on inside. If the school was safe, why would it need two armed guards? If parents hadn't been paying attention to the news and didn't understand that the police presence was probably precautionary and related to the recent nearby tragedy, they might wonder if there was something bad going on at the school at that very moment.

He wondered if the witness mentioned on the news was the woman who left or if it was Bridget, possibly pretending to have not been a part of it at all. She was the most likely one to have survived. Literally the last one standing. Would the police figure out she had been there? Had they gone to her strangely vacant townhouse, or to her parents' house? Would she have gone to the police or had they gone looking for her? It would have been a smart move for her to go to the police, to tell them she was there only as the event planner and explain that once the event got started, she left.

What did that mean for Seth? Would Bridget be looking for him? Or doing her best to avoid him?

Seth wanted to stay as far away from it as possible. There wasn't anything good that could come of it. Hiding out in the Parent Center sounded like the perfect way to spend his day.

The first bell was ringing as he stepped into the administrative hall. There were a couple of parents in the main office, and a couple of students in the attendance office, but it was quiet—the loudest sound was from the air conditioning, and the calm was a relief. It felt as if the havoc of the world was locked outside, and while that meant that all the middle school torments were locked inside, it turned out they were relatively benign in comparison.

He stepped into the office and saw Sarah and Mr. Owen, and the feeling was magnified—the world outside felt even further away. He thought right then that he would like to sit at the extra desk in the office that was sometimes occupied by a student taking a service class for credit, and he would possibly sit there all day long, sorting papers and answering the phones and not stepping outside until the school day was done. Let the police keep the outside world where it belonged.

Neither Sarah nor Mr. Owen acknowledged his presence, although he thought he could feel them noticing him as he checked his inbox for parent group bills or checks. He understood it better now—as a parent and not an employee, he was, to a certain extent, an outsider, regardless of the effort he may or may not have put into his volunteer job. In their minds, he could turn on them at any time in a number of ways that could make their lives miserable, even put their jobs at risk. There was nothing equal about the relationship, no matter how cordial. Even when it seemed, with the existing state of mutual cooperation that characterized their relationship, that they were friends, that just wasn't the case—at least as long as his kid or kids were attending the school. His mother and father liked to joke that fences made for the best neighbors. In middle school, it generally seemed like padlocked gates made for the best parents.

Still, even if they weren't friends, Seth thought, at the very least he and the other Ashbury's Friends parents put in some effort to contribute. It wasn't that difficult to greet someone. When he looked their way again, both Sarah and Mr. Owen were watching him, and as he turned in their direction to say hello, he found himself facing the principal.

Her face was impossible to read, but this looked serious.

"Can we speak in my office," she said to Seth.

"Absolutely." Sarah and Mr. Owen didn't even bother to try to hide that they were staring as he walked across the room just a few steps ahead of the principal and then into her office where, after she entered behind him, she closed the door.

There was never anything comfortable about being in a principal's office, whether it was as a kid or as an adult. Something about being in that space, with the door closed, made the person behind the desk seem like boss and parent and judge. The power balance was completely askew.

"Seth, I'm going to be straightforward with you. There is a lot of scrutiny of the goings-on at this school. My predecessor was removed for financial mismanagement, and the result has been that the campus has been watched more closely by the district. There was a phone call we received last week from a former student. She claimed, in essence, that you and or your children used information gathered at the roller-skating fundraiser hosted by the Friends to contact her. To ask her on a date? She suggested that you planned the roller-skating party solely for the purpose of re-establishing contact with her."

The easy answer here, Seth thought, was to say that he didn't think Bridget would be contacting the school again. That was too flippant. Why would she have called the school and said that? Why had she waited so long to do it?

"I don't know what to say about that. I didn't plan it just to meet her," he lied, "but when I did see her at the event I traded information with her. We did go on a date last December."

Where she did something to my head, he thought.

"At this point," the principal continued, "it's all hearsay, but I feel it would be best if you left the campus and stayed away until it is resolved. Dion and Frank can finish out your job duties for the year." She stood up, and he thought she was going to at least offer her hand for him to shake. She didn't.

"You can gather your thoughts before you leave," she said before she walked out of the room.

Seth returned to his car, stunned. He couldn't believe it. He'd screwed it up again.

This way of living these last few months, week after week of just normal, that was what he'd been wanting for years, every day thinking about nothing but taking care of his home and his kids and everything that emanated from those central concerns. He'd shopped, cleaned, cooked, driven them around, filled out forms, made appointments, nearly every day wondering when it was that he'd had so much time or inclination to worry about what might be lurking inside his own head.

On top of that he had been immersed in school and had developed some appreciation not only for the teachers and their methods of motivating their students, but also he'd found himself at times not minding the kids at all. When the bell rang and they all poured out of their classes, he no longer panicked. His impression of middle school had been modified from hellish to at best a place of awkward discomfort for the students wherein the teachers were continually trying to channel adolescent energy to better purposes.

It stung that it was Bridget who had given him that gift of forgetting and then taken it away. What had he done to her? Why had she called the school? Was it because of Jessica?

His phone rang. The caller ID said that it was Aaron.

Have to update her contact info, he thought.

"Hello?"

"Seth! It's Erin. How are you, Mr. Adams?"

"Hi, Erin. I've been better. Is everything okay?"

"You tell me! I told myself I was going to call you later this week but after I heard that people died in Ashbury Hills I had to check in. Then, when the word OCareRx was floated on the news, I decided it couldn't wait."

"Make sure I wasn't one of them?"

"Oh, gosh no! That didn't cross my mind. I thought it might be upsetting to you. I wanted to make sure you're okay."

"So, not only did I get a visit from you, but now I'm going to get random calls to see how I'm doing? To chat about things? How did I get so lucky?"

"You aren't trying to get me to say 'Poor you,' are you?"

"Not at all. It's really great to hear from you. Especially right now."

"Are you okay?"

"No. I think I just got banned from campus." Seth thought it was possible he remembered mentioning both the roller-skating event and Bridget to Erin. He was cloudy about a lot of the previous months. He described the conversation he'd had with the principal.

"You two went on a date, and then four months later she calls to complain. You haven't talked to her since?"

"No."

"What do you think made her complain?"

"I think maybe Jess was poking around, trying to find out more about her."

"Well, can the principal ban you from campus?"

"I don't know. There's probably a process to follow. I'll have to look it up in the magic notebook when I get home."

"Can she kick you out of the parent group?"

"No. You're right. She can't."

"She still needs you a little, right?"

"She needs our money. It makes things easier for her, but

if we don't help out, they'll figure out a way to do with less. That's the story of middle school."

"Well, figure out a way to use that. I think you should put up a fight, Seth. You can't be the first parent group leader who didn't get along with a principal. Like that never happens? Come on. Twist up a new ending."

"I'll try," he said.

"So," Erin said, "about the dead people. That's the same drug that was involved with your sister?"

"Yes."

"Do you think it was anyone you knew?"

"I think one of them was Doug Hanshaw."

"Wait. Doug? From high school Doug?"

"Yes."

"No way! He did not like me. He was part of it? What are the freaking chances? My God. I'm sorry, Seth. That's terrible! But . . . was he an OCareRx kid?"

"I don't know. If he was, I had no idea."

"I remember you guys had that extra bond. It always seemed like, I don't know, like you must have been on a sports team together outside of school hours. He didn't give a shit about me, that was for sure."

Back in the day, Aaron did anything he could every day to get out of participating in P.E.

Seth said, "I'm shocked to hear that."

"I hated gym, I know I've made that clear. Regardless, it's weird that you two ended up being such good friends. What are the chances?"

"I'm still sort of processing what it all means. Doug never said anything to me that I could connect to anything he might have been involved in that would turn out like that."

"What about your parents? Have you called them? They must be freaking out."

"Jess talked to them over the weekend. Not about this, but they were doing fine. They know I'm alive."

"Do you think the police will contact them?"

"I don't think there's a master list of all the OCareRx parents out there. Not the ones they would want, at least. There was a lawsuit, but the couples involved were the people whose babies died, not the ones who lived." He was thinking out loud. "The police would be looking for the people who did have children." He thought he was going to say something that would freak Erin out if he didn't stop talking. "It doesn't matter. They weren't part of this. Even if they are contacted, they won't know anything."

"Hmm," she said.

"What?"

"What do you think they were doing there?"

"I don't know," he lied. "I don't know what to think."

"I'm sorry, Seth."

"Thanks. It's all confusing, and I kind of feel like I'm waiting for the other shoe to drop. I'm wondering like everybody else what it was all about."

After they both let that sit without further comment, Erin said, "So twenty-something years after our little conversation about our true selves, look at where we are. Finally comfortable with ourselves. Do you remember how much fun we had dancing and drinking that night?"

Seth sang lightly, "Free, Free, Nelson Mandela."

"Exactly," Erin said. "You know, that night, after you passed out, at some point that night I did start to wonder if you were right—if we should just do it so I would have a better idea of what I was going to be dealing with. I thought about waking you up, but you were such a wounded bird that night, with your shaved head and all the confusing things going on inside of it. And then, how many years later? Honestly, I wasn't sure what I was going to find when I came to see you, but it wasn't that you would have crafted a homey little nook for your children where you are cooking and cleaning and caring for yourself and them. That's as weird as you being an alien."

"I get that," Seth said.

"Would you and the kids like a visitor again? I miss having that sort of touchstone in my life. Someone who has known me long enough to know where I came from. Someone like family."

"Like family? You're my sister," Seth said. It sounded too sentimental to him. As soon as the words were out of his mouth he wondered where they had come from and he almost wanted them back.

There was a pause in the conversation. He wondered if had been the wrong thing to say.

"I want to do family things," Erin finally said, buying into it. "I want to go to a little league baseball game."

"Maybe you could come to your niece's graduation."

"I love that."

"A visit, a phone call, and then another visit?"

"You know, Seth, it makes me feel really sad when you keep saying that. I feel bad that we weren't really talking when you were going through tough times. With the relationships I've had, maybe I internalized your behavior in your relationship too much. It felt almost like you had cheated on me. I was going through things myself, all these big changes, and I needed to separate myself from any and all negativity. It was much more about me than it was about you. I'm sorry."

"I wasn't looking for an apology. I'm the one who's sorry for being the kind of person that people feel like they have to put up with just to get along. I'm sorry I couldn't be there for you. Just so we're clear: I don't have any sort of social life, so I'm genuinely glad to hear from you or see you whenever that happens. I'm happy for a visit, a phone call, and then another visit. I'll take whatever I can get."

"Me, too! I'll let you know when I can set it up."

"Great. And you know what? I'm going back into school to argue my case."

"Good for you! Text me later." The feeling of gratitude that came over Seth was familiar. He was lucky to have a friend like Erin. Drunk or not, he should never have done anything that would have put that friendship at risk.

"You're a patient friend, Erin. Thank you for that."

"Good luck, Seth. It doesn't hurt to push back a little."

Chapter 21

He was thinking of Doug and Bridget as he got out of the car. Not just Doug and Bridget, but the other people whose faces were soon going to be appearing on the front pages of newspapers. Had he recognized any of them? At the time, none of them had looked familiar, but now, with his mind continuing to clear, he was less sure that was true.

The problem, Seth could hear Doug saying to him at some point in the past, is that you were born outside of the window. Your sister would have been in the window, but remnants of the drug could have still been in your mother's system.

When did he say that? When did Seth talk about this with Doug?

The police officers were like Buckingham Palace guards, perfect posture, staring ahead without acknowledging Seth as he passed them by on his way back in. He opened one of the double doors into the administrative hall and again was relieved to find it quiet inside, not a person in sight. However, when he stepped into the main office and no one was there, it seemed very odd. No Sarah, no Mr. Owen. He walked around the front desk and peeked into the principal's office. Also empty.

Maybe they were having an assembly? He walked back around to the other side of the desk, and sat down in one of the chairs to wait and think about what he might say. What would he say? What argument could he make?

He got up and left the office, heading up the hall to the Parent Center. The door was propped open, so he pulled it closed behind him as he entered the room.

First, he thought, he would need an excuse for being here. He would tell them that after speaking with the principal he had gone into the Parent Center to do some parent group things before he left the campus as the principal had instructed. Then he reconsidered his whole plan. Instead, he decided that he should just leave here, think of how to respond, talk to a lawyer maybe, and then come back. Before anyone saw him here. He cracked the door open, peeked back into the hallway. Across the hall, the Dean's office was silent. There still didn't seem to be anyone around. He wondered again where they were.

He'd only taken a step or two when he noticed that the police officers outside the entrance doors had repositioned themselves so that they were standing side by side with their backs to the double doors. He could see them through the glass. No one in, no one out was how he interpreted it. Maybe they'd asked the police to not let anyone in until the assembly was over?

Seth turned around and headed the other way down the hallway. He would use another exit to leave campus, possibly the exit at the back of the library.

"The problem," Doug said in a memory that intruded into Seth's head, "is that you were born outside of the window." This was a younger Doug speaking, maybe in his twenties. "Your sister would have been in the window. The drug could have still been present in your mother's system when you were conceived, which allowed you in, but there wasn't enough left to neutralize all of the body's systems, which is what we think has given rise to your . . . internal conflicts."

"I think what you're saying," Seth said, some snark in his voice, "is that I have some kind of human soul that doesn't like my alien parts, and you don't."

"Arguable, I think, on several levels," Doug said. "Regardless, it hasn't made you a better person."

They were at the Buccaneer, a family-type restaurant located a few miles from his college apartment, the restaurant that Seth faintly remembered Doug bringing him to after Doug found him in the park. Except this memory wasn't from after the park—he knew that because in his reflection in one of the restaurant's windows he could see that he still had a full head of hair. How was that possible?

"My first argument for you is always that it's easy to adjust," Doug said. He set down his cup of coffee, he opened and closed his right hand, stretching his fingers. "I'm getting better at this. Learning some new tricks. It doesn't hold forever with someone like you, but it does work with the regular folk." Seth remembered realizing at that moment that Doug had done this to him before. In fact, he was realizing that he'd come to the same realization many times before.

Doug recognized Seth's expression and said, "You're catching up now. This happens every time. Give it a minute."

As he'd stared at Doug over the table, he'd been able to remember many similar conversations he and Doug had shared since high school. Doug had been doing this to him since high school. The sense of déjà vu was nearly overwhelming.

"What if I don't want to adjust it? What if I let it ride?"

Doug studied Seth.

"Listen," he said, "this is a long game. We've been trying to locate people, establishing communication, planning, but we're still building. You can't be acting out and speaking out too much before someone notices. The problem is that when you let yourself get too worn down, and the adjustment begins wearing off, you start to spiral. Some people get worried that you might lose it."

"Some people," Seth repeated.

"You only have a few more weeks of school, Seth. "

"Two. One final to go."

"You don't want to get distracted by this. You're in a different place than the rest of us. This isn't you. It's just an aspect of you. You're more them than us. You really can't help us. Since it turned out this way, your only mission is to not do anything that draws attention. If you want to do your part and support the mission, this is what you have to do."

Seth leaned back from the table.

"The more we talk, the more overbearing you sound. This is life. You're making your own choices. I get to, too. I think I'm going to go."

"You don't want to do that, Seth. You wouldn't even be here if you weren't starting to bottom out. You're going to get wound up, you're going to get paranoid. This part of you only takes over when you've got nothing left, when you're bottoming out. We don't need to go through this every time, do we?"

"Don't say anything else, Doug. I don't think you or anyone else is ready to hurt me because all that's going to do is draw attention to you. Maybe you can afford to lose me, but you can't lose one or more of you."

"There's the paranoia."

Seth stood up. Doug, exasperated, said, "Seth, sit down."

Seth walked out of the diner.

Outside, it was night, and he only had to see one car pass by before he started wondering about Doug's "some people" and whether or not they were around at that moment. He couldn't remember how he'd gotten there. Had someone dropped him off? Had he taken the bus? He walked through the Buccaneer parking lot and started moving up the sidewalk, thinking that the more public, the better. But he found himself looking up a nearly empty, poorly lit Mason Boulevard. A car on the far side of the street drove by, and . . . did it slow a little? Did they look at him?

Immediately, everyone seemed suspicious to him, from the guy walking his dog across the street to the two bike riders who appeared out of nowhere and sped by him to the hooded transient sleeping beside his grocery cart on a bus bench. There was a certain level of security a person needed to feel to make their way comfortably through public spaces at night alone and normally, he felt some confidence in his ability to look after himself. This was one of those situations where that delusion—the idea that a person was completely safe anywhere at any time—could not be sustained. He was just a speck in the night, alone, basically defenseless other than his hands. Who knew if they'd be willing to kill him or not? Where could he go to feel safe?

There wasn't any place he could think of going that sounded very secure. A public place, like a store, would only be good until the store closed, but it would give him time to think. A public bus, headed toward his place, if only one were around. There was always the police station, which was closer than his place, if he didn't mind the chance that he might be committed. The police would likely call his parents, which might give him both a safe haven and a documented interaction with the police, which in turn would be one more consideration Doug would have to mull over before he did anything to Seth.

Then there was reality, where none of that was within an easily walkable distance. No stores, no gas stations. A few generic businesses, all closed, with empty parking lots. Real estate office, a print shop, a computer repair shop, windows all dark.

It was a couple of miles at least where he would be out in the open. He walked past one street that he knew would take him to Habner Park, which would be the first leg in a line toward his place. He didn't go that way because he still preferred the open boulevard where at least there might be occasional passerby and potential witnesses. He stayed on Mason for another few hundred feet before he noticed the car stopped at the next cross street ahead. It was the car that had first passed him outside the restaurant. The people inside were clearly watching him. Was he going to have to walk up there and cross right in front of them?

He turned around and returned to the street he'd passed. When he was around the corner, out of the sight line of the car, he started to jog toward the park. He crossed to the left side of the street, checking regularly behind him to see if the car was following. When it didn't seem to be, he wondered if he should be freaking out at the level he was. It was Doug, not the CIA. He should expect something blunt and direct.

Finally, Seth could see a well-lit path into the park not far ahead, and he already knew that he would stick to it across the whole park. He wanted to be visible, not hidden by the darkness. If he yelled for help, he wanted anyone who was out to be able to look in his direction and see what was going on. Soon he was on the path, and he slowed his pace to catch his breath. No one seemed to be following behind him, and he was in clear view of a row of houses across the street from the park.

He heard the sound of bike gears shifting, and up ahead saw there were two bikers headed in his direction. Were they the same two? Were they riding laps, doing circles around the park? Instead of going to one side of the path, they spread out across it, so that Seth had to step off to the side for them to pass. At the last moment, one of them swung closer and stuck out his or her foot, hitting Seth square in the chest and sending him tumbling down a lawn-covered slope.

Once he'd stopped rolling, he jumped up, wondering which direction they were going to be coming at him from. He realized a moment later there was a dog sniffing at his feet.

"I think you're under the impression that we'd hesitate to kill you," a man's voice said. It was the dog walker, standing on top of a mound of grass 10 feet away.

Seth raced back to the path and continued running along it. A parking lot was not far ahead. His body hurt. He wasn't in good shape. He saw a woman walking from the park office to the parking lot. She looked professional. She looked like she might work at the park. He jogged in her direction, and when he was close enough that he thought she would hear his voice he said, "Excuse me? I need help. I think . . . I think there are people chasing me." He stopped about five feet from her. "I lost my phone. Can you call the police?"

Seth remembered the woman's face clearly. It was Bridget. Twenty or so years younger, but very much the same.

She stared at him, as if considering whether or not she could believe him, whether or not she could help him.

"Okay," she said. "But you are going stay that distance away from me while I make the call. My car's over here. Come on. I love parks, but once it gets dark you never know how safe it is."

A car pulled into the lot. He thought it might be the same car that had been waiting at the intersection on Mason.

"That might be them," Seth said. "Can we hurry."

She looked up, seeming concerned, as the car turned down the row they were in. They walked quickly to the next row, where her car was. She gave him another hard look as if she was wondering if she could she trust him.

She unlocked the doors with her remote. She was in the driver's seat, and he was in the passenger seat when the car pulled up behind them and stopped, blocking Bridget from backing up. She could still go forward, Seth thought. Keys were in the ignition already. She started it up.

"Get us out," he said, pointing forward.

A pair of hands reached around from the back seat, settled on his shoulders, and then held him firmly in place.

"The long game," Doug said, breathing heavily and clearly done with Seth's behavior, "means longer than the next two months of your latest personal crisis. The long game means you build a life, you find a wife, you have children, you live the way your mother always told you to—not attracting attention to yourself, not making a hassle or raising questions about yourself. You live quietly and under the radar until we can do what we're here to do."

Seth found the seat release lever with his right hand, and the back dropped on Doug, making him grunt and freeing Seth from his grip. Doug cursed. Seth reached for the door handle . . . and found it locked.

Then there was that prickly feeling in his head. Bridget had tagged him. That was when everything went black.

He woke up under the wooden steps leading to the park bathroom, not knowing where he was or how he had gotten there. Someone was speaking to him.

"Seth, I'm ready to wait here all morning, but I'd rather not. Are you going to come out, buddy?"

It was Doug.

"Doug?"

"Yeah, Seth."

"Where are we?"

"We're at Habner Park, Seth. We've been here all night."

"How did I end up here? I don't remember being here."

"You were wandering around the park acting sort of strange. It was like you were having an episode. You kicked a biker, chased a dog and yelled at its owner, tried to get into some lady's car. I'm actually glad to hear you speaking without cussing or insulting me. Raving about crazy stuff."

Ouch, Seth thought. He felt guilty. Clearly Doug was not happy.

"I'm sorry. I don't remember any of that. What was I raving about?"

"Nothing that made any sense. Then at some point you didn't want anything to do with me, and you crawled under there. Said that was the sort of place a person like you belonged."

"How is it that you're here?"

"I'm staying with a friend down here for a few days. I was jogging laps. I heard a woman in the parking lot calling for help, and when I ran over it was you trying to get into her car. I must be your guardian angel."

Seth felt confusion and shame, deep shame. What had he done? He tried to sort of run his fingers through his hair, and realized he didn't have much hair anymore. It felt like he'd gotten a crew cut.

"Oh, yeah. Sometime during your episode, before I got to you, you somehow got all your hair cut off." This amused him. "Doesn't look that bad." Seth felt with his hand all around his scalp. It felt like fuzz.

"I'm going to take you to your parents' house, all right, buddy?"

"All right," Seth said.

"We'll get you some food first," Doug said.

Previously, this last part was the only part of that whole night that Seth had been able to remember. He remembered believing that Doug had been a good friend to look after him. He remembered thanking Doug over and over, and then hours later getting ready to do the perp walk to the front door of his parents' house while they watched him through the window from inside. Doug had shaken his hand and wished him good luck.

But now, his memory of that moment had changed. When they shook hands and Seth tried to let go, Doug held on. He wasn't the younger version of Doug anymore.

He said, "Seth, the only reason you are remembering any of this at this very moment is that we want you to remember."

Seth pulled his hand away. He didn't remember this. What was he talking about? Then he realized this part wasn't a memory. This was Doug. Somehow, they were still in the restaurant back then, but he was having a conversation with Doug in the present.

"How are you making me see this?"

"This is your imagination interpreting everything you're experiencing to help you process and understand the signals it's receiving. It's helping you to understand the conversation we're having in your head. The main thing for you to understand is that after everything went wrong the other day," he said, lowering his voice, "most of us ended up in one place."

Most of us.

Seth asked, "If some of you are already gone, why are you trying to send a message home? Aren't your friends who didn't survive that shitshow plan of yours already awake back wherever it is they came from? They're back home, reporting in, right? You still need to send a message?"

Doug shook his head. "Seth. You've invented all of that."

This threw Seth further off his guard. He was wrong? How wrong? What parts had he gotten wrong? The obvious conclusion was that he really did not have a firm grasp on any aspect of his reality.

Speaking slowly, Seth said, "Maybe it's from people messing with my head."

"Yes, there is a learning curve when it comes to human minds. We learned a lot from you. Here's what's real, Seth. Right now, you are standing in the school library at Ashbury Hills Middle School. We are here because you brought this place to Bridget's attention. It fits all of our short-term needs."

"Did you always hate me, Doug?"

"We were expecting you all morning. Your children are ours, now, too. Well, one of them. We're going to send you after the other one. You know, 'Leave no witnesses.' She's a loose thread now. Some things only a father can fix."

"Oh, no," Seth said.

"We're telling you this," Doug said in his head, "because we all really want it to sink in before we take control of you, too. Listen carefully: This is exactly what you asked for. Phase one. Everything that happens here going forward is on you. You could never do what was best for all of us."

Seth was already frightened that they were able to get into his head so easily. The knowledge that he had no way to resist them filled him with panic.

"Perfect," was the last thing he heard Doug say.

Chapter 22

Nothing became clear until I felt that needle stab of pain in my arm. I didn't remember anything after walking inside the school gate, except maybe feeling a tiny bit of nausea. Everything felt fuzzy—my vision, my memories, my thoughts—but it felt like it was going to clear up, and that came with an incredible feeling of relief. It was like someone had been holding me underwater.

Coming out of it felt like waking up with amnesia, not knowing at first where I was or even who I was, and then, when that information started to come back, not being sure what was real and what was not real. Whatever it was that dragged me away was still present. It was in the air, just pulling at me, at everyone and everything that could feel it. I finally had it together enough that I recognized the feeling of disorientation as something I'd felt before, but it took me a minute to connect it to what I'd felt outside the church across the street from the conference hall when I came back to myself. This was that after-trance effect.

I was walking up the hall at school. There were other kids around me, all walking in the same direction. It was morning. Was I on my way to History? What day of the week was it? I looked at my arm, at what it was stinging me. There were two patches taped to my forearm, both of which had wires coming out of them. The wires were attached to a small black box that was sticking out of my pocket.

"Ouch."

Jason was walking next to me, holding my arm, watching me carefully.

"Jess."

"Jason? When did you get here?" I looked around. "When did I get here?"

I wanted to stop moving to pull myself together, but Jason said, "Keep moving," in a way that made me follow his direction.

He followed up with, "Low voices."

We took a few more steps, passing a hallway of classroom doors. Jason pulled me down the hall. When the first door came up on the left, Jason turned the door knob, pulled the door open enough for the two of us to get in, then closed it quickly behind us. My head was going wavy. Was I sick?

Then there was that feeling again in my arm, like a needle prick, and the waviness evaporated.

"I'm feeling it, too," Jason said. "It's kind of like when you're lying out in the sun and you're hovering somewhere between awake and asleep. Except this is nauseating. The stimulator rips right through it."

I looked at my arm, totally confused.

He said, "I had a backup in the nurse's office, which I went and nabbed as soon as I saw how weird everyone was acting and I realized that the zapping was keeping it from happening to me."

"I don't understand."

"Listen, Jess. Try to focus. One of them must be here. One of the people from Saturday. Everyone here is acting vacant and I can almost feel," he said, reacting to another zap, "what it is that's happening to them, but the stimulator holds it back." His reaction to the charge was different than mine. He took it as a relief.

I looked at his box. At him.

"How bad is your back exactly?"

"Not getting better. This helps. I'm probably going to have to have surgery this summer. They say it will be okay after that."

"The zapping helps you that much? It stings."

"That goes away. The effect from the zap lasts longer each time. Your body gets used to it, almost like it understands what you're trying to do and it learns to make the most of it."

I thought of Trevor. Instant dread.

"What are they doing in the gym? Do you know?"

"Yeah, I went there first. All the bus people walked into school and kind of all at once got quiet and started heading in that direction, *even though no one had said anything about any assembly. I thought it was maybe some school thing that everyone else knew about, so I went with it. But it was obvious pretty quick that everyone wasn't on the same level of awareness as me. Like, no one would talk to me or look at me in the hall. Once we were in the gym I just kind of stood there and acted like everyone else for a while, then walked back out."*

"They're just waiting there?"

"They're all there. Students, teachers, custodians, parents, aides, everyone."

"What are we going to do? We have to get Trevor out. Can we get off campus?"

"There are police out front."

"I saw them. To keep the alien people out. Right." We both knew they were there to keep us in.

There it was again, rising up in my head. That pulling feeling that made me feel like I needed to be moving along. I should be heading to the gym. It frightened me a little, knowing what it was. It was almost enough to cause me to panic.

And then there was the electric buzz again, and the tightness in my chest released. The leftover fear helped me focus.

"All I care about right now is getting Trevor and then getting out of here."

Doug was no longer present. Seth was no longer stuck in his memories. Instead, he was standing alone just inside the entrance to the school library. The weird thing was that to Seth, it seemed like he was watching himself standing alone at the entrance to the library. He was watching himself push open one of the doors that led out to the hallway. He was watching himself leave. When he watched Seth step through doorway, the movement was a little clumsy, and he bumped the door with his hip, though the part of him that was watching didn't feel a thing.

His body walked away without him.

What was going on?

It is an amazing machine, he remembered Doug saying. It's using your imagination to interpret everything you're experiencing to help you process and understand the signals it's receiving.

They had taken his body, and left his mind to wander. Thinking of the gray shadows that climbed out of the bodies at the conference hall, he wondered if that was what he had become, some partially alien ectoplasm existing outside of the spectrum detectable by human eyes. Would he linger in the library for the rest of his existence?

There was a part of him that understood this present state. A part that remained calm.

There you are, Seth thought. Stuck to my psyche like a bug. Not even capable of independent thought, but blended into me in a way that we're one and the same. A voice in my head that sounds a lot like me.

In response, a thought: *Let's find our friends.*

Jason and I had an easy time crossing the campus. There was no one to see us. We didn't have to go anyplace where we would be visible through the chain link fence to the police outside. Still, we kept low, below the level of the classroom windows, and when we moved, we moved quickly across the open spaces, ending up at the side entrance to the auditorium. For the first time ever, school was actually kind of exciting. The whole time, I was so glad for every electric shock I received that the sting of it stopped mattering. We went in and headed down the hallway straight to the Drama room, to the costume closet, where we started rifling through the wardrobe racks, finally ending up with black shirts and pants and two black ski masks with eye slots and mouth holes—last used as the undergarments for evil trees in the Wizard of Oz when I was in seventh grade.

"We could set off the fire alarm," I suggested. "Fire and police

would come."

Jason shot that down. "They can take over anyone who comes here."

I started pulling the black pants over my leggings, and he started changing into his costume.

"Are we going to be able to get into the gym?"

"The doors were unlocked. No one was doing anything. They were all zoned out. I don't think they would even react if we went in there. There was one area, a circle, where no one was standing, and then everyone everywhere in the room was standing there facing in toward that circle."

"Where are the bad people? It's her, isn't it? Bridget? Where is she?"

"I didn't see anyone in charge. Trevor was near the bleachers. I think we could go in through the coaches' office, come out behind everyone, grab him, and then run back out the way we came in. I'll carry Trevor and you can close the doors behind us." He went into the closet and came back with Cinderella's broom. "We can block the door with this to keep them from chasing us out."

He handed me the broom on his way to the tech closet, where he found a pair of plyers.

"We'll get out of the school through the P.E. field fence, in the back. We'll cut a hole to the street, and get out that way."

"Fine." I just wanted to get started.

"We have to get out of here. It's not vandalism if it's what we have to do to save our lives.

"No one will believe us," I reminded him.

"I know," he said. "We won't talk about us. We'll tell them one of the people from the mass suicide is sheltering in the gym." He thought about it. "Although that still doesn't solve the problem of what happens to the rescuers when they get here."

He wanted to think more. I didn't want to wait.

"Let's go get Trevor." I slid the mask over my head and then

over that the pair of goggles that covered the eye slot in the mask.

"Okay." He agreed. "Let's do it."

We turned to leave the Drama room, and we heard the sound of a door closing. Steps approaching. Someone was coming down the hall. There was no time to hide.

We both were staring at the doorway when my father stepped into the room.

"Uh oh," he said in a mocking tone. "It's my Dad."

The shift from the library was sudden. One moment he was hovering near a metal detector by the doorway, and the next he found himself back in that space where he'd been with Jessica two days before, the space where they had watched everything that happened in the conference hall. He'd thought then that he was in Bridget's head somehow, and despite knowing now that he wasn't in an actual place, that he wasn't actually in someone's head, it still felt that he was. Here he had a body again, hands and arms and legs, although his movements were limited. It felt like there was something weird about his back and his neck—they were too stiff to move easily. He wondered if he had scales or an alien hump.

The two great windows were closed.

He was not alone. Although he couldn't see them, he could hear the thoughts of all the others. He wondered briefly if they could hear what he was thinking. The space was filled with the chatter of their thoughts.

It took a few moments to realize that what he was "hearing" was coming from the dark edges of the space he was in. Drawn by curiosity, he found there was a barrier at that dark edge, a wall, soft and sticky in a way, rubbery but not wet. He touched it for only a moment, then pulled back in distaste.

Looking closer to see what it was, he realized it was a small section of a great body, twice as tall as him and three times as wide. He would have said it was a giant bug, but it was nothing like an insect, no head, no antenna, nothing to call a face, it was more like an amoeba with eye-like patches in places across its form. Seth wanted to draw away from it, but found he couldn't.

At the edges of its body, on either side of it, there was another body just like it attached to it. They were interlocked with each other, flattened like wall panels, and they formed the entire perimeter of the space. Most of him was repelled by them. He wanted to back away, but he could not. He wanted them not to notice him. They were the walls, and they were thinking out loud.

Don't just touch it.

Although he wanted to stop his hand, it seemed to move on its own. Fingers spread wide as he pressed his palm flat against the section he'd just touched. It was that voice in his head talking.

Feel it.

Something in my father's tone of voice struck a nerve. It was that same tone I'd grown up with, the one that arose unexpectedly, the one I had been expecting since the day my mom Ubered me over to his house, the one I had been expecting to hear for so many months that I'd started to doubt my own belief in its existence. It was more than the tone that hit me, though. It was the look in his eyes, the way his eyebrows straightened into a line, the thinning of his upper lip. This was the worst of my father's moods and behaviors. I felt the pressure of that creeping numbness pushing to overwhelm me, and instead of being afraid it was going to take control of my mind, I was worried it was going to dull my anger.

"There you are," I said. "There you are." I looked around for something to hold other than Cinderella's broom, and saw a baseball bat leaning against a wall. I grabbed it and squeezed it as the box stung me again, and then the numbness was gone and only the anger

was left. I pulled the bottom of the mask down over my chin.

"Time to go," he said.

"Oh, you're going to make me?" The anger was frightening, and it was deep. It was almost more than I could stand, staring at this thing who by my calculation had made my life so much harder than it had to be. I thought of all he'd put my mother through, our family through, and I wanted to knock him down. I touched the material covering my forehead. I knew it was there but I needed to confirm that he wasn't going to be able to touch my head.

"Maybe you're something big and terrible and gross wherever you came from," I said, "or maybe you're some tiny, nasty-ass mind-controlling spore, but in this world you're a skinny, weird, know-it-all infested asshole, and I'm telling you now that I'm not going anywhere with you. I'll break your hands if they come near me." I lifted the bat.

He looked unimpressed, but I knew he could at the very least see that I was as big as him.

Jason said cautiously, "Jess. They're controlling him."

My father took a step toward me and I was glad. I couldn't hold myself back. I went at him. If there was any surprise, it was that he came at me, too. He either thought I wouldn't use the bat or he didn't care if he got hurt. I knew what he would do, so first I swung weakly at him. He reacted exactly the way he did at the mall, ducking back, and then lunging for me. When those fingers were out there I brought the bat back around and knocked his hand down.

He grunted in what I thought was pain, but his other hand grabbed at my arm. I brought the bat down on his thigh, and he collapsed to the ground. He wasn't going to give up. He was pushing himself up when I decided I was going to have to break an arm to keep him down. Then Jason threw himself in there, bumping my father with his shoulder, grunting as he shoved him backward into the tech closet. Jason closed the door, and turned the deadbolt lock. My father wouldn't be able to unlock it from the inside, but just in case, Jason pulled up a chair and set the top of it under the doorknob.

"You'll have to work your shit out later," he said. He put his hand on his lower back as if it hurt. I stared at the door for a moment, still seething, before Jason said, "Let's get Trevor."

"Fine," I said. Was I crying? I couldn't tell under the mask.

We ran down the hall toward the auditorium.

He asked, "What do you think they're going to do with the people in the gym?" He had an idea about it, obviously.

"Something that will make whatever they were trying to do last time work this time," I guessed.

"I think they're going to be batteries," he said.

I suggested, "What if we set off the fire alarms and the sprinklers?" He breathed out a shaky breath, and she knew he had been zapped. Hers came shortly after.

"I don't know. You just hit your dad with a bat without waking him up. I don't think that water will do it."

"We flood it then we shock them all somehow."

"Yeah, we're not going to maybe electrocute the whole school. You're all agro now, Jess."

"Right. No, we can't do that. We only want to get the bugs."

Chapter 23

When Seth pushed his hand into the wall, he knew it wasn't sound that instantly swallowed him, and that it didn't involve hearing, but at first it seemed like he was immersed in chaotic layers of noise. He was in the midst of voices locked in conversations that played out among the shared thoughts and memories from the forty-eight hours since this new form of theirs came into existence. Although none of it emerged in a manner that could be described as a linear narrative, all the pieces of their brief lifetime were there in that swirling cloud for Seth to assemble.

There was the memory of them pulling themselves using only their arms through the bodies collapsed across the conference room floor. They dragged their legs—which were more complicated to move than they, as a group, would have suspected—along a sidewalk. Although they weren't sure what had gone wrong, they hadn't panicked at their new state. The act of their colony joining together in their first attempt to send a message had served to refine their focus on their mission. It had been more than fifty Earth years since they had been able to meld. In these forms, it was not something that could be accomplished by one, or two, or even a dozen on their own. They had believed that the machinery of their bodies would keep their hearts beating and their lungs breathing when they separated from their forms, but it seemed in retrospect that they had been providing the only charge for the machinery at work inside.

However badly awry that had gone, the act had brought them back to the true selves hidden inside those human forms. In their present state, in a body, they weren't joined in the same way as they were when they had joined together outside of their bodies into a singular form to try to send their message. Instead, they were more of a group forced into a shared space, and even they knew that situation was not tenable. Their purpose in remaining a part of this existence was their only focus.

An approaching car had slowed as the driver noticed them on the sidewalk. The driver rolled down the passenger window to ask if they needed help, and they realized that they could lock down the driver's mind and control him without ever having to make physical contact. However, controlling someone this way required more effort than touch.

Feeling depleted, they'd instinctively tried to feast on the driver's thoughts, drain it all out of him, but found this still wasn't something they were capable of in one of these bodies, regardless of the number of minds wishing it so. They had to settle for whatever it was exuding from the man for the duration of the ride to the school, a whiff of panic, a shade of fear, perhaps from a deep, subconscious awareness of his body's hijacking. It felt almost like sustenance.

They needed a place nearby to make a second attempt to send their signal before their window to act closed, a place that offered a captive pool of bodies they could draw on. Someplace like the school, which Seth had recently described to Bridget as a place no one in the outside world paid any attention. "The only people who care about the school are the people who are forced to be there."

They gained a sense of their range when their ride reached campus. There was a custodian on campus to unlock a gate for the weekend soccer league, and they were able to reach out to him in his workroom and bring him to the front of the school. The two men carried their body to the nurse's office and placed them in one of the cots. With a touch to each of their heads, the men went back to whatever it was they had been doing before the interruption, with no memory of the interruption.

They'd slept for most of the day and night. The next day, they learned to walk again, eventually making their way to the gym and seating themselves on a spot on the floor underneath the tower on the roof. On Monday morning, as the staff had arrived, they had begun drawing everyone to the gym. The larger the crowd grew, the stronger they felt, the more firmly they could reach out across the whole campus. Seth saw flashes of the view from the eyes of teachers and students whose minds had been seized.

He caught quick glimpses of Bridget. She wasn't Bridget anymore. Swollen eyes, covered with dirt and sweat, flattened curls, pants torn from dragging herself across the street. She looked dehydrated and hungry, as if they had forgotten about a body needing water and food.

They had walked Bridget's body out of the gym and out to the ladder outside of the building. They needed to be able to see the sky. They managed to push the body to climb to the roof in a complicated effort, where they sat, depleted, and then restored their strength, continuing through it all to draw on those standing in the gym below them. As the morning drop-offs continued, hundreds of students flowed into the gym.

While under Bridget's influence, Seth had, for the last few months, embraced the challenge of working for the students, the teachers, and the school. During that time, he had spoken with another parent group leader from another middle school, and in that conversation, Seth remembered referring to the Ashbury kids as "my kids," and the teachers as "our teachers," and the school's parents as "my parents." He'd said something like, "My kids and my parents are really supportive of our teachers." He'd said it with a genuine feeling of ownership that now mostly eluded him but, regardless, he found that he didn't really like that they were being treated this way.

They were keeping everyone in the gym subdued, controlling the police, and preparing to send their signal. Manipulating a person, moving a person around, that required more of them than they were willing to expend in the effort. It was easier to keep them in place and focus on drawing what they could from them.

Why had they bothered with the morning's little bit of theater involving Seth and the principal? It seemed clear that one of the shared feelings among those assembled was that they did not like Seth at all. He wondered if in that other place they came from he might have been their boss.

They were considering their options, planning for possibilities. What their future here would be, should they survive. How would they escape? Where would they hide? Some wanted to stay right where they were, on the campus, imagining that they could maintain a level of control that would shield them from discovery and also give them access to humans to attend to their needs, a budget to work with, and minimal oversight. We'll turn it into an independent charter. Others thought that with their increased ability to influence minds, they might not need to hide. These wanted to assume a position of control elsewhere, with a group of humans who had more influence and power than children. We'll live among them and they'll never know.

There were concerns about making this second attempt so soon. Could they instead find a way to improve their situation before the next window in sixty months so that they could improve their chances of succeeding?

There were also areas of dissension in regards to the amount of damage they could leave in their wake. This was all supposed to have happened out of sight to minimize the chances not only of being discovered, but also the risk of other OCareRx kids still out there being revealed. They did not want this world to have any forewarning or any witnesses to question. The miscalculation that led to their current condition had made some of them more wary, but there was also a fatalistic streak in their group, no longer caring for subtlety because this was likely to be their last chance.

Points were debated and critiqued. Some arguments were more sound than others, some voices more emotional and extreme. Seth was struck by the fact that, regardless of being fixed on their mission and being separated from the machinery of their individual bodies, their human personalities were still at play. The lives they had lived here were imprinted on them.

It was almost hypnotic and close to overwhelming, being exposed to it all. He was struck by their determination, the lengths they had already gone to in order to try once then to try again. There were very few thoughts that seemed to be connected to who they were before this happened. No thoughts of families, jobs, friends, regrets, worries. It was about what they had become and what they still had to accomplish. Seth had suspected, perhaps hoped, that Bridget would be dominant, and that he might be able to communicate with her, but she blended into the rest. Forty-eight hours was the whole of their new existence. That hadn't been Doug before. It had been all of them playing Doug. They were all meshed together in a way that none of them were exactly who they were before, and their only intent was to make another attempt before they were dead.

Join them.

Idiot, Seth thought to himself. It occurred to Seth that without this slice of alien conscience in him, he would likely be out of commission like the rest of the school. This was what it was supposed to do—its function and purpose. It wanted to join the torrent of thoughts. It wanted to be one with its colony, to be of one mind and one purpose with them. It wanted not only to listen to them, but also to be a part of them. There should have been a switch somewhere inside his mind, a tether he would be able to untie, a restraint its friends had managed to overcome, but when Seth tried to do the same, to release his mind so it could be a part of them, nothing happened. He wasn't fully one of them, and never would be.

It was not to be.

More them than us.

Seth almost felt sorry for himself.

In the relative dark of the Drama room, the back hallways, and our auditorium, our outfits seemed like a good idea. We blended in with the shadows. When we stepped out of the auditorium into daylight, not so much.

"Not as stealth as I thought," Jason said, reading my mind.

"I noticed."

"The purpose was also to cover our exposed skin. It still works for that."

"Okay."

We heard the echo of the gym doors opening. Watching from behind the trash bins, the first thing we both noticed was that four of the police officers were inside the school. Two were on our side of the gym, one was standing beside a ladder that went to the roof of the gym, and the fourth was over by the gym's front door, at the top of the gym stairs. We also saw Mr. Owen heading in our direction. He looked like he was sleepwalking. We waited where we were until he passed us.

"He's going to let your Dad out."

"I don't think we can get around to the back of the gym," I said. "Not with the guard police there."

"We can't stay out here too long," Jason said nervously. "We're not safe anywhere that doesn't lock."

I pointed at the classrooms closest to the gym, and then pointed out the trail I thought we should take to get to them, which involved cutting around and behind buildings so we could stay out of sight.

As before, it wasn't hard to avoid being seen. There was no one around. In ten minutes, we were inside what had once been the home economics classroom and was now a history classroom with a stove vent in the ceiling at the side of the room, but no stove. Jason figured out how to do something with the door that made it lock when it closed.

On one side of the room were windows that faced another classroom building. We went straight there and closed all the shades. We both turned around and were looking out through more windows that faced the gym building, and behind it, the athletic field.

"Yikes," I said. It felt like we were exposed. We ran across the room and closed those shades, too, and then peeked out between the slats.

The steps leading up to the gym entrance were about 300 feet away. The officer there was to the left of the top of the steps. I hoped he hadn't seen us closing the shades. The other officer was still next to the gym building ladder. I'd literally never noticed that ladder before today, and I had walked up to the building every school day for three years. It didn't look like anything dramatic was happening outside. Literally nothing was happening. The cops weren't even moving. They seemed frozen in place.

I asked, "Do you think that if we walked up like we were being mind controlled that they would just let us pass?"

"I don't think there are any rules. We might get by or they might stop us. Or they might shoot us."

"My father's out there looking for us, too. I just know it."

Jason had an odd look on his face.

Irritated, I said, "What? Say it."

"I've been thinking about your dad finding us in the Drama room. How did he find us there? I mean, Mr. Owen walked past us without noticing us. He couldn't tell we were there. So how would your dad know to look for us in the Drama room?"

I didn't like where this was going.

"I didn't tell him. I was with you the whole time."

"Right, but maybe he's able to track you."

"I changed my phone ID the night after he followed us."

"You put his hand on your forehead. Maybe you're still connected."

"Uch." I threw up a little in my mouth. "Gross. Oh, no." I thought about it. "Maybe you're right. He is going to find us." I started to panic. Our safe spot now seemed like a trap. "We have to keep moving. Or wait . . . " What could we do? I was this close to Trevor. How to get the rest of the way? Should we just give up and run to get help?

Jason was reading my mind again. "Should we run?"

"No. I mean, I want to, but we have to get Trevor."

Jason offered, "I think you might be right. Maybe we can just walk in there and grab him. If they can't find us without your Dad, maybe they won't even notice us."

"Do you think?"

"Maybe so."

"Otherwise, we have to wait for my father to find us. The only way we're going to get into the gym is if he brings us."

"For real?"

"Yes," I said. "We'll pretend we're giving up. He doesn't know about the boxes. When we get inside we'll find Trevor, grab him, and then we'll run out the back of the gym. It's almost the same plan."

We were both silent as we thought our ways through those scenarios.

"I think I'm going to want to kill him again when he says my name that asshole way."

"Jessica," Jason said, imitating my father's tone.

"Jessica," I repeated. A better imitation.

"Doesn't sound like him at all," Jason said. He said it again, doing his best to straighten his eyebrows into the angry line. "Jessica."

"You're right, that sounds like President Seth. I copied Jason's last try. "Jessica."

He said, "Nailed it."

I rolled my eyes. "Who knows who he'll be when he gets here?"

Chapter 24

It wasn't too long before we heard him approaching the building. Not his voice, just the sound of his footsteps. We saw him trying to look in through the windows. He tried to see inside through the cracks at the sides of the blinds. Finally, our ninja outfits were useful. We could hide in plain sight, as long as we stood still. Maybe he would move along.

Then the doorknob started to turn. It was locked and it took him a little bit of trying to figure that out. Jason and I both started to panic. He shot over to the other side of the room, went flat against the wall next to the door. We heard a key sliding into the lock. Someone had obviously given the parent group president a master key. The knob turned, the door pulled open, and in stepped my father.

His eyes settled right on me.

"Jessica." There it was.

"Yeah," I said.

"You're going to join everyone in the gym now." He didn't sound like my father.

"Right," I said.

"Let's go. Time's running out."

"Got it." I didn't move. He didn't seem to be aware of Jason being in the room or stepping up behind him. I looked away from both of them and out the window so my father wouldn't see any hint in my expression.

All three of us were wary as he took a step toward me.

"Let's go," my father said, indicating which door I could use.

"Oh, no—you go first."

Jason mouthed something that I thought was Grab his arm. After a beat, I jumped at my father, grabbed his arm, and with surprising ease twisted it behind his back. I was thinking that I should just knock him down and tie him up, but Jason was there in a flash, sticking something to my father's arm and, I realized, attaching my father to his box. Jason pressed the button.

"What?" I was shocked. "No." I reached for one of the pieces of tape, but Jason blocked my hand.

"You and he are going to have a better chance than you and me," he said. My father was struggling, but he was awkward and no challenge for me, like he had lost some of his coordination.

"He's weak. We could tie him up. Why didn't you talk to me first?" Then I felt the first shock go into him—I felt his body react to the jolt. I hardly noticed mine anymore, but I was encouraged that my father reacted at all. Maybe I could believe they were controlling him.

"I can't stop this," Jason said. "My back hurts. You and I can't stop this. Maybe he can."

"Put it back on you." I was ready to move onto twisting Jason's arm, too, because my father had stopped fighting.

"The other choice is that you give him yours." He started backing to the door.

"What are you doing?"

"I've got to leave the room now, Jess, so that they can't send me after you. Your Dad had a key. I don't have a key."

He opened the door, reset whatever it was that made the door lock before, stepped out. The door closed. I heard him going down the steps. I turned to my father. He looked confused for a minute, and then worried.

"Hold on," he said to me. "I'm getting there, but still." Which I understood. "And I hurt. My leg hurts and my hand. They must have smashed my hand." He sounded normal. Eyebrows relaxed.

I knew it helped if someone explained things, so I said, "You just tracked down your daughter so you could force her into your bug hive, and Jason just sacrificed himself so I could tell you what a shitty father you are."

"Oh. Okay," he said.

"I just want you to know that's why your hand and leg hurt."

"It's bad. It's bad."

"I guess that depends on whose side you're really on."

"They just took me over. How did you make it stop?"

"Jason plugged his nerve stimulator into you. It shocks you. It breaks through it. I have one also."

Next he asked, "What did I do?"

"Stalked us, mostly."

We heard someone trying to turn the door knob, and I froze again.

"Oh, no."

I was sure it was Jason, but tried to tell myself it wasn't, really. Whoever it was didn't have a key, and couldn't open it.

My father said, "They're running things. They didn't flip a switch and make me someone else. They just took me over and pushed me out. I guess I'm too human for them." Was he bummed about it, or just thinking out loud? I wasn't sure what kind of expression was on my face, but because of it he added, "I'm on your side, Jess."

"Now you are."

"This is . . . ," he sounded like he wanted to explain something, "I didn't know any of this . . . "

"I don't know what I believe when you say things. I don't think you're a liar—I just don't think you're the most reliable source." I peeked out the window and saw Jason crossing the street, then heading up the gym stairs. "Great." My voice cracked. "Jason's going in there, too."

"Too?"

"Trevor, you amazing father."

"Not now with that," he said. "It's not just Bridget. A bunch of them all ended up inside her head. It's not like what happened at the conference hall. That thing they do, when they merged in the air, that's something like a colony mind. But what ended up in her head are all these different minds . . . " I had no idea what he was talking about.

He thought about it.

I said, "How are we having this conversation now?"

"We'll have to go into the gym," he said.

"I figured that out already, thanks. I was going to let you bring us in. But Jason," my voice quivered again. "Jason."

"You're going to have to give me your . . . whatever this is," he said, pointing at the stimulator box.

"What? No way. Why?"

"Otherwise, they'll find it and take it. If you give it to me, I'll put it back on as soon as I can."

"I'm just going to stay here then."

He looked at me. I expected him to call me a pain in the ass. Instead, "Okay. I understand."

"You do?"

"Yeah. Why should you trust me? I don't trust me. We'll figure something out."

"I think we should just run in there, grab him, grab Jason, and go," I said. "Your reactions and timing were off. I think everyone else's will be, too."

"There's a learning curve, I guess. People are more complicated than you'd think. I was going to use you to convince them that I was on their side."

"Then what? Trade me away? Sorry, don't like your plan."

"I don't know. I don't know how it's set up in there. I don't know where Trevor is. I have to figure those things out before we can make a plan."

"Jason said Trevor's at the back of the gym, near the coaches' office." I stopped myself, looking at him intensely. He was still holding onto his first idea. "I'm not giving up the box."

"I get that. I didn't know about any of this. I didn't know about the conference hall, Bridget, Doug. I don't know what I might have known because they've messed with my head so much. If there's information about all this in there, it doesn't ring any bells now. My take on it was, you know, that Earth was supposed to be, I don't know, sort of a vacation spot for aliens, right? I guess I don't know shit."

"I get it. You're like, clueless on so many levels."

"I feel like at least part of me can honestly say I never asked for this. But I don't trust me, either."

"That helps." It didn't.

"It's honest."

"Fine," I said after the box zapped me. My voice trembled again, darn it. "Please let's get Trevor and Jason. I want to go back to our crappy home tonight and sleep in my bed and not be afraid of people reading my mind or taking control of it."

Seth looked out through the shutters. Nothing was moving, including the two cops stationed on this side of the gym, who were still as statues, one at the side of the building, next to the ladder to the gym roof, and the other near the top of the stairs about fifty feet from the gym doors. Seth's gaze lifted from the doors to the roof of the gym building. Bridget was up there. He couldn't see her from this angle, although he could see the rectangular structure on top of the building that he had listened to the principal climbing the night she changed the circuit breaker. There were also black bars on the side of it—another ladder—that someone could climb to get to the top.

"All right, let's just do it," he said as he turned to her. Jessica looked worried, but that quickly turned to intent.

"Fine."

They let themselves out of the room, and slowly walked toward the end of the building. Seth had a slight limp. There was the sound of the classroom door closing behind them, and then it was completely quiet except for their shoes on the concrete. No teachers' voices carrying between the buildings, no bells, no rattling of the custodians' carts, no students. When they reached the hallway at the end of the building, they looked around the corner, up to the end of the hallway. There was a service road to cross, then they would head up the stairs and right into the gym.

Jessica said, "We'll go up the stairs and then go right into the gym. I don't know if that cop is going to move, but if he says something then we'll ignore him and pretend we're under their control. We get in there, we grab Trevor and Jason, and then we run out the back. Jason has wire cutters in his back pocket so we can cut through the fence on the P.E. field to get out."

It was a thin plan, but the idea of running in and running out actually seemed doable. They hadn't walked far before it became apparent that it didn't matter anyway. As they neared the end of the hallway, Seth felt something that made his skin prickle, followed by a wave of pressure that almost made his ears hurt. He looked at Jessica as she was covering her ears with her hands. When that didn't have any effect, she said, "It's not a noise. It's just pressure in my head."

He thought he heard the sound of impacts, possibly cars crashing into each other on the boulevard to the west of the school. His box zapped him, and he sighed in relief even as the sounds continued and grew more pronounced. He thought it was also cars crashing on the freeway to the north, and he struggled to understand the cause of those sounds.

Speaking louder than necessary, Jessica said, "When I start hearing their voices, I'm afraid it's going to be like the conference hall and I won't be able to move or speak. This is so much stronger than it has been all morning. It feels like they're going to suck me in. I wish we could speed up the zappers."

"It's starting," he said. He looked up at the roof of the gym. He could not see the concrete rectangle tower from this angle. What he could see was a shape forming in the air above the gym building. Much larger than it had been in the conference room.

"Do you see that?" He pointed up at the sky.

She looked up. "Yes. It's flickering, like it's there, then it's not, then it's back. The further it pulls me in, the clearer it is." He could tell by her next expression that her box had shocked her.

"See, now I can't see it. The box pushes it back but I can still feel it building up again. Let's go now."

They must not only be pulling in the people in the school, Seth thought, but also everyone in their range. As they drew more into their influence, their range grew and they drew in even more. That was why he was hearing crashing cars but no skidding tires. No horns. They were shutting down everyone they could reach to draw off of them whatever they could get. There was the boulevard, there was the freeway, there were homes all around the school. He was sure Bridget's body was perched atop that tower and that they were reaching out in every direction around her.

If an earthworm were cut into three equal pieces, and each of the wriggling, thrashing sections were laid on top of each other, that was what the shape in the sky looked like, Seth thought. Giant flailing segments joined at the center. One segment would grow so long that its ends would lash against the center mass and then get reabsorbed while another would begin to extend in its place. It was repulsive and terrifying and impossible not to watch.

They started up the gym steps.

The police officer to the left began to react when they were halfway to the top. He looked awkward as he moved stiffly to intercept them. The box gave Seth a zap.

"Uh, oh," Seth said in a low voice. "Changing the plan. You ignore him. You head into the gym."

She turned right at the top of the steps and he turned to face the officer.

"You know what you have to do now, Seth," they said using the officer's voice.

The thing in the sky was moving even faster.

"Young lady, stop where you are this moment," the officer said to Jessica in a raised voice.

She was halfway to the gym doors. She slowed her pace but otherwise ignored him.

"Jessica. This is your last warning."

She slowed even more. She wasn't far from the door.

The officer moved his arm, and it was such an awkward movement that it took Seth a moment to realize he was actually trying to pull out his gun. They were ready to kill her now.

Leave no witnesses.

Seth threw himself against the officer. He was bigger than Seth, thicker, more muscular, and Seth was only able to push him slightly off-balance, but he did knock the gun out of his hand, and when it hit the ground, Seth kicked it across the asphalt, in the direction opposite the gym doors. He was about to chase after it when the cop put his hands on Seth's sides, picked him up off the ground, and shook him.

Even with poor motor skills, size and density made a difference. Seth couldn't hit the man hard enough to hurt him. As Seth struggled, the cop grabbed at his neck but ended up with a handful of shirt, and Seth was able to slip out of the shirt and free of the officer's grip, falling to the ground. Seth started to crawl in the direction of the gun, rising to his feet, managing to avoid two grasping swings of the cop's arms. He was a step or two ahead, which wasn't far enough for him to stop and pick up the gun without getting grabbed again, so he kicked it further away and ran even faster after it.

When he got to the gun first, he picked it up before the cop managed to shove him forward, where he splayed onto his stomach. He picked up Seth again. Seth twisted in his grasp, and saw above the gym that the thing had stopped flailing around in the sky. Three of the round segments were pointed upward, and beams of grey light were shooting out of the ends of each.

It's done now, Seth.

It was too late.

Staring at it, Seth was robbed of his momentum. It drew him in. It was glorious. Bridget was on top of that concrete rectangle, arms outstretched, hands open as if they were channeling all that power through her fingers instead of their combined minds. Their individual minds were subsumed by this unified form, and they were nearly one with the organism that gave rise to them despite being separated by space and time from that original colony. One day every living world would be part of that colony. It was their manifest destiny. This was a message that would be received across the universe.

The box zapped him as the cop, still holding him off the ground, took the gun from his aching hand.

Sirens could be heard approaching seemingly from every direction, but their sounds were still distant. It sounded as if there might be helicopters coming, too. Otherwise, inside the zone covered by their influence, it was still very quiet. No more cars crashing.

There was an impact, hard, as something slammed into the cop from behind, sending the two of them spinning. Jessica, he realized, had just thrown herself into them. It wasn't enough to knock Seth entirely free, but he did get one hand loose.

Do it.

In an instant, he was pressing two fingers against the cop's forehead and whispering, "I'm sorry."

Chapter 25

When I rammed into them, it was like running into a padded wall. The officer just kind of shrugged me away, because he was that strong, and I landed on the ground, and when I did I heard the stimulator box crack and break.

I pulled out the pieces and said, "Oh, no." That phantom tentacled amoeba was flickering and flailing, shooting beams of light into the sky.

There were two loud shots. I jumped up from the ground at the noise. I looked over at my father, expecting he might dead on the ground and that I would be next. Instead what I saw was him stuffing his hand into his pocket while standing next to the officer, who was slowly lowering his gun.

I heard something hit the gym roof with a loud thud.

Bodies fall that fast, I thought.

The gun went back into the holster. I got up and ran for the gym doors. I still thought that they were going to take me over again, even though the intensity of the pressure in the air had lessened. It didn't go away completely, but it was definitely less. It was still strong enough to be pulling at me, but the thing in the sky was gone.

I expected chaos when I opened the doors. It was the opposite. Total silence. The entire school was in there, jammed onto the stands and standing packed across the floor, everywhere except for a circle in the middle of the room, and everyone was facing that empty circle. Jason was right by the door, totally out of it.

I grabbed his hand and pulled him after me, surprised that he didn't put up that much resistance. I still felt that force pulling on me. They weren't dead up there. They wanted me or someone else to do something, but the feeling was losing strength. I looked at Jason's face as we moved, hoping for some kind of recognition to show in his eyes. I thought I saw something there, some kind of stirring, and was expecting him to say something acknowledging me.

Instead, he said, "Help us."

I shrieked a little, but I didn't stop pulling him.

"Yikes. Stop that." I saw Toi and Valimar. I saw Ms. Payne. Then I stopped looking at people's faces, because I thought I wouldn't want to remember them this way.

Mr. Gillum's head turned to me when I passed by him and he said, "You can help us. Call for help."

I didn't look at him. I said, "Go away. Go away." There had to be a reason they weren't just making someone climb up to help them. Maybe they weren't strong enough to make someone do it.

There were slight movements in the crowd, eye flickers, lip twitches that I thought meant that maybe their minds were starting to break free of it. We reached Trevor and I grabbed his hand. We went straight up the hallway, passed by the coaches' office, then out the back door, and we came out facing the field.

Trevor pulled away his hand and then rubbed his eyes.

"Come on," I said, "We have to meet Dad."

They were coming out of it. We went around the side of the building and saw my father seated near the top of the gym steps, where it seemed like he was keeping out of the sight line of the officer he'd fought with. He had his shirt back on. The gym doors were still closed. The officer was seated on the ground, looking very much out of it. I tried to move us along quickly even though he didn't react to us at all.

"He's going to lose his job," I said quietly when we reached my father. I felt bad for the officer.

Seth was more than ready to leave by the time Jessica appeared with Trevor and Jason in tow. He jumped to his feet and they all headed down the gym stairs. He didn't know how long the cop he had touched would be out of it, but the other officer, the one who'd been standing at the bottom of the ladder to the roof, had started to show signs of coming about. He hadn't yet seemed to take much notice of his present surroundings, but Seth thought that wouldn't last.

When they reached the last couple of steps, they heard the gym doors opening. It didn't sound like mass pandemonium.

"We should get out of sight," he said.

Jason was starting to come out of it.

Jessica told him, "It's okay. We're at school. We've got my dad. Hopefully, he still has your box."

Seth felt around for it, then started peeling the tape off of his arm.

"Yes," Jason said. He put his hands on the sides of his head. Seth felt some sympathy. Still unsure, Jason asked. "Are we okay? Is your Dad okay?"

Jessica said, "Who freakin' knows, really?" She threw Seth a sharp look as she continued. "You, me, and Trevor are okay."

Seth handed her the box. She quickly attached it to Jason. Trevor was slower to come all the way out it, and had no clue about anything when he did. Jessica helped nudge him the same way she had Jason.

"How are you feeling, Trev? I usually see you during the day, but I haven't seen you since drop-off today."

Trevor obviously wasn't going to bother with trying to put things together himself. "Why are we here? Why are we together at school?" He sounded like he'd been awoken from a nap.

"We're going home," Seth said.

Jessica asked, "You're sure no one will remember we were here?" She was thinking of the cop, Seth thought.

"The one with the gun won't remember anything."

"I remember some things. You remember some things."

"I might have some level of immunity, and you were connected through me."

"Still. You don't know that for sure."

"Jess, give me a break. I'm doing my best."

"Still."

"The touch is stronger than what they were doing."

She said, "It doesn't feel like the problem is necessarily over when you talk like that. Don't touch people anymore." She paused, thought about it. "Someone on your planet is going to be really pissed at you when you get home." At the moment, he didn't see a point in explaining again that his alien theories needed to be revisited. He wasn't in the mood to be reminded that she didn't believe that he knew what he was talking about.

He looked back at the gym building. No one seemed to have come outside yet. He looked up at the roof, truly expecting to see Bridget at the edge looking back at him, or maybe a grey ghost version of her lingering there.

There was nothing there.

Of course, he'd heard them in their last moments, begging for help. He'd heard that voice inside him telling him he could help. He'd told that voice to shut the fuck up. Maybe he'd even said it out loud. Then he'd listened until all the other voices that weren't his own went silent.

Trevor and Jason were watching me and my father silently. I couldn't tell how much of everything they were understanding.

I said, "So we just leave her there?"

"They're gone now. She's gone. Someone will find her. Hopefully it'll be a day or two before that happens."

Jason said, "We're leaving the campus?"

Always ready to slip off unnoticed, my father said, "I think that's best. We're not going to have that option for long."

We walked down the maintenance road to the gate, which wasn't locked. The chain with the lock on it had been wrapped to make it appear locked. We let ourselves out and headed toward the front parking lot. Three empty police cars were parked in front. There were no people in the rest of the school or in the parking lot, but on the street outside the lot there were cars locked together in a pile in the middle of the road. There was another car crashed into the chain-link fence next to the bus stop. There were groups of people at or approaching each of the different crash sites. The air was filled with the sounds of sirens.

Trevor said, "Whoa."

We went straight to our car. Once inside, my father started it up and slowly pulled out, then headed to the parking lot exit. We turned to the right, away from the boulevard, heading instead down a street into the neighborhood around the school. In the first few blocks there were signs that the effects had also been felt here. A crashed car here. A man there lying on the driveway next to his ladder, with three people crouched around him, two on their phones.

We kept our windows up. My father kept his eyes on the road.

Chapter 26

There was a lot of commotion around Ashbury Hills Middle School and Ashbury Hills in general in the following weeks. With media outlets already setting up in town to cover the initial story about the deaths at the conference hall, news stories about the devastating cluster of car accidents became companion pieces that emphasized the sense that Ashbury Hills was under siege. A local channel's evening news broadcast aerial footage of the affected area that had been filmed in the early afternoon, not long after the series of pileups. Several hundred viewers called in to point out that there appeared to be a body atop the gym building at the school adjacent to the crash area.

The mounting toll from the car accidents was pushed to a corner graphic in national coverage once the shooting victim on the school gymnasium roof was identified as the last and only unaccounted for person thought to have been connected to the eighteen still-unexplained deaths at the conference hall a few days earlier.

Although none of the media knew there had even been a nineteenth person being sought, the discovery of the body and the revelation of its connection was presented as the finale of the story, the other shoe dropping, while the cause of death— Was it a suicide? Was it murder?—was put on a backburner pending the outcome of an investigation. At that point, the media wasn't aware of the goings-on at school earlier in the day or the presence of police on campus, so wild conjecture also became part of the story: Why was there no weapon near the body? Was there another armed suspect still on the loose? Had she been shot from afar? Had she killed herself? Did she have a role in the deaths of all the others?

There was a lot of activity online regarding both the

happenings at the conference hall and the middle school. What was it that killed the eighteen people in the conference hall? Why did none of the car drivers involved in accidents that day—or anyone else in the affected vicinity—have any memory of what happened? What was the bigger picture that tied the two scenes together? Seth found it fascinating that a few of the wildly speculative conspiracy theories thrown out by online commentators were fairly close to describing exactly what had occurred.

He watched the system slowly turning its focus on these happenings, trying to assess the scope of the problem and whether or not it hinted at a greater threat. It wasn't just the eyes of the media and everyone who paid attention to the media who were investigating, but also all the unseen forces at work in this world's operation. The story would eventually vanish from the headlines, but the system's tendrils would quietly continue to reach for answers, to revisit and re-examine the incidents. He felt sure that at some point down the line, someone—a journalist, a researcher, an online detective, maybe even a police investigator— was going to be contacting him to ask him about his multiple connections to those involved. He was from an OCareRx family. He'd worked in the same office as Bridget for three months more than a year ago. He'd known Doug for twenty-plus years. He was the parent group president at the school where Bridget's body was found. He'd gone on a date with her last December. The system might pick up on any one of those threads. It might be in a week and it might be in five years, but someday it was likely to happen. He would need to plan for that moment.

Telling the truth was no more an option than it had ever been. He knew, and he thought that Jessica knew, that no one would believe the truth. Not only would it not solve anything, it would likely make their lives worse. On the other hand, there were more OCareRx children out there, and for all he knew there might be some kind of alien host headed toward the planet. Did he have an obligation to try to alert the system? That argument didn't sway him. Would anyone listen? He would rather lie low.

School was closed for two days, after which time classes resumed as if nothing had happened. A week later, when Seth stepped hesitantly into the school office, he was generally ignored, but in a good way, as if there had never been a conversation about any improper actions on his part. Mr. Owen might have nodded at him to acknowledge his presence.

A bit surprised and greatly relieved, Seth quietly went about his parent group work.

One morning a few weeks later, to Seth's amazement, it was somehow suddenly the day of the commencement ceremony.

He was there, guiding other parents to their seats. People he didn't quite remember surprised him with friendly greetings. Teachers whose names he couldn't quite recall smiled and thanked him. As parent group president, he had been offered four front row seats, which were filled by Trevor, Marina, and Seth's parents. When the ceremony finally started, Seth took his seat farther back, between Erin and Jason's mother, whose name he also didn't remember.

Everyone at school seemed to be fine. No word of bad memories or seeming aftereffects, although Seth was most certain every student and staff member on campus that day had experienced an occasional flash of confused distaste at some random moment which they could not explain. When Jessica was onstage, before crossing to receive her diploma, she waved at her mom and then caught Seth's eye and almost smiled.

Check and mate. He'd won this round.

My life at the end of middle school was surprisingly not terrible. I didn't spend my nights staring at the night sky worrying about when the aliens were going to get here, and not just because I had no idea which part of the sky I should be watching. They were here already, right? As Jason said, "Those were the ones we know about. You know there's gotta be more."

Not that it didn't cross my mind from time to time, but the day-to-day eventually took precedence.

The weirdest part was the first day back at school. It felt strange to be at school acting as if everything was just normal—because even if it all seemed normal, it wasn't. It was weird seeing people and knowing that I knew something about them that they didn't know. The fact that Jason was in on the secret was the only thing that made it manageable. But it got better every day after that, until we got to the weekend of the play and for a while I stopped thinking about it at all.

Mom came home in time to be part of grad week activities. She was surprisingly low key. She didn't try to shake things up or make us move back in with her before the school year was over. She didn't fight with my Dad. She showed up for every grad week school event and she set up times to hang out with Trevor or me or both of us, and when she wasn't with us, she just went about getting her life in California back in running order. Neither of us ever really told each other what we'd been through while she was gone, and that turned out to be fine. She promised never to leave us like that again. We'll see.

At some point, it might have even been at graduation, I realized that I had never told my father about my mailing his signed paperwork to the Framework Foundation. Every time it came up in my mind after that, I told myself I would tell him at the next opportunity, but that moment hadn't yet presented itself.

To be sure, for the next few months, whenever the topic of aliens came up in conversation, Bridget and her friends weren't far from my mind. If or when alien invaders did arrive, they weren't necessarily going to be coming in spaceships armed with laser beams and future weapons. They were just as likely to be raining down on us like a storm of splat toys. Or hiding inside someone standing not six feet away. However it was that they traveled, Jason and I figured it was going to take them some time to get here. Maybe we'd be dead by the time they got here. There was time to prepare. We just had to be on the lookout for the ones that were already here.

I ordered a six-pack of nerve stimulators online. Two for Trevor, two for me, and one each for my parents. Jason talked his dad into giving him a Taser for one of his graduation gifts.

Jason and I went back to Splendor near the end of summer, shortly before we started high school and six weeks after Jason's back surgery. He still had to wear his brace, but was done with his crutches.

It was a nice street to walk on. It had sidewalks, and lots of trees, and it felt just a little bit like it was maybe a little farther off from the rest of town than it was. This time we got the ice cream cones first and ate them while we walked there.

There was a moving truck outside of my old house. The new people had only lasted a little more than a year. I wondered if my parents knew, and if either of them would want to try to buy the place back. It wasn't that I disliked either of the new homes—it was that neither of those places were ever going to feel like home the way our house on Splendor did.

We walked around the circle of the cul-de-sac and came back down, and were right across the street from Ms. Angela's house when the front door opened. Ms. Angela walked out, kind of looking around carefully before she stepped out too far and then, deciding it was safe, she walked out to her mailbox. She saw us when she reached the sidewalk.

"Hi, Ms. Angela."

This time, she looked exactly as I thought she should. She was older than the woman we saw last time, a bit wider at the sides but thinner at the middle. Her hair was tinged with gray, and her clothes were more drapey, looser.

"No way," Jason said quietly as we stared at her. She was wearing those big, black-framed glasses.

"Is that you Jessica? And Jason? Look at how tall you both have grown. How nice to see you." Her greeting seemed genuine, but I noticed that it stopped short of inviting us over. I also noticed she said it as if she hadn't seen us in years.

"It's great to see you, too. We were here a little bit ago and worried that you'd sold the house."

"Oh, no dear, I'd never sell this place."

"Does your daughter live with you?"

"No, she moved out of state years ago. Just me, myself, and I right now."

I wanted to ask who it was that answered the door the last time we were here, but felt weird calling it out across the street. Instead, I said, "Remember how you used to tell us it was an even stranger world than it seemed?"

"Yes, I do."

"Do you realize what an understatement that was?"

"No one really understands it until it's their turn to learn it," she said. "Then they have to figure out how to live with it. The real trick is learning to live a good life despite what you know about the world."

"Right? How do you do that?"

"Jessie, honey, your guess is as good mine. I just try to keep moving. When you figure it out, let me know."

.

At one of his sessions over the summer, while she trimmed his eyebrows, Dr. Penny said, "You've given up on this idea of your situation being 'fixed.' That's done?"

Although he still had many questions, Seth also had answers enough to have a better understanding of who he was inside and who he wasn't. There might be something else mixed in with his psychic DNA, but it didn't own him. He owned it. He was convinced the remaining questions weren't that different than any other person on the planet: Why was he the way he was? Where was it that whatever it was that made him this way existed? Seth also believed that this newfound self-understanding was the reason that the other someone in his head had gone silent since that morning at the school. Maybe that other Seth was gone. Maybe he was just blending in for now. Regardless, Seth developed a habit of correcting himself whenever a particularly arch or alien thought cropped up in his mind, which happened less and less as time went by. Just shut the fuck up, he'd say to himself. It would become his mantra.

"I don't think I can be fixed. My best bet is probably to focus on taking care of myself. Put myself in situations that encourage my better side. Spend less time thinking about myself."

"That's true for most people."

"I've got to find my niche. Well, I mean, for a few months there I had a niche, but now I've got to find another niche. I need to surround myself with the right kind of influences."

"What do you have in mind?"

The long game means you build a life.

"I think I want to be a middle school teacher."

:

REVIEW: A NEW FRAMEWORK?

It was in the midst of the effort to update and revise *God Myth*, on the impending tenth anniversary of its initial publication, that I weighed upon adding a section on "star god" theologies—those myths which rely on an entity identifiably not born of the soil of this planet. That categorization did not seem specific enough—at the center of many theologies can be found a godhead whose power and identity clearly originate outside of the earthly biosphere. Granted, too, was the point that many long-lived religions that embrace a star god theology have flourished—although I have dealt with these cults in other chapters of my book, and I think appropriately, as the hucksterism they embody at their core.

I might have arrived at a different conclusion a few short months later, when I came across Doug Callas' *Intelligent Designers*. First, it is a remarkable story for its timing. The events described took place in a small Kansas town decades before the country openly tangled with the Intelligent Design movement from which the title is derived.

There was no press coverage of the events that occurred in Whilton Creek, and it was not until the publication of Callas' book 20 years afterward that anyone was tipped off that anything had gone amiss. It is, in fact, the void of information for twenty years, the slow rebuilding of the scene from what imperfect witnesses remain willing to step forward, the sense that the picture is not complete, that lends itself to the sort of myth-building required to inspire a following, and then a movement. Human nature abhors a void, and lurking nearby every such moment stands one con person or another, ready to fill it, often with the most improbable of explanations.

The tale is a cautionary one for those so eager to open

up our educational institutions to theology in the guise of the Intelligent Design movement. Years before that deceptive moniker gained its foothold, a young school teacher with strong Christian leanings longed to incorporate Christian mythology into her curriculum, in particular to provide "balance" and a "buffer" against the state-mandated coverage of evolution, which at one point, according to her students, she described as "the intellectual elite's founding lie." Because it was against the law at the time (inexplicably, as of this writing, and horrifically, it is no longer) to teach theology in the classroom as if it were actual history, she assigned a paper to her students asking them to describe the origins of the universe and of mankind.

Clearly, she did not expect purely scientific responses; this was before the Internet became widespread, and the state-mandated science text expended all of a paragraph on the origin of life on earth, preferring instead to proceed from the voyages of early American explorers, as if that were the start of the world. When the inevitable paper was read aloud describing human origins in ways mirroring the text of Genesis, she did prod along the ensuing discussion with what she would have described as non-biased questions. And thus it went, apparently, until it came time for the somewhat ironically named Joseph David Paul, the 15-year-old son of two church-going parents, to read his paper.

"First," he read, "there was a nearly endless nothingness. Everything was dark, and everything the universe had once been had contracted back into its center point, into a burning black ball in the middle of nothing. It might have been that way for millions of years, and it might have been that way for a fraction of a second, before the pressure on that contracting black heart exploded. And the universe has been rebuilding itself and spreading ever since."

By Paul's accounting, the first wave of the Big Bang, which created the oldest parts of the universe 14 billion years ago, formed worlds and beings that were billions of years old before our own solar system began to form. When their civilizations reached a certain level of celestial maturity, these beings took it upon themselves to begin seeding various parts of the universe younger than their own. They set upon it as a scientific enterprise, choosing different worlds—including our own blue speck, and seeding them by means of attaching the necessary formative elements to comets and meteors, which they flung Earth's way. Timeless beings, or else immortal, they continue to the present to monitor their experiments from afar.

This was Mr. Paul's response to the writing prompt. It was enough to leave the teacher aghast. But then, Paul launched into the meat of his report, describing the arrival of another alien race, these not nearly as ancient as the first. These arrived on planet Earth some 50,000 years ago, apparently with the intent of setting up residence.

There is some artistry in the effort, particularly considering the dearth of apparent resources to which the young man might turn for information—an issue which would come to head shortly. He did not have access to the works of Lovecraft or Asimov. He went back to Hebrew translations of Genesis— literally translated, "They breathed life"—not "He breathed life" to support the idea that it was these visitors, and not the mythic Yahweh, who created the first versions of man using what biological tools were available. From scientific studies, Paul supported the notion of humankind as laboratory product, noting that humans shared commonalities in physiology and genetics with a range of species, from birds to lizards to insects and fish. He cited evidence in ancient art and literature of extraterrestrial presences, and he did it with nary a whiff of conspiratorial sensation.

There was even a war included, between the high-minded first group of celestial gardeners, and the second group of scientist colonizers, leading to multiple conflicts and many attempts to eradicate not only these new invasive forces but also the altered life forms that resulted from their experiments—us humans included but also the like of unicorns and harpies—that had contaminated their experiments. After this war, the defeated remainders of the second, later group, eventually stranded and scattered across the globe, gave rise to the worldwide myths of the pantheons of gods and goddesses and their offspring that live with us today. In the membership of this last group Paul included Jesus and Buddha, as well as a host of figures I have mentioned elsewhere in this text, all of whom share the notable characteristics of having been born to virgin mothers on December 25: Dionysus, Horus, Krishna, Mithra, Thammuz, and Zoroaster, among others.

So ended the unit on the origins of life on Earth. But in Whilton Creek, the discussion was just getting started. As one would imagine, the perfidy that followed might have been scripted for an after-school special. A hastily called town meeting followed—whereupon it should be noted no mention was made of the young teacher's straying from curriculum, the true source of the "trouble" here—and book burnings after that, followed by the ransacking of a desperately meager town library as well as the ostracizing of the Paul family from the outside community, and then of young Joseph from within his family, ending, in tragic manner, with the suicide by hanging of the 14-year-old teen who dared to connect imaginary dots in a different way.

Of course, after his suicide, the mystery deepened. The original paper written by Paul disappeared from the safe in the mayor's office, removed, it would become apparent, by none other than the town minister's daughter. A set of journals Paul apparently left with her to safeguard went with her as well. Paul's parents, who have done as successful a job of hiding themselves as this reporter has ever seen, promptly left town, and haven't been heard from since.

And then, quietly, at the dawn of the Internet age, an apparently connected phenomena occurred. A curious icon appeared. You've probably seen it, if not directly then out of the corner of your eye, a 4 x 4 x 4 grid, white lines against a dark background. Only one of the 64 squares is colored blue, this representing planet Earth. This logo has appeared on billboards and in commercials, in magazine advertisements, and on the sides of buses, most often in the context of supporting scientifically based initiatives, such as stem cell research, and sponsoring grants for projects in areas as far and wide as genome research, spaceflight technology, solar flares, and modern weaponry. What seemed to be a corporate logo turned out to be a sketch from one of Paul's journals. From Paul's notes, this grid represented the framework by which the first group of aliens perceived the universe. Not only as a linear composition, as we see it from our world view (which would require only one grid level) but with higher and lower parallel dimensions stacked above and below.

It would not be readily apparent that the current holder of those journals and that high school essay had joined forces with a law firm and a public relations firm, much less that the owners of said firms had established records as profiteering charlatans. Out of respect to my publisher's legal department, I shall not name them here. Suffice to say that when the first Framework-sponsored website appeared sharing Paul's story, his essay, and his journals (all seemingly, shall we say, edited for persuasive purposes), the texts were presented alongside an appeal soliciting information related to evidence that might support Paul's theories—i.e., of extraterrestrial visitation, past or present, or say, of extra-dimensional events. The most prominent piece of information displayed is the one soliciting donations to support the effort to "share the truth of Paul's vision." Both charlatans, seeing gold in the hills, sold their respective firms for grossly inflated sums and fully invested themselves in The Framework Foundation Incorporated.

First established was the Framework Collective, whose mission was to sift through all the data drawn by their solicitations, a project which continues to this day, with the research offices worldwide processing more than 4,500 claims per week related to supposed extraterrestrial or extradimensional occurrences—most of them, surprisingly (or not), deemed fraudulent and/or redundant.

Then came a sleek museum housing wings that represent the random groups into which they've divided their data: Antiquities, Aerial, Terrestrial, Sub-terrestrial, Oceanic, Psychic, Purpose. Each wing houses displays on enough supposed extraterrestrial material, present-day and historical, to back a 20-year revival of *The X-Files*. The Framework Museum's collection of earthly objects and images puts to shame its country cousin, the New Genesis Museum in Kentucky, and would seem to clearly cross a line in the sand between the religionists and the extraterrestrialists. Where the approach of one has been to catalog information and posit unsupportable theories to explain the evidence it has found in the litter and detritus of ages of men; the other has determined to preserve its fixed theology despite the ever-increasing evidence against its plausibility and historical accuracy. I'll leave it to you to determine which is which.

It is the last museum hall, Purpose, which signals the founders' aspirations—their desire to create a new faith. They're inviting you to help them do it by combining their multiple Internet presences into one multilingual portal that catalogues their Framework research and then asks the viewer/reader to explain what he or she believes is the intended purpose of humankind. If Paul's theory were proved to be true, what do you believe the space entities' intentions are for humanity? What are we intended to be, and why?

After incorporation as a non-profit, the Framework took its considerable fortune and began to amass impressive troves of "evidence" that humankind has been interacting with alien cultures, witnessing their existence, and recording their interactions, for thousands of years. What they couldn't buy from already existing extraterrestrial museums around the world, they've recreated. The art displays in the Aerial hall include recreations of 10,000-year-old cave drawings from six far-flung and diverse regions of the world featuring nearly identically rendered, helmeted alien creatures; these appear next to a series of original German and French paintings dated to the late 1500s that would seem to depict warring armadas of saucer-shaped spaceships, next to poster-size recreations of the more exotic of Leonardo Da Vinci's sketches of aerial machines. An ingenious mix-and-match display allows you view sophisticated, life-size recreations of the dozens of alien races testified to by various witnesses throughout history. You can combine the races with each other, or with prototypes of "average" men and women from different periods in time, to see what the progeny of human and alien mingling might look like.

A projected image of the Crucifixion (the original hangs above the altar of the Visoki DeCani Monastery in Kosovo), which, similar to many paintings from the period, does seem to include a sort of space vehicle, seemingly with pilot included, hanging in the air above and behind the Christian idol, fills one wall. On the wall next to it, a photo collection of Nazca line images appears near *Baptism of Christ* by Flemish artist Art De Belder from 1710, which appears to depict a saucer beaming light down on Jesus and John the Baptist. In the middle of the room is a replica of a sarcophagus lid of a Mayan ruler depicting what are known as ancient astronauts—beings who appear to be dressed as astronauts who are featured in a large range of art and objects from the previous millennia.

In the Antiquities Hall, lined by downsized Easter Island moai, there is a fabrication of *Book of the Monoliths,* by Aveldo Sofir, beside a reproduction of an 8th-century illuminated manuscript depicting what appears to be a crashed spacecraft, and the list goes on, perhaps in the belief that repeating the same argument over and over helps to make the claim more true.

My favorite display was a small unnamed hall wherein were presented rather elaborate theories of the evolution of the cosmos in variations on the Framework theology. One, by Schreiber Esse, posited that the earliest alien visitors were there to install equipment in the planet's core and in our moon and sun that would allow them to control the planet's environment and operate it as a sort of Second Life for far-off alien races, an idea surely toyed with by Phillip Dick. In a galaxy millions of light years away, an evolutionarily advanced alien that wishes to experience life in a more basic form signs up and pays a fee. Then the alien is plugged into a machine that transports their conscience into a newborn life on backwater Earth, and so the adventure begins. The fee the alien pays for the session determines how long the session lasts, with that particular body's death occurring when the session ends. By Mr. Esse's estimation, there have been some 50 billion aliens who have played Life on Earth since the first prototype human vessels were developed. He has posited that many aliens have returned multiple times to repeat the experience, giving rise to our human belief in reincarnation.

The sheer mass of the objects on display in the Framework Museum is overwhelming, as are the movie galleries that run, on continuous loop, several thousands of hours of video footage alleged to be of encounters with alien spacecraft—in the sky, in the ocean, in sinkholes in the earth, and in some cases, even at airports around the world. Most of the footage is from the cockpit, or with the camera pointed at a radar screen, and is available due to the support of governments other than the

United States, where a president has not yet been elected who has courted the vote of the cult of the ancient astronaut fervently enough to convincingly pretend it is worth the effort.

To walk through this warehouse of human homage to alien couture will convince you of one thing, whether or not you leave the place believing in visitors from the outer reaches. That is that humanity would really, really, really like to believe we are not alone in the universe.

The Framework Foundation, as it were, is a group of people, many of them scientists, who subscribe to theories supporting an extraterrestrial explanation to the question of the origin of life on Earth. That answer, which became their credo, seems to have unified under one umbrella believers of many stripes, from science fiction fanatics to Wiccans. They insist their approach is to gather and analyze information, and to see each thing outside the norm as a clue and a piece to be assembled into the puzzle that explains our purpose here on Earth. Critics suggest that their scientific method would seem to be lacking. Fittingly, The Framework does not comment on its method.

To date, I am told, they have received over 200 million responses in 110 languages in their call for a purpose. The submissions are posted online and can be viewed easily, and bi-weekly releases provide updates that summarize polling results. My favorite answer viewed so far as to our Purpose: "to eat, to drink, to fuck, to sleep, all to contentment, and then to die. The star people aren't part of my picture." That results can now be found posted in establishments across the planet reminds how thoroughly The Framework has penetrated its target market. The museum, the foundation, and the campus receive over 2 million visitors a year, some of them "scholars" of such phenomena who are part of a continuing seminar series that fills the campus auditorium on a bi-weekly basis.

Tickets for these talks cost extra, of course.

Also by James T. Riley

THE CHAMBER CHILDREN

MY NAME IS JARED

HILL PEOPLE

www.ingramcontent.com/pod-product-compliance
Lightning Source LLC
Chambersburg PA
CBHW070446030726
47503CB00004B/924